Jayne Ann Krentz is the critically acclaimed creator of the Arcane Society world, Dark Legacy series and Rainshadow series. She also writes as **Amanda Quick** and **Jayne Castle**. Jayne has written more than fifty *New York Times* bestsellers under various pseudonyms and lives in the Pacific Northwest.

The historical novels she writes as Amanda Quick all feature her customary irresistible mix of passion and mystery, and also have a strong psychic/paranormal twist.

Visit her online:
www.jayneannkrentz.com
www.facebook.com/JayneAnnKrentz
@JayneAnnKrentz

D0228458

Books by Jayne Ann Krentz

* Not published by Piatkus

CLOSE UP

AMANDA QUICK

PIATKUS

PIATKUS

First published in the US in 2020 by Berkley,
an imprint of Penguin Random House LLC
First published in Great Britain in 2020 by Piatkus
This paperback edition published in 2020 by Piatkus

1 3 5 7 9 10 8 6 4 2

A CIP catalogue record for this book
is available from the British Library.

ISBN 978-0-349-42447-7

Printed and bound in Great Britain by Clays Ltd, Elcograf S.p.A.

Papers used by Piatkus are from well-managed forests
and other responsible sources.

Piatkus
An imprint of
Little, Brown Book Group
Carmelite House
50 Victoria Embankment
London EC4Y 0DZ

An Hachette UK Company
www.hachette.co.uk

www.littlebrown.co.uk

For my brother, Stephen B. Castle,
with thanks for the photography insights.
I am so glad we are family!

And, as always, for Frank, with love.

CLOSE UP

Chapter 1

ere comes Cinderella," Toby Flint said. "She's out after midnight again. I don't see any glass slippers, and those trousers sure don't look like a fancy ball gown."

"Still looking for Prince Charming?" Larry Burns said with a sly grin.

Vivian Brazier hurried up the front steps of the mansion and flashed a breezy smile at the small group of men in fedoras and frumpy jackets loitering around the closed door of the Carstairs mansion.

"Gosh, I was told I'd find Prince Charming here," she said. "Looks like I was given wrong information. Again."

Toby clapped a hand over his heart. "Now you've gone and hurt our feelings."

"What feelings?" Vivian asked. "You gentlemen are all spot news photographers, remember? You don't have feelings."

"Cinderella's got a point," Larry said.

There were several snorts of laughter. The uniformed officer guarding the front door chuckled.

She had been labeled *Cinderella* several months earlier when she had arrived at her first late-night crime scene wearing house slippers. She had rushed out the door so fast she had forgotten to put on her shoes. After that she had purchased slip-ons she could step into in a hurry but the *Cinderella* name had stuck.

Toby and the other local freelancers had found her to be a novelty at first. News photography was largely a man's world. But they had come to accept her because they knew she paid her bills the same way they did—by sleeping with the radio tuned to the police band all night long.

Freelancers were usually the first to arrive at crime-and-fire scenes because the *salaried* photographers—the guys who held genuine press passes from the newspapers and the syndicates—didn't show up until their night editors roused them from their beds with phone calls. Time was everything in the photojournalism business, especially at night.

Vivian looked at Toby. "How did you get the word?"

"I was sitting on a bench at the station, drinking coffee with some of the officers, when the call came in," Toby said.

Toby often spent his nights on a bench at the station waiting for the crime-and-fire reports. He was somewhere in his forties, single, rumpled, and perennially broke. Whenever Vivian opened her senses and looked at him the way she did when she studied a subject before she took a portrait, she was invariably aware of the jittery, nervous energy in the atmosphere around him.

She was pretty sure she knew why he always seemed to be poised on the edge of an invisible cliff. Toby could—and probably did—make a living selling photos of crime scenes, fires, and automobile accidents, but he was an inveterate gambler.

His addiction to dice and cards was no secret among his colleagues because he was always trying to borrow film or flashbulbs or gas money for his beat-up Ford sedan. Everyone knew that loans to Toby were never repaid. Vivian sometimes, but not always, gave him a couple of bucks or some supplies. She was on a tight budget but she felt she owed him. Several months ago, back at the start of her career as a freelancer, he had been a mentor of sorts. He had taught her many of the tricks of the trade and introduced her to the photo editor of the *Adelina Beach Courier.*

Like every other news photographer in the country, Toby dreamed of getting an assignment from *Life*, one that would make him famous and pay off his debts, but that had never happened. Vivian understood dreams. She had a few of her own.

"Any details on this one?" she asked.

"Fancy antique dagger found at the scene," Larry offered. "Same as the Washfield and Attenbury murders."

Vivian felt a ghostly whisper of cold energy on the back of her neck. "That's the third one in the past six months. The last Dagger Killer murder was only a month ago."

"This one is gonna be a real moneymaker for all of us," Larry said.

The other photographers muttered in agreement and checked their Speed Graphics to make sure they were loaded with film and fresh flashbulbs.

"Only thing that sells better than a movie star murder is a movie star who was stabbed by the Dagger Killer," Toby said, grimly cheerful. "Nice of the guy to do it here on our home turf this time. Gives us locals first crack at the front-page shots. We don't get a lot of this kind of action here in Adelina Beach."

Adelina Beach had a carefully manicured reputation for exclusivity, at least the classy neighborhood on the bluffs where the Carstairs mansion was located did. Several Hollywood stars and socialites had grand homes on the winding lanes overlooking the vast expanse of the bay and the Pacific Ocean. Murders were not supposed to happen in this part of town. Crime, what there was of it, usually took place down below on the streets near the beach where regular people lived.

Vivian's insides were already twisted tight with tension. Toby's words made her queasy. She liked to think she had become somewhat accustomed to crime scenes. She had learned how to brace herself for the shock long enough to do her job. But she knew she was never going to develop the invisible emotional armor that seemed to protect most news photographers from the horror and the deep sense of sadness generated by terrible crimes.

The front door opened. Light spilled out of the hallway. A plain-clothes detective appeared. Vivian recognized him. Joe Archer was the head of Adelina Beach's tiny homicide squad. He surveyed the cluster of photographers and grunted.

"Let 'em in," he said to the uniformed officer. "One shot each. I don't want them messing up the scene."

Vivian surged through the doorway with the other photographers. Her Speed Graphic was as good as a genuine press pass. The big camera was the badge of the news photographer. Cops rarely questioned a freelancer who carried one. The trick for getting past the police line, Toby had explained early on, was attitude.

Vivian had quickly discovered that the sturdy Speed Graphic also made a handy defense weapon that could be used to keep the competition from jostling her aside. The male photographers might joke or flirt or talk about their craft with her when they were all standing around waiting for a picture, but when it came time to grab the shot a photo editor would buy, she was on her own. News photography was a competitive business.

The body lay on a high-backed, red-velvet-and-gilt sofa. Clara Carstairs looked much smaller in death than she did when she dazzled audiences on the silver screen. Her slender figure, clad in a formfitting gold satin evening gown, was gracefully posed on the crimson cushions. Her dark hair flowed in deep waves around her bare shoulders. Her makeup, from the delicately drawn eyebrows to the fashionable shade of red lipstick, was flawless.

One gold high-heeled sandal had fallen to the carpet, revealing a dainty foot clad in a silk stocking. The hem of the gown was hiked high up on one thigh. Crystals sparkled in her ears and around her wrists. An empty glass tipped on its side and a bottle of cognac sat on a black lacquer coffee table.

If not for the blood that soaked the bodice of the gown and the jeweled dagger on the coffee table, it would have looked as if Carstairs had returned from a night on the town, poured herself a nightcap, and fallen asleep on the sofa.

The lighting was almost perfect. Mysterious shadows cloaked the background. The victim and her gold gown were luminous against the red velvet cushions.

Vivian and the others halted about ten feet from the scene, close enough to make the body the dramatic focal point but far enough away to get the surrounding elements for a touch of context. The ten-foot rule of thumb was one of the reasons why most of the pictures on the front pages would look the same in tomorrow's papers. The trick, Vivian had discovered, was to find an angle or an element that added that extra something to the final image, a hint that the victim had possessed deeply held secrets, secrets she had taken to the grave.

Two more photographers rushed into the room just as the first flashbulbs flared. The space was suddenly illuminated in a blaze of hot, blinding light. In the aftermath the used bulbs were swiftly ejected, landing on the carpet where they got crunched underfoot. They were immediately replaced as everyone ignored Archer's orders and prepared for a second shot.

Vivian held her fire, searching for the picture that would stand out from the others, one with the emotional impact that would make a photo editor seize on it. She would know it when she found it. That was the way it always worked for her.

Tires squealed outside in the street. A moment later a reporter strode into the room, fedora pushed back on his head, notebook at the ready. The space was filling up fast.

Vivian prowled the edge of the crowd, pausing near a potted palm.

From where she stood Clara Carstairs no longer appeared to have fallen asleep. The knife, the overturned sandal, the lifeless, outflung hand told the sad story of a beautiful young woman who had come to Hollywood with dreams in her eyes only to die like the tragic heroine she had played in her last film, *Farewell at Dawn*.

The subject's secrets were always there if you knew how to look for them.

There was a lull in the blaze of lights. Several photographers, including Toby, headed for the door. One or two hung back, hoping for one more good picture.

Vivian grabbed her shot.

And then she, too, sprinted for the door. The race was on to get the film into a darkroom where it could be developed and printed in time for the morning editions of the papers. The photographers who carried real press passes would be able to use their papers' darkrooms. Vivian and the others had to do their own developing and printing.

She reached her little red speedster and was about to get behind the wheel when something made her pause.

She glanced back at the front door of the mansion. The angled light from the hallway appeared ominous. The lone officer still stood at the entrance. As she watched, the remaining photographers hurried outside to their cars.

It occurred to her that there might be a market for a photo of the scene of the crime. The big house was a Hollywood legend in its own right. Clara Carstairs was not the first famous resident. She could envision a caption. *Mansion of Doom?*

She slapped a fresh film holder into the camera, popped in a new flashbulb, and went back up the front walk. It might be a mistake to waste time on an outdoor shot but her intuition told her that it would sell. She would include the officer. Pictures with people always sold best.

She stood in the shadows of the front entrance and prepared to shoot the doorway. The low rumble of a powerful engine stopped her. She turned and saw headlights spearing the night. An expensive convertible braked to a halt at the curb. A man got out. He was not wearing a hat. When she saw his famous profile in the light of the streetlamp she held her breath and retreated deeper into the shadows. Ripley Fleming was one of the hottest stars in Hollywood.

Fleming moved swiftly along the stone walk, the wings of his elegant overcoat whipping around him. He went up the front steps and confronted the officer.

"What the hell is going on? Is Miss Carstairs all right?"

The officer, stunned by the realization that he was speaking to a famous actor, had to try a couple of times before he could string words into a coherent sentence.

"Miss Carstairs is dead, sir," he mumbled.

"Dead?" Ripley said, as if he was not familiar with the word.

"Murdered, sir. They're saying it's the work of the Dagger Killer."

"Murdered," Ripley repeated. He sounded dazed.

He turned to gaze through the partially open door. Vivian knew that from where he stood he could see a portion of the body on the crimson sofa. There was something about his expression that was vaguely familiar. In the glow of the hallway light, Fleming's chiseled features were set in the same dramatic mask of shock that had made for a riveting scene in his last film, *Dead End Alley*.

And there it was, another golden shot for her camera. A picture of Ripley Fleming's arrival at the scene of the Carstairs murder shortly after the body had been discovered would be worth more than the photo of the dead woman because there were no other photographers around to capture the expression on the actor's face. *Exclusive.*

Vivian quietly readied her camera. Ripley must have heard her moving in the shadows. He whipped around and saw her. Something akin to panic replaced the horror on his memorable face.

"Please, no," he whispered. "No pictures. I'll pay you—"

She hesitated a second but she knew she had already made the decision. She lowered the camera.

"Forget it," she said. "You don't need to pay me not to take your photo, Mr. Fleming. I'm very sorry about Miss Carstairs."

"Thank you," Fleming said. He hesitated. "I owe you."

"No," she said. "You don't."

He fled down the steps and jumped into his convertible. Tires shrieked when he pulled away from the curb and raced down the street.

"Reckon the rumors in the Hollywood papers are true," the officer mused. "Looks like Mr. Fleming and Miss Carstairs were having an affair. I'd better tell Detective Archer about this."

The cop disappeared inside the house.

Vivian shot the house and hurried back to her car. This was why she was never going to have a great career in photojournalism, she thought. Taking a picture of the body at a crime scene was one thing. Photographing the shocked lover after he had begged her not to take his picture was beyond her. It would have felt wrong, indecent.

She jumped into the speedster and drove quickly down the winding lanes of the ritzy neighborhood and through the quiet streets of the town below. She parked in front of the beach house and hurried inside with her camera.

She headed straight for her darkroom—a converted pantry off the kitchen—grabbed the bottle of developer, and filled up the first tray. Next she prepared the stop bath and finally the fixer tray.

When she had everything ready she turned off the lights, closed the heavy black curtain as an extra precaution against light, and went to work.

An hour and twenty minutes later she was in the office of the photo editor of the *Adelina Beach Courier*. Eddy Banks—middle-aged, reeking

of cigar smoke, and endowed with extremely poor taste in clothes—
studied the prints of the Carstairs murder.

"These are damn good," he said. "Her fans are gonna be in tears
tomorrow when they see this shot." He narrowed his eyes. "Carstairs
will go on the front page. I'll use the house for page two. Nice bit of
atmosphere. Did you give either of these to one of the syndicates?"

"No," Vivian said. "They're all yours if you want them. But these
aren't my five-dollar celebrity-seen-in-a-nightclub shots. I want seventy-
five for those two pictures."

"I'll give you thirty bucks for both."

"Fifty."

"Consider 'em sold." Eddy eyed her. "These photos are going to go
national. You ought to demand a photo credit as well as the cash."

"You know the last thing I want is to have my name associated with
newspaper photos."

"Still dreaming of making it big in the art world, huh?" Eddy shook
his head. "You're wasting your time."

"Because I'm not good enough to be an art photographer?"

"Hell, no." Eddy snorted. "Because the art world is never going to
take photography seriously, especially not the kind you do."

"Times are changing."

"Some things never change." Eddy took another look at the picture
of Clara Carstairs on the sofa. "She was a real beauty, wasn't she? She
looks so young. Downright tragic. Do the cops have any leads?"

"I don't think so, not unless Archer found something at the scene
tonight. From what I could see it was the same setup as the Washfield
and Attenbury murders. No signs of a struggle. Celebrity victim in a
dramatic pose. Bloodstained antique dagger at the scene."

Eddy shook his head. "Can't be that many expensive old daggers
around."

"According to the cops, none of the museums or antiques galleries in the Los Angeles area have reported any thefts of daggers. Whoever is doing this probably has access to a private collection."

"Sounds like it."

"He must be wealthy, too," Vivian added. "Rich enough not to care about leaving a valuable antique at the scene of a murder."

"Good point." Eddy planted his cigar in his mouth. "Well, looks like we've got our headline."

"*Clara Carstairs Murdered by Dagger Killer, Police Baffled* for the front-page shot," Vivian suggested. "*Mansion of Doom* for the second photo?"

"You're getting real good at the news photo business."

"I've been hanging around you too long, Eddy."

Eddy glanced at the picture again and shook his head. "Like a scene from one of her own movies."

Vivian studied the print. Her inner vision stirred and whispered to her. *There are always secrets. You just have to look for them.*

"Yes," she said. "It almost looks like a scene from one of her own films."

Secrets.

Chapter 2

Exhaustion finally hit on the drive back to the beach house. Vivian parked the speedster in the small attached garage and let herself in through the kitchen door.

She headed for the bedroom. The night shift was over. She needed sleep because she had a busy day ahead.

She kicked off the slip-ons, undressed, and fell into bed. She contemplated the shadowed ceiling while she reviewed her schedule. She had a studio portrait booked at ten o'clock. Like her crime-and-fire pictures, portraits were bread-and-butter business, albeit far more respectable. Successful art photographers often did portraits. Charged a lot for them, too.

She had cleared her afternoon to devote to her art. A model was due at two for the next picture in her new series.

It took about twenty minutes of staring at the ceiling before she abandoned the attempt to sleep. She was tired but every time she closed her eyes she saw the scene of the Carstairs murder. As Eddy had pointed out, it could have been a stage set from one of the actress's own movies.

No, not a stage set. The lighting and the sight lines were not right, not for a movie.

But they were perfect for a photograph.

She pushed the covers aside, stepped into her slippers, pulled on a robe, and made her way down the hall to the living room. She paused to turn on a lamp.

Shortly after moving in a few months ago she had converted the front room into a studio. Lights, cords, tripods, and a variety of props littered the space. Black cases containing her precious lenses, light meters, film, flashbulbs, and all the rest of the equipment required for her work were lined up against one wall. Backdrops and swaths of fabric were suspended from a series of movable rails. A large, freestanding mirror stood in a corner. She had discovered early on that it was easier to get a good portrait if the sitter could see his or her own reflection.

She left the studio, went into the small dining room that now served as her office, and switched on a lamp. The table was covered with folders filled with photos and newspaper clippings. Most were her own work but some were pictures taken by other photographers that she deemed worth a closer study. Photography was an art. There was always something to learn, always a new way to see beneath the surface. A way to discover and reveal secrets.

She opened the file labeled WASHFIELD MURDER and dumped the contents onto the table. Leonard Washfield had been a wealthy and well-connected socialite. The family money had come from the railroads. Leonard had been born and raised in San Francisco but he had moved to Hollywood after graduating from college. He had financed a couple of successful motion pictures and soon became known for his extravagant parties. He had been photographed at the hottest nightclubs, where he always seemed to have a beautiful actress on his arm. A month ago his dramatic death had been front-page news.

For a moment she stood looking down at the little pile of photos and clippings. There was a certain sameness to them because the photographers were mostly using the same kind of camera and had shot mostly from a distance of about ten feet. But there were some pictures, including her own, that had taken advantage of the unique lighting at the scene.

After a while she picked up the folder labeled ATTENBURY MURDER and examined the pictures. Sarah Attenbury had been a glittering fixture on the Los Angeles social scene. Invitations to her parties were coveted by everyone who moved in high-flying circles in Hollywood and Beverly Hills.

The first faint light of a foggy dawn was illuminating the sky when Vivian concluded that she was certain of what she was seeing in the pictures. She went back into the living room and picked up the phone.

"Operator, please connect me with the police," she said. "Yes, I'll hold."

A short time later a gruff voice came on the line. "Adelina Beach Police Department."

"Detective Archer, please. Tell him it's about the Carstairs murder."

"He just left. Been a long night. Hang on, I'll see if I can catch him."

The phone on the other end clattered on a desktop. After a couple of moments a man with a smoker's rough voice came on the line.

"This is Archer."

"Detective Archer, my name is Vivian Brazier. I'm a photographer. I was at the Carstairs house earlier this evening taking news photos."

"I remember you. The lady with the camera. What's this all about?"

"I have been looking at the pictures that appeared in the papers after the Washfield and Attenbury murders and there are some striking similarities between those two homicide scenes and the one at the Carstairs mansion."

"The fancy daggers." Archer's voice sharpened. "We think they came from a private collection. We're checking out that angle. Is that all you've got? Because if so, I'd really like to go home and get some sleep."

"I think the pictures were deliberately and carefully composed. Each element is intentional. The lighting was staged for a dramatic shot. Your killer considers himself an artist."

"What the hell? You think he stopped to paint a couple of pictures after he murdered Washfield, Attenbury, and Carstairs?"

"No, I think he photographed the scenes."

"Are you serious? We're looking for a *photographer*? That means my suspect list is approximately the size of the telephone book. Everyone and his kid sister has a Brownie."

"You're looking for a pro, not an amateur. He'll be using expensive equipment, fine-grained film, and pricey paper. There aren't a lot of camera shops that carry high-quality lenses, film, and paper. Trust me, those shops will remember their best customers."

"Paper?" Archer sounded thoughtful. "You think he's printing his photographs?"

"Of course. I told you, he considers himself an artist. Find him and you'll find his equipment and negatives as well as the prints."

"What about those old knives?"

"I can't be absolutely positive but I suspect they may be his way of marking each murder scene as part of a series."

Archer whistled softly. "You saw all that just by looking at the crime scenes?"

"I spend my days composing pictures. I know what to look for. Oh, one more thing."

"Hang on, I need to make some notes." There were some rustling sounds. A moment later Archer came back on the line. "All right, go ahead. What else do you think you saw at the scenes?"

Vivian picked up a newspaper clipping of the Washfield murder. "Do you know anything about photography, Detective?"

"Evidently not as much as I thought I did."

"For the past couple of decades there has been an argument going on in the art world over the issue of whether or not photography should be considered an art or just a means of documenting reality."

"Who cares?"

"The art world cares. Museums and galleries that hang photographs care. So do photographers who are trying to use their cameras to create art."

Photographers like me, she thought. But she did not say that aloud.

"This battle about whether photography deserves to be called an art is a big deal?" Archer said.

"A very big deal. There are two aesthetic approaches involved, pictorialism and modernism."

"I'm not really interested in art. I'm trying to stop a crazy killer."

"Fine. I won't bore you with the details, Detective. All you need to know is that the older school is called pictorialism. It's all about making a photograph look like a painting."

"How do you do that?"

"You shoot for a painterly look. Soft focus, maybe. You use all sorts of tricks and tints to manipulate the photograph when you print it. You're not trying to capture reality, you're going for an abstract vision. Modernism is the new tradition. It's all about clean lines and a sharp focus. It's about revealing reality."

"You're losing me."

"I think the killer you are hunting sees himself as working in the older tradition. His pictures will be pictorial in style and that means he'll be purchasing supplies that only a photographer working in that genre would want. That should help narrow down your suspect list."

"You really think he's taking pictures of the scene after he kills someone?"

Vivian studied the pictures of the Washfield murder.

"Oh, yes," she said. "When you find him, I'm sure you'll find his collection."

"If you're right you've given me the lead I've been looking for. I'll get my people out on the street first thing this morning to start talking to camera shops."

"Expensive camera shops. The kind that sell professional equipment and the best film."

"Got it. Anything else?"

"One thing," Vivian said. "Whatever you do, please keep my name out of this. Photographers, especially those who shoot murders and fires, don't get much respect from the art world."

Archer snorted. "I get it, believe me. Same goes for cops. People call us when they get robbed but no one sends us engraved invitations to the big charity ball."

"Thank you, Detective," Vivian said. "I appreciate it."

"Don't worry," Archer said. "Your secret is safe with me."

Chapter 3

Vivian did not sleep late. She got up early, bathed, dressed, and rushed out the front door and down the street to the news-stand. Screaming headlines announced the Carstairs murder. Her picture was on the front page of the *Adelina Beach Courier.*

She grabbed copies of every morning paper the vendor stocked. Arms full, she hurried back to her house, brewed some strong coffee, and started reading.

All of the morning papers carried photos and lurid accounts of the newest Dagger Killer murder. The papers that considered themselves to be family papers were careful to paint out all traces of blood and ran the images of the body on page two. Others, such as *Hollywood Whispers* and the *Adelina Beach Courier,* slapped the most graphic pictures on the front page.

She read all of the articles carefully, curious to see if any of the reporters had discovered that Ripley Fleming had arrived at the scene of the murder.

By the time she finished her coffee it was clear that Fleming had escaped relatively unscathed. *Hollywood Whispers* and a few of the other movie gossip papers reminded readers that he and Carstairs were rumored to have been intimately involved but that was no more than what had already been printed.

Talk of a romantic connection between an actor and an actress was an excellent way to keep their names and photos in the press. A picture of the shocked lover arriving at the scene of the murder, however, would have invited a very different kind of speculation.

The phone rang, startling her. She glanced at her watch. It was almost nine. Her heart sank. Her ten o'clock portrait client was probably calling to cancel. She got to her feet and went into the living room to pick up the receiver.

"Hello." She kept her voice cool and businesslike.

"I'm calling for Miss Vivian Brazier."

The voice on the other end was female, brisk, and professional. The client's secretary, most likely.

"This is Vivian Brazier," Vivian said.

"I'm calling from the Penfield Gallery. Miss Penfield had an appointment with an artist to review some of his paintings at one o'clock today. However, that meeting has been canceled. I do realize this is very short notice but, if you're still interested in showing some of your pictures to Miss Penfield, she will be willing to take a look at them at one o'clock."

Vivian's mood soared skyward with near-miraculous speed. Excitement and hope sparked. Shortly after moving to Adelina Beach she had managed to place two of her limited-edition art photos with a local gallery. The pictures, both landscapes, had been exhibited in a show and had sold for modest prices. But afterward her career had stalled. She had not been able to get any more of her photographs into the local galleries.

"Yes, of course, I'll be happy to show Miss Penfield some of my recent work today," she said. "I'll be there at one."

She hung up and went into her bedroom, opened the door of her closet, and contemplated her wardrobe. She had several smart suits that she had brought with her when she had moved from San Francisco to Adelina Beach but they had been designed to be worn to charity luncheons and garden club teas. They required gloves, hats, and handbags that matched the shoes—not at all the sort of thing an up-and-coming photographer wore to a fashionable gallery.

She pushed the suits to the back of her closet, where they were lost in the shadows along with a couple of dramatic evening gowns. She had not worn any of them since her arrival in Adelina Beach. The clothes belonged to her other life, the life she had lived as the eldest daughter of the fashionable, socially connected San Francisco Braziers. That life had gone down in flames following the scandalous liaison with an artist and then her subsequent refusal to marry the man her parents had handpicked for her.

It had been almost a year since she had sat down with her family and announced her decision to pursue a career as an art photographer. The news had landed with the force of a grenade in the Brazier household, although she was at a loss to understand why. It should have been obvious that she was passionate about taking pictures. She had been an avid photographer since her father had given her a Brownie on her eighth birthday. She'd moved on to her first view camera and set up her first darkroom at the age of twelve. She had been enthralled by the magic she could create in the dark.

But the scene in the elegantly appointed living room of the Brazier home on the night of her announcement still rang in her ears. "But, dear, photography is just a hobby," her mother had said. "There's no reason you can't continue to do it after you're married. I'm sure Hamilton won't mind."

At that point Vivian had pulled the pin out of another grenade. She had informed her parents that she had turned down Hamilton Merrick's offer of marriage. Her mother had been first horrified and then distraught and, finally, furious.

Her father had warned her that if she continued with her crazed plan to become a professional photographer he would cut off all financial support until she came to her senses.

Her sister, Lyra, had watched the drama in silence, a speculative expression in her eyes.

Later that night Lyra had come to Vivian's room and sat down on the velvet-covered dressing table stool. She had watched Vivian fill the two suitcases sitting on the bed.

"You're serious about your art photography, aren't you?" Lyra asked.

"You know I am."

"You're sure you don't love Hamilton?"

"Absolutely certain. I suppose if I had to marry someone, Hamilton would probably do as well as any other man." Vivian took a pile of lingerie out of a drawer and dumped it into a suitcase. "Mother and Father approve of him. He's in line to take control of his father's business. He goes to all the right social affairs and we do have a few things in common. I certainly enjoyed the outings on his yacht and he's an excellent dancer. He was even willing to overlook the scandal. But I'm not in love with him and, frankly, I'm sure he doesn't love me."

"You're positive about that?" Lyra said.

"Yep." Vivian paused in the act of taking a hatbox down from the closet shelf. She eyed Lyra closely and then she smiled. "I see. I hadn't realized you liked him so much, at least not in that way. You did a very good job of concealing your feelings."

Lyra flushed. "Mother was so sure you were going to marry him. I did not want to let anyone know I found him attractive. Besides, Hamilton has always treated me as if I were his kid sister."

Hamilton was, indeed, a handsome, charming man, Vivian reflected. On the surface he appeared to be everything a woman in her world could ask for in a husband. They had known each other most of their lives because they had grown up in the same social circles. When she was in her teens she'd had a mad crush on him, but when they had gone their separate ways to college she had not really missed him.

After graduation Hamilton had taken a position in his father's law firm. He had dated a lot of women, including her, but he had not shown any interest in marriage until quite recently. It had come as a shock when he had asked her to marry him. Talk about a quick way to kill a perfectly good relationship.

She dropped the hatbox on the bed and walked across the room to hug Lyra.

"Trust me, neither my heart nor Hamilton's will be broken when I move to Adelina Beach," she said.

"Must you leave San Francisco to pursue your art?" Lyra asked.

"For now I think it's best. If I set up a studio here, Mother and Father will be embarrassed. Or, even worse, they would pressure their friends to ask me to do portraits and wedding photography. I don't want to do that kind of work, at least not as a career. I want to do the kind of pictures that hang in museums and galleries. Pictures that make people stop and take a second look. I want to create art."

"Why Adelina Beach? Why not Hollywood or Beverly Hills?"

"Adelina Beach is adjacent to L.A. It has all the advantages of being close to the city but it has a reputation as an art town. The best and most exclusive galleries in Southern California have shops there. It's the place to be for someone like me, an artist trying to establish a career."

"I will miss you so much," Lyra said. Tears filled her eyes.

"It's not as if I'm moving to New York or the moon," Vivian said. "You can come and see me as often as you like. All you have to do is get on the train. And I will come back to San Francisco on holidays and birthdays."

"I know, but it won't be the same." Lyra used the sleeve of her robe to wipe her eyes. She managed a shaky smile. "But I will admit I have always wanted to see Hollywood."

"We will tour Hollywood together the first time you come to visit me."

Lyra's visits had occurred with increasing frequency in the past several months. She had loved the sun and the beach and she had enjoyed acting as an assistant in the studio. Aware of Vivian's financial circumstances—Gordon Brazier had followed through with his threat to cut off all funding—Lyra invariably showed up at the beach house with a gift of a new dress or a fashionable hat. Vivian's mother had recovered from her initial emotional reaction and had begun to send lavish presents—shoes, jewelry, or a smart new handbag.

The result was that Vivian possessed a rather extensive wardrobe for a struggling photographer.

She pushed aside a new tennis outfit—unworn—and settled on what she had decided to make her signature professional style—a pair of black slacks with wide, flowy legs, a black silk blouse, and a jaunty little turquoise scarf. Square-toed, stacked-heel shoes fashioned of perforated black patent leather finished the look.

She crossed the bedroom to the dressing table and brushed her shoulder-length whiskey-brown hair so that it fell in deep waves. Next she uncapped her new crimson lipstick. There would be no hat and no gloves today. Hats and gloves were too formal, too traditional. She was an *artist*. She had to project the right image—that of a modern, unconventional woman; a free spirit. A woman who did not conform to the rules.

She had concluded early on that in art photography, as in every other area of life, looking the part was 75 percent of the challenge. Most of the rest involved the same quality it took to walk boldly past a police line armed with only her Speed Graphic—attitude.

Chapter 4

At precisely one o'clock that afternoon she stood in the back room of the Penfield Gallery trying to conceal her tension, afraid to let herself get too hopeful. Fenella Penfield was acknowledged as a force of nature in the Southern California art world. Her verdicts were treated as law by serious collectors and fashionable members of the public.

At the moment, she was bent over the first of the three prints Vivian had brought to show her. She studied it for a long moment and then straightened abruptly.

"Forget the landscape," Fenella said. She pushed the picture of the storm-tossed Pacific aside as if it were yesterday's newspaper. "It's dramatic enough but unless you're Ansel Adams, no one is interested in landscapes. They're inherently boring."

Vivian winced inwardly but she had been brought up in the hothouse social world of San Francisco. She knew how to conceal strong emotions. There was no point arguing about the marketability of the picture. It was Fenella Penfield's gallery, after all. Her opinion was the only one that mattered.

Penfield was in her mid-thirties, a tall, thin, angular woman with a razor-sharp profile and the tight face of a dedicated smoker. She wore her dark hair in a severe chignon that emphasized her dramatically made-up eyes. She clearly relished the process of savaging the delicate feelings of vulnerable artists. She was well aware that she could make or break a career and seemed to believe that she had a divinely inspired mission to purify the art world.

The Penfield Gallery was located in a fashionable shopping district. The area had once been an exclusive neighborhood of large, two-story homes built in the Spanish colonial style. Fenella knew how to cater to her wealthy clientele. She always took care to park her elegant red Duesenberg directly in front of the entrance. The expensive vehicle, with its long lines and miles of gleaming chrome, was a visible symbol of class and luxury. It might as well have spelled out the message *Don't Even Think of Entering This Gallery Unless You Are Rich* in neon letters. The upscale tone was carried through to the grand entrance and the stark white-walled showroom.

The back room of the gallery looked as if it had once been part of a grand reception hall designed to host large parties and social gatherings. Unlike the showroom in front, however, it was a typical gallery back room. Vivian had seen enough of them in the course of showing her portfolio to know. Framed and unframed paintings were stacked against the walls. Cartons and crates were piled on the floor. Large sculptures loomed in the shadows. The workbenches were littered with framing tools and materials.

At the rear of the shop a handsome staircase led upstairs to a balcony that ran the width of the room. There were more pictures and boxes stacked on that level.

Vivian understood why clients were impressed with the Penfield Gallery and she could certainly appreciate the smart marketing. But she had been raised in a wealthy household, a home filled with genuine Old World antiques, fine carpets, and beautifully polished furniture. It took a lot more than a handsome car out front and the severe, ultra-modern décor of the showroom to impress her.

Fenella contemplated the image of the Adelina Beach pier in the morning light. An aging, dust-coated Ford was parked near the beach. A man and a woman stood next to the vehicle, gripping the hands of their two small, barefoot children. Everything about the couple radiated a mix of exhaustion and resolute determination. The children were wide-eyed and excited by the sight of the ocean.

It was clear that the family had not come to California on a vacation. They were there for the same reasons so many others had made the journey. Whatever lay behind them was worse than the uncertainty of their future in the West. They had come to find a new start; a new life.

"I call it *Finding California*," Vivian said.

The photo had been entirely unscripted. She had come across the family on her way home after selling a late-night murder scene to Eddy at the *Adelina Beach Courier.* The sight of the weary family gazing out at the pier and the horizon beyond had made her pull over to the curb. The couple had agreed to let her take the picture. Afterward she had given them the twenty dollars she had just collected for the crime scene shots. They had acted as if it was a small fortune.

"I'm not the Farm Security Administration," Fenella announced. "I have no interest in hanging pictures designed to promote Mr. Roosevelt's New Deal." She tossed the photo aside. "Besides, everyone who arrives in California on Route Sixty-Six takes a picture of the beach and the pier. I was hoping you would have something more interesting to show me."

Vivian braced herself and reached into her portfolio. She took out the last picture and put it on the table. It was the first in her new series of experimental photographs.

Fenella's face tightened. Her bony shoulders tensed. Her eyes narrowed. For a long moment she stared at the picture. Vivian told herself that might be a good sign.

"It's the first in a series of limited editions," she ventured. "I'm calling it *Men*."

When Fenella did not reply, just continued to gaze, transfixed, at the picture, Vivian took the risk of opening her inner vision a little, just enough to get some notion of what to expect.

The back room of the gallery and everything in it blurred as she focused on Fenella. She caught a fleeting glimpse of energy shivering around the other woman. It was the color of a hot sunset on the eve of a violent storm. Rage.

Stunned, Vivian hastily shut down her sixth sense and gripped the edge of the table for support. Her pulse was skittering and she was breathing too quickly. She had been braced for a dismissive rejection but not for red-hot anger.

This was the problem with using her other vision outside the controlled environment of her studio. Glimpsing the raw energy of someone else's emotions was always unnerving.

Well, at least she now knew for certain that she would not be launching a career in art photography at the Penfield Gallery.

"You can't be serious," Fenella said at last. Anger and disgust etched each word. She flipped the picture of a nude male figure aside. "This is nothing short of pornography. They sell pictures like this from behind the counter in cheap magazine shops. Really, I am extremely disappointed, Miss Brazier. I have an opening in my upcoming exhibition. I thought I might be able to fit in one of your photographs but obviously that's not possible."

"Sorry to waste your time," Vivian said.

She started to gather up the prints.

A salesclerk appeared in the doorway. She was elegant and refined in a prim black suit. As far as Vivian had been able to determine, every member of Fenella's staff came from the same mold. Male or female, they were all elegant and refined. They all wore formal black suits.

"Yes, Miss Curry," Fenella said. "What is it?"

"I apologize for interrupting you, Miss Penfield, but Mr. Deverell is here."

Fenella frowned. "He doesn't have an appointment."

"No," Miss Curry said. "But he insists upon seeing you. He says it's about the Winston Bancroft photograph, the one from Bancroft's Woman in the Window series. He's decided that he wants to acquire it for his collection, after all."

Fenella shook her head. "Collectors. They can be so difficult. Very well, Miss Curry. Ask him to wait in my office. I'll be there in a moment."

"Yes, ma'am."

The clerk vanished.

Fenella looked at Vivian. "Morris Deverell is one of my best clients. He is obsessed with art photography."

"Photographs in the pictorial style, I take it," Vivian said. She did not bother to conceal her disapproval. "That's Winston Bancroft's style. He does mostly nude female figures, I might add."

"Bancroft's nudes are art, not porn."

"Just because he doctors his photographs in an effort to make them resemble paintings doesn't make his pictures art. No matter what he does he can't make a photograph an abstract painting. In any case, what's the point of trying to imitate another kind of art?"

Fenella gave her a stern look. "You would do well to study Bancroft's work, Miss Brazier. At least some museums and galleries such as mine are willing to hang works from the pictorial school of photography. I'm afraid the modernist style is doomed to fail." She smiled coldly. "When all is said and done it is nothing more than a form of journalism, isn't it?"

Vivian's mouth went dry. If Fenella Penfield had learned of her newspaper work, her career was truly doomed. Still . . . Fenella had not actually accused her of debasing her art by doing photojournalism. Fenella was not exactly the subtle type. If she did know the truth or if she had heard rumors, she would not have asked Vivian to show her some work.

Would she?

Not that it mattered now. Fenella had just accused her of doing pornography. That was probably lower than news photography on the respectability scale.

A figure loomed in the doorway of the back room, a man this time. He was in his mid-thirties, tall, slender, attractive in a distinguished sort of way, and athletically built. From his sleekly oiled hair to his well-cut blue blazer, expertly knotted tie, and neatly creased and cuffed trousers he was the picture of upper-class sophistication. He looked like the sort of man who played polo and golf in his spare time.

He had a folded newspaper tucked under one arm.

"Well, well, well," he said in a voice that managed to combine amused curiosity with just the right edge of ennui. "What do we have here? An artist, I suspect. The scarf is a nice touch, if I may say so. It adds a certain, shall we say, flair?"

"Mr. Deverell," Fenella said. "I wasn't expecting you this afternoon."

"I happened to be driving past the gallery and decided to pop in to see if the Bancroft was still available. I'm told it is."

"Yes, it is," Fenella said. "I asked Miss Curry to show you to my office."

"Don't blame your clerk," Morris said. "When I heard that you were talking to an artist I couldn't resist having a look for myself. I find artists fascinating."

Fenella hesitated. Vivian got the impression that she did not particularly want to make the appropriate introductions but it was obvious she had no alternative.

"This is Miss Brazier," Fenella said. "She's a photographer. Miss

Brazier, Mr. Deverell. He's an avid collector of fine art photography. The pictorial tradition."

"Miss Brazier is a photographer?" Morris's eyes glittered. "What a coincidence."

"I beg your pardon?" Vivian said.

"Under the circumstances, meeting you gives me a bit of a cold chill. A rather exciting cold chill but a chill nonetheless."

Vivian stared at him. And then she looked at Fenella, seeking guidance. Collectors were known to be an eccentric lot. She had met a few, mostly wealthy acquaintances of her parents, but the feverish excitement in Morris's eyes and his strange comment indicated that *eccentric* might not be a strong enough word to describe him. *Mentally unstable* would be more accurate.

Even Fenella, notoriously unflappable and believed to have ice in her veins, looked a little wary.

"What an odd thing to say, Mr. Deverell." She gave him a cool smile. "Please wait for me in my office. I will be with you in a moment."

Morris chuckled. "I gather you haven't seen the afternoon papers, Fenella. The Dagger Killer struck again last night."

"Yes, I heard the news on the radio this morning while I was having breakfast," Fenella said. "Ghastly business. But I don't understand what that has to do with Miss Brazier's photography."

"I see you haven't heard the latest." Morris did not take his gaze off Vivian. "According to the afternoon papers, the police have concluded that the killer is most likely a photographer. A very good photographer. An artist."

Vivian could not tell if it was lust or sick excitement she saw in his eyes. She opened her senses for a split second and glimpsed a hellish mix of toxic, twisted energy. She suddenly wanted to escape Fenella's back room as quickly as possible.

Fenella looked startled. "What on earth are you talking about, Mr. Deverell? How could the authorities possibly conclude such a thing?"

"I doubt if they figured it out on their own," Morris said. He finally took his attention off Vivian and smiled at Fenella. "Don't forget there are always a number of news photographers at a murder scene. Got a hunch one of them gave the idea to the detective in charge of the investigation. Whatever the case, the newspapers are running with the story."

"That's the press for you," Fenella said. Disdain dripped from every word. "Always happy to print the wildest speculations."

"If you will both excuse me," Vivian said, "I'll be on my way." She fastened her portfolio case and tucked it under her arm. "Thank you for your time, Miss Penfield."

"One more thing, Miss Brazier," Fenella said.

Vivian hesitated. She really did not want to hear any more about her failure as an artist but running away might make her look like a coward. Her parents had taught her to stand her ground.

"I realize you are somewhat discouraged at the moment," Fenella said, her voice gentling a little. "I'm sorry about that but I am only trying to give you some advice."

Vivian took a step toward the door. "Right. Thanks."

"I suggest you take a look at Bancroft's Woman in the Window on the way out. If you decide to change your style, I would be interested in looking at more of your work."

Vivian suppressed the urge to say, "Go to hell." It would not only be an unladylike response, it would not be very smart. Fenella Penfield, after all, ruled the art world in Adelina Beach and beyond, and she had just said that she would be willing to look at more pictures.

"I appreciate that," Vivian said.

Clutching the portfolio very tightly, she went briskly toward the doorway. Morris Deverell smiled and got out of her path.

"The world of art photographers is a small one," he said as she went past. "Wouldn't it be an interesting coincidence if the killer turns out to be someone of your acquaintance?"

"I don't think that's very likely," Vivian said.

She forced herself to walk, not run, through the showroom of the Penfield Gallery. She did not pause to study the Winston Bancroft photograph.

She did not take a deep breath until she was outside on the sidewalk.

Chapter 5

Vivian could read the headlines on the papers at the corner newsstand from halfway down the block.

DAGGER KILLER A PHOTOGRAPHER?

EXTRA: COPS THINK DAGGER KILLER
PHOTOGRAPHS HIS VICTIMS

DAGGER KILLER DERANGED PHOTOGRAPHER?

She bought a copy of every early-afternoon paper she could find and took them back to the beach house. She sat down at the small kitchen table and read each story with great care, searching for her name. The article on the front page of the *Adelina Beach Courier* was typical of the others.

Detective Archer of the Adelina Beach Police Department told reporters that the Homicide Division has a new lead in the gruesome murders that have claimed the lives of a movie star and two wealthy socialites in recent months. His investigators have concluded the killer is most likely a skilled photographer who takes pictures of his victims.

The detective went on to point out that the three people who were murdered evidently were acquainted with the killer and trusted him enough to allow him into their homes. "There was no sign of forced entry," he said. He added, "We now know a great deal about the murderer. An arrest is expected soon."

Vivian put down the last paper and half collapsed in relief. Her name had not been revealed.

But she could not get the memory of Morris Deverell's chilling words out of her head. *"Wouldn't it be an interesting coincidence if the killer turns out to be someone of your acquaintance?"*

After a while she got up and locked the front door.

Chapter 6

San Francisco

Nick Sundridge went to the window of his Victorian town house and looked out at the fog-shrouded city of San Francisco. Mentally he counted backward from ten. When he reached the number one, he went into a light trance.

He was still aware of the room and the scene on the other side of the glass, but he saw the real world in a remote, detached way, as if he was in another dimension. In a manner of speaking that was the case. He was in a waking dream, examining the scene of a murder.

The bride looked at him with her dead eyes. There was a long silk scarf wrapped around her throat. Her gown was drenched in seawater. Her hair hung in wet tendrils.

"The thing about drowning is that there is never any evidence," the dead bride said, "except for the scarf, of course. And the money. There is always a pattern, isn't there?"

Nick came out of the trance with the sure knowledge that time was running out. He glanced at the clock. He had been under for only a few minutes but he was already damp with sweat. It was always that way with the fever dreams. He dreaded the aftermath. True, it left him energized but it was not a good energy. It was the ominous rush that came with the knowledge he might already be too late. The sensation haunted him on every new case these days, regardless of whether it was warranted, a legacy of the near disaster on the rooftop of the hotel a year earlier.

He reminded himself that on this occasion he had a little time. Not much, however. A couple of hours maybe.

He grabbed a towel to mop his forehead while he took slow, steady, deep breaths and forced himself to think strategically, not with his emotions. He was actually pretty good when it came to the logic of a case. Emotions, not so much. Speed was critical, but if he made the wrong move, the new bride would die.

When he was sure he had his senses under control he draped the towel around his neck and moved barefoot across the carpet to one of the two long tables that comprised the only furniture in the meditation chamber. The space had originally been designed as a dining room but a man who lived alone and did his own cooking had no need of a formal dining room.

He was not alone in the chamber. Rex was stretched out under the table, waiting patiently. Now he bounded to his feet, ears pricked, and trotted forward. Ready to hunt.

"It's okay, pal." Nick rubbed the special spot behind the dog's ears. "Dreamtime is over. I'm awake."

In the shadows of the darkened room Rex looked more like a wolf than a dog. He had arrived in Nick's life almost a year earlier, not long after Patricia had left. Nick had been driving to Santa Rosa to visit his uncle and had stopped at a gas station. Rex had appeared from behind the garage. He had padded up to Nick and thrust his nose into Nick's hand.

Nick gave the dog a couple of pats and figured that was the end of it. But Rex had evidently made a decision. When Nick opened the driver's side door of the car the dog jumped up onto the leather seat, stepped over the gearshift, and took up a position on the passenger's side of the vehicle.

Nick looked at the gas station attendant. "Your dog?"

"Nope." The attendant adjusted his billed cap and grunted. "Stray. Someone probably wanted to get rid of him so they took him for a long ride and dumped him out on the side of the road. Happens a lot. Costs money to feed a dog. What with the bad economy and all no one wants to waste food on a mutt that can't earn his keep. Besides, it's not like he's Rin-Tin-Tin."

"What do you mean?" Nick asked.

The attendant shrugged. "Seems smart enough but as far as I can tell he doesn't do any tricks. Won't even sit up and beg. Just stares at you like you're not real bright. I feed him occasionally and keep a bowl of water for him but mostly he eats out of garbage cans. He sleeps around back of the garage. Comes out every time a car pulls into the station. It's like he's been waiting for someone to show up."

Nick opened the passenger side door, silently inviting Rex to vacate the vehicle. Rex ignored him. Nick reached into the car with the intention of hauling the dog out. He changed his mind as soon as his hand settled on the scruff of Rex's neck. He got the sensation that he and the dog had a few things in common. A couple of misfits looking for the place they belonged.

Nick closed the passenger side door.

"Looks like whoever he was waiting for just showed up," he said to the attendant.

He climbed behind the wheel and got back on the road to Santa Rosa.

Unlike Patricia, Rex didn't have a problem with the trances. He didn't look at Nick as if he thought Nick was mentally unbalanced. He accepted the fever dreams with the equanimity that only a dog could summon.

Nick wished that he could deal with the trances in the same casual manner. But the truth was they sometimes scared him. Every time he went into a dream meditation he sensed he was playing with fire. Uncle Pete had explained the visions were a manifestation of the Sundridge family curse.

Pete Sundridge had raised him after his parents had been killed in a car crash. Nick had been thirteen when he had gone to live with his uncle. The weird trances had begun striking at odd moments. Back at the start they had been unpredictable and terrifying. Pete had sat down with him and explained the problem in a straightforward fashion.

❦

"You've got to figure out how to deal with them because they're going to make your life a living hell if you don't. Actually, they'll probably make your life a living hell at times anyway. Here's the thing you need to remember: You can't tell anyone else about them. People will think you're crazy."

"Maybe I am crazy," Nick said.

"The dreams could drive you straight into an asylum but it doesn't have to be that way. You can control them if you put your mind to it. You're not the first Sundridge man to get the curse. The others survived. Mostly."

❦

Nick switched on a lamp and contemplated the items that he had arranged on the surface of the workbench. There was a long silk scarf, a brochure advertising the delights of a transatlantic voyage from New York to London, a couple of photos of smiling brides, and several newspaper clippings covering two East Coast society weddings that had taken place in the past three years.

Next he studied the reports of the tragic deaths of the two brides.

Both had died in the course of transatlantic voyages from New York to London. Both had been swept overboard during a storm. The grieving husbands had inherited a great deal of money thanks to insurance policies that had been taken out shortly after the weddings.

There were no photos of the husbands in the papers, but in the modern age everyone had a camera. Sure enough, the families of both brides had a few snapshots of their daughters that included their fiancés. Yesterday copies of the photos had been delivered to Nick. He had examined them closely with the aid of a magnifying glass. There was no question but that the groom in both pictures was the same man.

The brides were all descended from quietly respectable families. They did not move in the most exclusive circles. Weddings at the apex of the social world were scrutinized by a great many people, including family lawyers who knew how to verify the finances of both sides. Engagements frequently lasted a year and there were always a lot of extravagant parties and photographs of the future groom along the way.

Nick was sure the man he was hunting preferred to remain out of sight as much as possible. Gilford Norburn stalked his prey in the backwaters of society.

Nick contemplated the scenes he had summoned in the trance and then he went to the other table. Another smiling bride. This time the wedding was in San Francisco. The local papers had dutifully recorded it with a small picture of the bride. Again there was no photo of the husband.

He glanced at the calendar and confirmed a couple of critical dates. Then he picked up the phone and called the client. It was just after dawn but Eleanor Barrows answered on the first ring. It was evident that she had not been asleep.

"Yes?" she said. Anxiety vibrated in her voice.

"You're right, Mrs. Barrows," Nick said. "Your niece's new husband is bad news. I'm very certain that he plans to kill Linda and soon."

"*Kill Linda?* Dear heaven, I knew there was something off about Gilford Norburn. I was sure he was just after the house and the money her father left me. I took steps to protect both, at least until I'm gone. At that point she inherits everything, of course. It didn't occur to me Norburn might murder Linda. I assumed I was the one he might try to get rid of."

"He doesn't need to get rid of you because, if he followed his pattern, he took out a large insurance policy on Linda." Nick looked at the items scattered across the workbenches. "There is *always* a life insurance policy."

"I don't know what to say. I never considered he might insure her life."

"I wouldn't be surprised if the policy is for an amount that is worth more than Linda's future inheritance. They are scheduled to sail for Hawaii today."

"Yes. At noon."

"At some point along the way Norburn will use a scarf to throttle Linda and then he will toss her overboard. The ship may be able to recover the body but it won't matter. There won't be enough evidence to arrest Norburn."

"Dear heavens. How can you possibly know all this?"

"Because he has done this before. At least twice back East. Perhaps more often. He's established a pattern. I saw it when I—" He stopped because any attempt to describe how he had tracked down the two East Coast brides would involve trying to explain the fever dreams. "I saw it when I examined the evidence," he said smoothly.

Nothing out of the ordinary, ma'am. Just the usual private investigation methods and a little help from the Sundridge family curse.

But he didn't say that aloud. Thanks to crime fiction magazines such as *Black Mask* and Hollywood's version of the private investigator, the public had developed two distinct images of the profession. There was the sophisticated, fast-talking couple who moved in elite circles and amused themselves solving crimes at the highest level of society.

The other image, the one that was rapidly taking hold, was that of the tough, ruthless loner who did it for the money and whose methods did not stand close scrutiny. He was pretty sure his clients put him in that category, which was a good thing because they didn't ask too many questions.

"This is ghastly news," Eleanor said. "How can I convince Linda she's married to a murderer before she boards the ship? She will never believe me."

"I might be able to persuade her husband to betray himself," Nick said.

As understatements went, that was a big one. But there was no reason to alarm the client further. Eleanor Barrows was already upset. If he explained what he planned to do, she might fly into an outright panic. She might even conclude that she had hired a mentally unbalanced private investigator.

"Why would he confess?" Mrs. Barrows was in tears now. "He has no reason to do that. He's a monster."

He'll talk because I know his weak point now and I will apply pressure, Nick thought. But he did not say that aloud.

"I can be very persuasive," he said instead. "I'm going to hang up now, Mrs. Barrows. I have to get to your niece's house before she and her husband leave for the port. It would be much more difficult to deal with this situation there. Norburn might be able to slip away in the crowd."

He put down the receiver, stuffed the photos and newspaper clippings into an envelope, and took his gun and shoulder holster off the top shelf of the kitchen cupboard. He buckled on the holster, selected a blazer that was cut in the fashionable drape style so that it concealed the gun, and headed for the door.

Rex bounded after him. Nick opened the passenger side door of the custom-built maroon Packard convertible. The dog leaped up onto the leather seat. He was vibrating with eagerness.

Nick got behind the wheel and fired up the powerful engine.

It was still very early when he arrived in the quiet residential neighborhood a short time later. He cruised slowly past the house where Linda and Gilford Norburn lived. There was a light on in the kitchen and in one of the upstairs bedrooms. The couple was awake but the shades were still closed. There was no vehicle in the driveway. Eleanor had mentioned that Norburn drove an expensive European speedster. It was most likely still parked in the garage behind the house.

Nick continued to the corner and pulled over on a side street. He shut off the engine and opened the door. Rex followed him out. Nick hesitated and then reached back into the car for the leash. Rex often made people uneasy but sometimes that proved a useful distraction. Nick hooked the leather lead to the dog's collar.

"Try to look adorable," Nick said. "We don't want to frighten the neighbors."

Rex ignored him.

"You aren't exactly the adorable type, are you?" Nick said. "Neither am I. Probably why we ended up together. All right, let's case the joint. It's always good to get the lay of the land before you confront a guy who has no problem killing women."

A service lane ran behind the house. Nick and Rex made their way along the path and gained access to the grounds by means of a garden gate. There was an unattached garage. Judging from the size and the barn door–style entrance, it had probably once served as a carriage house.

Nick went inside the garage. A sleek speedster loomed in the shadows. In Nick's experience most people left the key in the ignition. It turned out that Gilford Norburn was no exception.

Nick pocketed the key. In addition to housing the speedster, the garage served as a tool and gardening shed. Rakes, trowels, shears, and watering cans were neatly arranged on a workbench that stood against one wall.

A roll of heavy garden twine caught his eye. He used a pair of shears to cut off a long length of it.

A few minutes later, satisfied with the arrangements he had made, he and Rex went around to the front of the house. Nick pressed the bell. Footsteps sounded in the hall. The door opened. The man who looked out was in his late thirties. He was mostly dressed for the day in a pair of buff-colored trousers and a white shirt. He had not yet put on a tie.

He eyed Rex with an expression that was somewhere between wariness and irritation. Either Rex was not doing a very good job of looking adorable or else Norburn did not like dogs in general. Nick was willing to bet on the latter.

"Gilford Norburn?" Nick said in the tone he used when he was playing the role of a salesman or a messenger.

"I'm Norburn. Who are you and what are you doing on my front step at this hour? If you're selling something you can get lost."

Gilford started to close the door.

"I have a message for Mrs. Linda Norburn," Nick said. "It concerns a member of her family."

Gilford paused in the act of shutting the door. He narrowed his eyes. "Mrs. Norburn is my wife. She's upstairs, packing for a voyage to Hawaii. She doesn't have time to talk to you. Give me the message. I'll see that she gets it."

"I was instructed to give the message to Mrs. Norburn personally," Nick said. "It concerns an inheritance from a distant relative."

That got Gilford's attention. He opened the door wide. There was an avid glint of excitement in his eyes.

"I was under the impression my wife had only one living relative," he said. "Her aunt."

"Your information is wrong. I'm afraid I'm not at liberty to discuss the particulars with anyone except Linda Norburn."

Light footsteps sounded in the hall behind Gilford. A woman appeared. She peered past Gilford's shoulder.

"I'm Linda Norburn," she said. "I heard something about a message for me."

Gilford looked annoyed. "It's all right, darling. I'm sure it's not important."

"The message concerns a death in the family," Nick said. "And an inheritance."

Linda stared at him, horrified. "Not Aunt Eleanor. I talked to her yesterday. She was in excellent health."

"If I might come inside?" Nick said. "This isn't the sort of news that should be delivered on the front step."

"Yes, of course, please come in."

"We don't know who this man is," Gilford said. He was starting to appear uneasy again.

"My name is Nick Sundridge," Nick said. "Mrs. Norburn, your aunt, Eleanor Barrows, is fine. But she sent me to tell you some very important news."

"Let him in, Gilford," Linda said.

Nick was relieved to hear the firm edge of authority in her voice. Linda was not a weak-willed individual. Norburn evidently realized he would not win the small skirmish. Reluctantly he stepped out of the way.

"The living room," Linda said. "Follow me, please."

Nick moved into the hallway. Rex accompanied him.

"The dog stays outside," Gilford ordered. "He looks vicious."

Nick motioned Rex outside. Rex obeyed. Nick dropped the leash on the front step. Rex sat down.

"Stay," Nick said.

Rex whined but he sank down on the step.

Gilford shut the door. Rex's low growl could be heard through the wooden panels.

Nick walked into the living room behind Linda. She stopped and turned to face him, her hands knotted tightly together, eyes huge with fear.

"Please tell me who died," she said.

"The good news is that the death has not yet occurred," Nick said.

"What?" Linda stared at him.

"But if I can't make you believe me, you're going to be the victim of a tragic accident at sea," Nick added.

"What the hell is going on here?" Gilford demanded. "Linda, he's crazy. We've let a madman into our house."

Nick opened the envelope and dropped the contents on the coffee table.

"Did your husband tell you that he has been married and widowed twice?" he asked.

Linda shook her head, dumbfounded. "I have no idea what you are talking about. You must have the wrong address."

"Damn right, he's got the wrong address," Gilford roared. "He's a con artist or a thief who talked his way in here to rob us. Sundridge, you had better get out of here before I call the cops."

"Go ahead and call them," Nick said. "I'm sure they'll be interested in these photos." He picked up the pictures and held them in front of Linda's face. "Meet Norburn's first two wives. Both drowned within a few months after they were married, just as you're going to drown somewhere en route to Hawaii. Did you know that your husband took out a life insurance policy on you recently?"

"You're lying," Gilford snarled. "You can't possibly know that. Furthermore, that isn't me in those pictures."

He lunged forward in an effort to grab the photos. Nick snapped them out of the way and then gave them to Linda.

Bewildered, she stared at the pictures. "Gilford, is this you in these pictures?"

"Of course not," Gilford said.

"Look at the eyes and then look at the ring on his little finger," Nick said. "It's the same one he's wearing now."

Linda inhaled, a sharp, shocked breath. She looked up from the photos. "It is you, Gilford. What is going on here? I don't understand."

"I told you, the man in those photos isn't me," Gilford said.

"I've got the telephone number of the insurance agent who sold your husband the policy on your life," Nick said to Linda. "The office opens at nine so you'll be able to verify what I'm telling you. Your husband bought the policy a month after you were married. Payable on your death. *Accidental* death, I might add. Which is why you're scheduled to go overboard. Murder isn't covered."

"All lies," Gilford snarled.

True. The part about having tracked down the insurance agent was a lie. The best you could say about it was that it was a bluff. Just one of the tactics that gave private investigators a less-than-respectable reputation. There hadn't been time to start making phone calls to every insurance company in the Los Angeles area. But there was bound to be one because it was part of the pattern.

Linda turned to Nick. "My aunt asked you to investigate Gilford, didn't she?"

"Darling, your aunt disapproves of me," Gilford said. "You know that. This is some kind of setup. She's trying to make you distrust me."

Outside a car screeched to a stop in the street. Linda rushed to the window and pulled the shade aside.

"It's Aunt Eleanor," she said.

"The police will be able to verify the identity of the man in those photographs," Nick said. "They might not be able to prove that Norburn murdered his first two wives but they can certainly confirm his first two marriages."

"That proves nothing," Gilford raged.

"Among other things it proves fraud." Nick paused. "Unless you disclosed those first two marriages to Linda?"

"No," Linda said. She turned away from the window to stare at Gilford. The photos in her hands shook a little. "He never told me that he had been married."

Gilford made fists of his hands. His eyes were very hard and very cold. "My past has nothing to do with us, Linda. Sundridge can't prove anything."

"I don't need to prove anything," Nick said. "The police will handle that end of things. In a couple of days the story will be front-page news on every paper in the country. The press loves a good society murder story. A court of law might not be able to get a conviction but that won't be necessary. You'll be tried and convicted in the press."

A loud pounding sounded on the door. Rex started barking furiously.

"Linda," Eleanor shouted, her voice muffled. "You must listen to me. Norburn intends to murder you at sea. I've called the police. They'll be here in a few minutes."

Linda started down the hall toward the front door. Unfortunately her path took her very close to Norburn.

"No," Nick said.

Why in hell couldn't things ever go according to plan? Why did there always have to be a miscalculation?

Even as he asked the question, he knew the answer. People. They were invariably the problem. Unfortunately for a man in his line of work, people—specifically clients—were the ones who paid the bills.

He moved quickly, trying to intercept Linda, but it was too late. Norburn grabbed her and pinned her close with an arm around her throat. At the same time he took a folding pocketknife out of his trousers. He flicked the blade open and put the tip to Linda's throat.

It was not a big knife but it didn't take a large blade to do lethal damage.

The front door opened. Eleanor appeared. Rex raced inside.

"Rex," Nick said quietly.

The dog rushed to his side and took up a position next to him.

"The door was unlocked," Eleanor said. She stopped, taking in the situation at a glance. "Let her go, you bastard."

Rex growled.

"Keep that damned dog away from me or I'll cut Linda's throat," Norburn said.

"Rex," Nick said. "Stay."

Rex obeyed but he shivered with battle-ready tension.

"Linda and I are leaving," Norburn said. He backed away, Linda locked against him, the blade of the pocketknife at her throat. He edged toward the rear of the house.

"I assume you're going to try to get away in your car," Nick said.

"That's right," Norburn said. "My speedster can outrun any police car. If anyone tries to stop me, Linda will be a dead woman."

"You'll be needing your key," Nick said. He held up the key he had taken from the ignition.

Norburn stared at the key in disbelief. "You son of a bitch. Give the key to Linda. Go on, give it to her, you bastard."

"Sure," Nick said.

He walked forward. Rex paced beside him.

"Stop," Norburn yelped. "Don't come any closer."

"Make up your mind," Nick said.

Norburn angled his jaw toward a console table. "Put the key on top of that table. Linda will pick it up."

Nick set the key down on the polished wooden table. Norburn edged toward the table. He did not loosen his hold on Linda.

"Get it," he told her.

She reached out and picked up the key, fingers visibly shaking.

Gilford dragged her out of the living room. They both disappeared down the hall.

Eleanor turned to Nick, stricken. "He'll kill her."

"No," Nick said. "He won't. She's his insurance policy. She's no good to him dead."

But he knew he was taking chances now. He had a talent for predicting actions and calculating outcomes but Norburn was wound up very tight. Rage and panic created an explosive tension. People who lost control were highly volatile, less predictable.

Nick and Rex reached the kitchen just in time to see Norburn and Linda at the back door. Norburn no longer had Linda by the throat. Securing a captive in that way was awkward, after all, especially when you were trying to run. He now had his fist clamped around Linda's upper right arm.

"Open the door," Norburn ordered.

She obeyed. Norburn charged through first, intent on pulling her after him.

The toe of his shoe caught on the garden twine that Nick had strung across the back door a few inches off the floor.

Norburn yelped. In a frantic effort to keep his balance, he released Linda, dropped the pocketknife, and flailed wildly. But it was too late. He had too much momentum.

He toppled forward, slamming chest-first on the floor of the porch with enough force to send a shudder through the wooden boards.

"Guard," Nick said to Rex.

The dog leaped forward and took up a threatening post near Gilford's head.

"Get that dog away from me," Gilford said.

Everyone, including Rex, ignored him.

Nick stripped off his necktie and crouched to bind Norburn's wrists behind his back.

Wailing sirens shattered the early-morning silence of the neighborhood.

"The police are here," Eleanor said. "Thank heavens. Linda, are you all right, dear?"

"Yes." Linda wrapped her arms around her midsection. She gazed at Gilford. Shock and disbelief were starting to give way to fury. "You were right about him, Aunt Eleanor."

Eleanor put a comforting arm around her. "I'm so sorry, darling."

Nick got to his feet.

"You can't prove anything," Gilford hissed.

But his voice was weaker now, as if he was trying to convince himself.

"All I have to do is make sure that every newspaper in the city knows that you married Linda under false pretenses and took out a life insurance policy on her, just as you did after you married those other women," Nick said. "You lied about your name. You lied about your previous marriages. You lied about your finances."

"You don't know anything about my finances," Gilford roared. "That's private information."

"I'm sure Linda's lawyer will be able to get those details," Nick said.

Gilford's jaw clenched. "My wife doesn't have a lawyer."

"You're wrong, Norburn," Eleanor said. "Linda does have a lawyer—my personal attorney."

Two uniformed officers appeared around the corner of the house.

"No one answered the door," one of them said. "Thought we'd better have a look back here. What's going on?"

Eleanor pointed at Gilford. "That man on the floor is my niece's husband. He was planning to murder her for the insurance money. Mr. Sundridge stopped him."

The officer's eyes narrowed in a thoughtful expression. "Nick Sundridge?"

"That's right," Nick said.

"Heard Detective Teague talk about you. You're the private detective who was involved in that shoot-out on top of the hotel a year ago. Something about a fight over a woman."

"That's right," Nick said. There was no point trying to explain the nuances of what had happened on the hotel rooftop. The public's impressions had been fixed in stone, thanks to the press.

"I hired Mr. Sundridge to investigate my niece's husband," Eleanor explained.

Linda raised her chin. "My aunt is right. My husband was planning to kill me."

"Don't listen to my wife," Norburn said. "She's mentally unstable. She needs help. I'm going to arrange for her to enter an asylum."

"Nonsense," Eleanor said. "The only crazy thing she ever did was fall for your lies."

"Linda is my wife," Norburn said. "She can't be made to testify against me."

"That's actually not entirely accurate," Nick said.

But no one was listening to him.

Linda glared at Norburn. "I won't be your wife for much longer, Gilford."

"You can't divorce me," Gilford said. "You don't have any grounds. I'll fight you every step of the way. All I have to do is prove you're mentally unbalanced."

"There is no need for a messy divorce," Eleanor said coldly. "My lawyer will file for an annulment immediately."

"On what grounds?" Gilford yelled, his voice rising.

"Fraud," Nick said. "Among other things, you married Linda under false pretenses."

"Don't worry, Linda," Eleanor said. "With an annulment it will be as if the marriage never happened."

Not quite, Nick thought.

The annulment of his short marriage to Patricia hadn't been exactly magical. The problem was that, while the proceedings in such matters were always handled privately, everyone knew there were only a handful of legal grounds that could be used to annul a marriage. Fraud was one of them. So were bigamy and incest.

But there was another qualifying reason, the one that inevitably invited the most speculation and gossip: *incapacity*. It could imply insanity. It could also be interpreted as the husband's inability to consummate the marriage.

In the past year he had discovered that rumors of either condition were pretty much guaranteed to destroy a man's personal life.

He rested a hand on Rex's head and watched the officers lead Gilford Norburn away in handcuffs.

"Maybe we should think about moving," he said to the dog.

Chapter 7

Adelina Beach

The picture was perfect. Just what the client had ordered.

Vivian released the shutter. She stepped back from the tripod and the large view camera and smiled at the woman posing in the big, fan-back wicker chair.

"I think you will be very pleased with your portrait, Miss Frampton," she said. "I'll have it ready for you on Wednesday."

Anna Frampton rose from the thronelike chair. She had requested something in the modern style. *I don't want to look stiff and straitlaced like my grandmother,* she said when she booked the sitting.

Vivian had opened her inner eye while they discussed the effect that Anna wished to project. She had sensed a daring, defiant energy shimmering in the atmosphere around the woman. At the end of the meeting Vivian had directed Anna to return for the sitting dressed in menswear-style trousers, a leather flight jacket, and a pair of boots.

Vivian had done the makeup, going for movie-star drama. She had posed Anna lounging in the corner of the big chair, one leg thrown casually over an arm, and then she had fiddled with the lights and made tiny adjustments to the drape of the trousers while she coaxed Anna into a sultry pout that would have done credit to Hepburn or Garbo.

When Vivian studied her subject through the viewfinder she saw an unconventional woman infused with an intense sensuality and a taste for adventure. The final picture would violate all the traditional rules of a formal portrait but she was sure the client would be thrilled.

"I can't wait to see it," Anna said. "You made me feel like Amelia Earhart."

Earhart and her navigator, Fred Noonan, had been lost at sea several months earlier. The search for the wreckage of Earhart's plane had been officially called off but hints that she and Noonan had survived continued to surface in the press. The public's interest showed no signs of waning. Dead or alive, it was clear the daring lady pilot was on her way to becoming a legend.

Anna unwrapped the borrowed scarf and handed it to Vivian. "It will be interesting to see how Jeremy reacts to the portrait."

"Jeremy?"

Anna grimaced. "Jeremy McKinnon, the man I'm supposed to marry. He's a banker. Swears he's madly in love with me. Maybe after he sees me in the aviator jacket he'll have second thoughts."

"You're hoping Jeremy will take one look at your portrait and decide you're not the woman he wants for a wife?"

"It will be easier if he's the one who changes his mind," Anna said. "I'd rather not be the one to do it this time."

"This time?"

"I've already wriggled out of two engagements. I'm afraid my family is starting to see a pattern. To be honest, Miss Brazier, I find the thought of marrying Jeremy or anyone else very depressing."

Vivian smiled. "I understand. Don't worry. When Jeremy sees this portrait, I can promise you that he will realize that if he goes through with the marriage he will have to deal with a very modern woman."

"That should do it," Anna said cheerfully. "Between you and me, I'm certain that Jeremy is terrified of modern women."

Vivian ushered her outside and watched her drive off in a racy little convertible. When the car disappeared around the corner she closed the door and, after a moment's hesitation, locked it.

It had been two days since the encounter with Morris Deverell in the Penfield Gallery but she was still feeling deeply uneasy. The fact that there had been no arrest in the Dagger Killer murders in spite of Detective Archer's optimism did nothing to calm her nerves.

She went back into the studio, took the film holder out of the camera, and hurried into the darkroom. She could not wait to see the results of the portrait. Anna Frampton was an important client who moved in fashionable circles. If she was pleased with the finished picture there would be referrals.

Vivian filled the trays with the chemicals and the stop bath, closed the door, pulled the black curtain around the workbench, and turned off the lamp. Working in the dark, using only her sense of touch, she started to open the holder to remove the film.

A draft of air under the door made her stop abruptly. Instinctively she closed the holder while she tried to understand what had just iced her nerves. The front door was locked. So was the kitchen door. But she had left some windows open. The studio would have been unbearably hot otherwise; the client would have been damp with perspiration halfway through the sitting.

I should have closed and locked the windows.

This was ridiculous. She was overreacting.

She stood very still, listening intently. She thought she heard a floorboard squeak. The sense that she was no longer alone in the house built rapidly until it became overpowering. She could hardly breathe. The urge to run, to hide, to escape surged through her. She was trapped in the darkroom. She had to get out. Now.

She put down the holder and reached for the edge of the heavy curtain.

The door of the darkroom crashed open just as she started to pull the thick fabric aside. A man loomed in the entrance, silhouetted against the daylight streaming through the windows of the kitchen behind him.

Morris Deverell had a dagger in one hand. She didn't need to employ her inner eye to sense the waves of sick excitement emanating from him. He smiled.

"How did you figure it out?" he said.

He did not wait for an answer. He lunged forward, the point of the dagger aimed at her midsection.

A strange sense of intense focus flashed through her. Time slowed. It was as if she was observing the scene through the lens of a camera.

She yanked the blackout curtain back into place just as Morris rushed toward her.

He yelped in fury when the point of the dagger ripped through the fabric. For a few seconds he struggled to free the blade even as he used his free hand to haul the curtain aside.

Vivian was waiting, the tray of developer in her hands. She hurled the strong chemicals straight into his face. Morris grunted and reared back, instinctively raising his free hand in a belated attempt to protect his eyes. She followed up with the tray of fixer.

"You crazy bitch," Morris roared. He wiped frantically at his eyes. "You're a dead woman. Do you understand? You're *dead*."

But he was partially blinded by the chemicals. He instinctively retreated a step and came up against the heavy curtain. He waved the blade in wide arcs, fending her off while he attempted to clear his vision.

Vivian seized the heavy steel enlarger easel and threw it, discus style, at Morris. The corner of the metal plate caught him in the chest.

Yowling in pain and rage, he managed to free himself from the blackout curtain.

He turned and staggered out the door and into the kitchen.

Vivian rushed after him because there was no other way out of the darkroom. She could not let him trap her there again.

She reached the kitchen in time to see Deverell stumbling out the door. The small backyard was enclosed with a waist-high wooden fence. It was doubtful he would try to scale it in his current panicky state. It was more likely he would use the garden gate that opened onto a walkway that led around the side of the house to the street.

The bastard was going to get away.

Driven by the violent energy of panic and fury, Vivian changed course and ran toward the front door. She got it open just in time to see Deverell emerge from the side of the house and veer toward the sidewalk in a shambling run. He was using both hands to wipe his eyes now. He had evidently dropped the dagger.

A tall, muscular young man was coming up the sidewalk, heading toward Vivian's front door. Roland Jennings had come directly from the lifeguard station. He wore only a pair of swimming trunks. He had the kind of body that made both men and women look twice. His chest appeared to have been hewn from granite, thanks to hours of exercise on the nearby stretch of sand known as Muscle Beach.

He was Vivian's afternoon client.

Roland stopped, bewildered by the sight of a half-blind Deverell staggering toward him.

"Stop him, Roland," Vivian shouted. "That's the Dagger Killer."

Roland Jennings did not hesitate. His job as a lifeguard had accustomed him to reacting swiftly in emergencies. He grabbed the back of Deverell's elegantly cut jacket and hoisted him off his feet.

"My eyes," Deverell shrieked. "I need a doctor."

Roland ignored him. "Are you okay, Miss Brazier?"

"Yes," she said, panting for breath. "He just tried to murder me. Hang on to him while I call the cops."

"Sure," Roland said.

He gave Deverell a ferocious shaking.

"My eyes," Morris shrieked again, his feet dangling several inches off the ground. "She tried to blind me."

Vivian's next-door neighbor Betty Spalding, a retired schoolteacher, came out onto the front step. She wiped her hands on her apron.

"What's going on?" she asked.

"It's the Dagger Killer," Vivian said.

Betty's eyes widened. "Good heavens. He looks like such a nice man."

A few more neighbors appeared.

"Whatever you do, don't let him get away," Vivian said to Roland.

"Don't worry, Miss Brazier," Roland said. "I've got him."

"My eyes," Morris yelled. He struggled in Roland's iron grip. "Get me some water. I'm going blind."

"Bring him over here," Mr. Anderson said. "I'll use my garden hose to wash out his eyes."

Vivian rushed back into the house and called the police. On the way out the front door she grabbed her Speed Graphic and an extra film holder. She would deal with the shock to her nerves later. In that moment she had to stay focused.

She might like to call herself an artist but she paid the bills with her photojournalism work. There was only one word to describe the golden opportunity that had just been presented to her.

Exclusive.

Chapter 8

DAGGER KILLER ESCAPES, FOUND DEAD

Morris Deverell, arrested yesterday afternoon on murder charges, escaped the hospital where he was taken for treatment. Early this morning his body was found on the rocks below Sunset Point. Authorities believe that Deverell was hitchhiking and was struck by a passing motorist traveling at high speed. The driver did not stop at the scene. The impact sent the body over the edge of the bluff, where it was discovered.

Detective Archer of the Adelina Beach Police Department announced that, in addition to an extensive collection of antique daggers, several pieces of expensive photography equipment were discovered in Deverell's large house on Pacific Lane.

When she finished the article in the *Adelina Beach Courier*, Vivian allowed herself a moment to admire the photo. It showed Roland Jennings in a classic Charles Atlas pose with his feet braced wide apart, one fist on his hip, the other holding Deverell aloft. She had written the caption for Eddy and he had used it unchanged. LOCAL HERO CATCHES DAGGER KILLER. Per her customary demand, there was no photo credit. She was pretty sure the picture would go national.

The phone rang just as Vivian was about to turn to page two of the newspaper. She got up from the breakfast table and went into the studio to pick up the receiver.

"Is it true?" Lyra asked. "Is that horrible man really dead?"

"Yes," Vivian said.

"Thank goodness. The San Francisco press is reporting that the police found a collection of daggers and a lot of expensive photography equipment in a locked room in his house. It's just as you predicted, Viv."

"I know. We can all relax now."

"Luckily Mother and Father are still in London. I doubt if the news will make it into the British papers. Even if it does, your name doesn't appear anywhere in the reports in the San Francisco papers. I checked all of them this morning. There's a reference to the fact that the killer was arrested in Adelina Beach but his intended victim is described as a single woman living alone. It says the woman bravely drove off her attacker by throwing some strong household cleaning agent into his eyes."

Vivian glanced at the front page of the *Adelina Beach Courier*. "That's what the local paper says, too. It was Detective Archer's idea to give the press that story. He was trying to protect me."

"From what?"

"Archer understands that if my name gets into the papers, one thing will lead to another and sooner or later my night shift work as a photo-journalist will become public knowledge. If that happens my art career will be doomed."

"Fingers crossed that you can keep this quiet," Lyra said.

"You sound doubtful."

"Let's just say I'm not hopeful."

Vivian sighed. "At least the parents don't know yet."

"Sooner or later they will have to be told the truth," Lyra warned.

"I know. I'll tell them when they get home. By then the story will be old news."

"That isn't going to lessen the shock."

"You know, I could really use a dose of optimism this morning. I didn't sleep well last night. Every time I closed my eyes I saw Deverell coming at me with that damned dagger."

"Oh, Viv, that's horrible. Maybe you should come home to San Francisco, just for a while."

Something in her voice sent a shiver of concern through Vivian.

"Lyra, what's wrong?"

"What's wrong?" Lyra's voice rose. "I'll tell you what's wrong. You were nearly murdered yesterday afternoon. In case you weren't aware of it, that sort of thing tends to rattle a sister's nerves."

"Okay, calm down." Vivian sought for a distraction. "How are the plans for the engagement party going?"

"Fine."

"Fine? That's all you can say? You're going to marry the man you've loved from afar ever since you were a young girl. You don't sound particularly excited."

"I'm still trying to deal with the fact that I almost lost my sister to a madman with a dagger yesterday. If our situations were reversed, how would you feel this morning?"

Vivian took a deep breath. "You're right. Sorry. I guess I'm still a little unnerved myself. I just want to be sure that marriage to Hamilton is what you really want."

"Hamilton is perfect," Lyra said. "Mother and Father adore him. Father says he's the right man to take control of the company someday."

"Father is wrong. You're the right person to take control of the business. We both know that."

"That is never going to happen," Lyra said. "Father is very old-fashioned about such things. He loves us but the idea of a woman running a shipping business is beyond him."

She sounded resigned, not bitter, Vivian thought. Lyra had evidently reconciled herself to her future.

"I know," Vivian said. She tried to think of something positive to say but nothing occurred.

"Hamilton does listen to me when I talk about business subjects," Lyra continued. She was very earnest now. "Unlike Father, he is very modern in his thinking, especially when it comes to women. He respects my opinions. He says he intends to consult with me on important matters when it comes to Brazier Pacific. I'm sure he will be open to my advice."

Alarm jolted through Vivian. "Lyra, please don't tell me you're marrying Hamilton because you want to help run Brazier Pacific. I really don't think that's a good idea."

"Don't be silly," Lyra said firmly. "I love Hamilton. He's absolutely perfect. Just ask the parents. Oh dear, I've got to run. I have a tennis game with Marsha this morning."

"Lyra, wait—"

There was a click and the line went dead.

Vivian placed the receiver gently in the cradle. She knew Lyra better than anyone. Something was wrong.

Chapter 9

Jonathan Treyherne read the headlines in the *Adelina Beach Courier* while he sipped his morning coffee from a fine china cup. Morris Deverell, the Dagger Killer, was dead. The public could relax, at least until the next insane murderer hit the front pages. There would always be another madman armed with a gun or a knife or a garrote who would arise to terrify the good citizens of the towns and cities across the nation.

There was never a shortage of crazies, Treyherne thought.

His elderly housekeeper appeared in the doorway. "More coffee, Mr. Treyherne?"

"No, thank you, Mrs. Geddes. That will be all this morning." Jonathan set the paper aside and rose from the table. "I will be working in my study this morning. Please see to it that I am not disturbed."

"Yes, sir."

Jonathan started to leave the dining room. He paused in the doorway.

"By the way, I will be lunching at my club today and dining out this evening. You and Mr. Geddes may leave whenever the usual house-keeping and gardening duties are completed."

"Yes, sir. Thank you, sir."

Mrs. Geddes retreated into the kitchen.

Jonathan went into his study, then closed and locked the door. For a moment he stood quietly, thinking about the new commission. He would execute it with his customary skill and grace. Murder was an art, after all.

He always took a month to complete one of his great works, never more, never less. He did not take on commissions that left him feeling rushed. He was doing art, after all. Timing and precision were critical to a successful outcome. Each stage of the project—from research and preparation to the final result—was important but, more to the point, each stage was to be savored.

It amused him to take the client's money, but the truth was he could not have cared less about the financial payoff of each commission. The extravagant fees he charged were merely a means of keeping score.

No, what he craved—what filled him with temporary ecstasy—was the thrill of the challenge and the hot satisfaction of carrying out the perfect crime, one in which murder was never suspected.

He always made it a point to attend the funeral. Knowing that he moved among the mourners without drawing so much as a second glance provided the final, exhilarating rush. He was not a wolf in sheep's clothing, nor was he mad like the Dagger Killer. He was a mod-ern example of the true Renaissance man, a scholar poet who was skilled in the violent arts.

The inevitable gray fog of acute ennui and the sensation of empti-ness would settle on him eventually in the aftermath of completing the commission. But the prospect of a month of rising anticipation culmi-nating in a deeply felt sense of satisfaction was irresistible.

Yes, there would be a letdown afterward but he took comfort in knowing that there would always be another project. He was the best at what he did.

He lit a cigarette and crossed the room to a painting that hung on the wall—a sensual scene of two reclining nudes by Tamara de Lempicka. It was one of the few works of art that he had brought with him when he left New York.

He took down the picture, set it aside, and opened the safe. Reaching inside, he took out the leather-bound notebook and carried it to the desk.

He switched on the lamp, sat down, and opened the notebook. The slender volume was filled with his poems. He had begun writing them after his first successful commission a few years earlier. The need to record the details of his work had become overpowering.

He understood that predictability was the greatest hazard in his work. He rarely repeated a strategy or a technique. Art was, after all, about originality and vision. He considered each project with the same care that he gave a new poem. There were rules, just as there were in writing poetry. But within those confines there was a great deal of room for creativity.

He turned to a blank page in the notebook, picked up the expensive fountain pen, and wrote the date. The new commission was somewhat different from the previous projects, but he began the poem the way he always did, with the particulars of the subject—name, occupation, address. That was all he had at the moment.

Vivian Brazier. Photographer. Number 12, Beachfront Lane, Adelina Beach, California.

He wrote it all down in the code that he had devised for the purpose. He would work on the poem as he set about observing the subject and crafting a strategy. The remaining verses would detail his impressions and observations. Inspiration would come. It always did.

Someday, perhaps when he retired, he would decode the poems and publish them. Anonymously, of course. Better yet, he might present it to a potential publisher as a work of fiction.

He even had a title: *Memoirs of a Gentleman Assassin.*

Chapter 10

Adelina Beach
Three weeks later . . .

Please move your left thigh a bit more to the right," Vivian said. "Just an inch. Yes, that's perfect. Chin angled toward the light. Head tilted. I want to emphasize your profile. Now look directly into the camera. Seduce me with your eyes, Norman."

Norman Proctor gave her a slight smile and half lowered his very long lashes. He was posed amid a cluster of potted palms that Vivian had rented from a local nursery. Norman had explained that he wanted to look like Johnny Weissmuller. He was certainly built like Weissmuller, and at the moment he was wearing even less than Weissmuller had in the latest Tarzan film, just a very tiny loincloth. But Norman was having difficulty looking appropriately seductive.

He was another new client in a steady stream of good-looking, vigorous young men from Muscle Beach. She had already photographed some of them for her new series, Men, but after the picture of Roland Jennings capturing the Dagger Killer hit the front pages she had been inundated with requests for glamour shot portraits. That was because, twenty-four hours after the photo on the front page of the *Adelina Beach*

Courier went national, Roland had been invited to do a screen test at a major studio. Some of his friends at the gym had begged for the name of the photographer who had captured the magic shot. Roland had provided the information. Word spread fast in the bodybuilder world. Now every strongman who spent hours exercising and showing off his well-toned body on Muscle Beach had dreams of becoming a star.

She knew that most of her new portrait clients were barely getting by working as bellhops and valets and lifeguards so she gave them a special price. She had also invested in a variety of wardrobes suitable for the images they wanted her to capture. She could pose them as rugged cowboys, swashbuckling pirates, or glamorous leading men.

Norman had opted for the most popular costume, the one that displayed the most of his undeniably attractive physique. But the picture was not yet right.

"Pretend I'm Maureen O'Sullivan," Vivian instructed.

She got nothing but fake sensuality in response. She opened her senses and studied Norman for a moment. There was plenty of latent heat in the man. The problem was that she was using the wrong image to bring it forth for the camera.

"All right, Norman, let's try this," she said. "Pretend you've received an invitation to join Cary Grant and Randolph Scott for cocktails at Bachelor Hall."

It was as if she had flipped a light switch. Norman sucked in a deep breath. His eyes took on a hot, sultry sheen. There was a definite fullness in the vicinity of the loincloth that had not been there a moment ago. It was a wonder he didn't ignite the film inside the camera.

"Oh, yes," Vivian said softly. "That's it. That's perfect." She released the shutter and stepped back, triumph sparkling through her. "You're going to love this shot, Norman."

Norman exhaled slowly and relaxed a little. "Thanks, Miss Brazier. When can I pick it up?"

"I'll have it ready for you next week."

The doorbell chimed. She glanced at the clock. It was too early for her next shoot. A new client, perhaps. At the rate she was doing Muscle Beach portraits she was going to have trouble getting back to her art photography. But at least she had not had to sleep with the radio tuned to the police channel lately. There was enough money coming in now to pay the rent and keep her darkroom well stocked so that she could pursue her art.

"Excuse me," she said. She paused at the doorway. "You can get dressed now."

"Sure." Norman stepped out from the fronds and reached for his swimming trunks.

Vivian swiftly averted her gaze. It was one thing to view a nearly nude man with an eye toward composition and lighting. Watching one walk around almost stark naked, even if he was more interested in the two most glamorous leading men in Hollywood than in Maureen, was another thing entirely.

She went into the front hall and paused to glance through the narrow pane of decorative amber glass that bordered the door on one side.

A man stood on the front step. He was not alone. He had a large dog with him. The dog was a handsome beast with a decidedly feral edge. Definitely not the cute and cuddly type.

The stranger waiting for her to open the door was a lot harder to classify but the words *cute* and *cuddly* did not come to mind. She opened her senses a little but she couldn't get a proper read on him while peering through the glass. All she could see were the superficial, easily cataloged elements—dark hair cut short in the current style and strong, rather fierce features that were far too interesting to be labeled handsome. A stern, grim expression implied a severe lack of a sense of humor. He looked like a warrior doomed to fight a never-ending battle.

She knew one thing—she couldn't wait to get the new client in front of a camera. She wanted to know his secrets.

She opened the door and smiled her best professional smile.

"Good afternoon," she said. "If you're here to request a portrait I'm afraid I'm fully booked today but I can give you an appointment first thing in the morning."

"My name is Nick Sundridge," he said. "I'm not a client. May I come in?"

The voice, she decided, went with the man—dark and resonant and compelling. It was a midnight-and-moonlight voice, full of shadows and unspoken promises. A voice that could lead a woman into—or out of—hell. She absolutely had to photograph the man.

But he had just said he was not a client. A tiny shiver of alarm flashed through her. She was suddenly very glad that Norman—big, muscular Norman—was still in the studio.

She dropped her professional smile.

"What do you want?" she said. "If you're a traveling salesman—"

"I'm going to have to work on my image. People keep mistaking me for a salesman."

"Is that right? Would that be because you are one?"

"I'm more of a messenger."

"Western Union?"

"No, this message was delivered by telephone, not telegram, late last night. I was in San Francisco at the time. I've been on the road ever since. Long drive."

"Who sent the message?"

"You don't know the sender but I assure you he has your best interests at heart. I've got a character witness you can call."

Before she could respond Norman emerged from the studio and ambled down the hall. He was wearing the very snug swimming trunks and his hair was still tousled. He looked like a man who had just rolled out of bed.

He noticed Nick, gave him a brief, polite nod, and then looked at Vivian.

"You can reach me at the gym when my photos are ready, Miss Brazier," he said.

"Right," she said.

She tried to think of an excuse to make him linger for a few minutes, but before she could come up with something plausible he was halfway out the door.

"Got to get going," he said. "I'll be late to work at the lifeguard station."

He went past Nick Sundridge and strode briskly down the front walk.

Vivian's next-door neighbor Mrs. Spalding magically appeared and made a show of walking to her mailbox. The elderly Miss Graham across the street emerged from her house. She, too, headed for her mailbox.

The mail for that day had not yet been delivered. Neither Mrs. Spalding nor Miss Graham cared. Vivian's new Muscle Beach clients had become a source of great interest in the small neighborhood.

Nick's brows rose ever so slightly. "About my message, Miss Brazier."

She moved deliberately out of the doorway and onto the front step. Nick and the dog made room for her.

"You can deliver your message here," she said.

"I'm a private investigator, Miss Brazier. I've been hired to protect you. I suppose you should think of me as your bodyguard, although in fairness, I ought to warn you that I haven't had a lot of experience—"

She froze. "What on earth are you talking about?"

"Someone wants you dead," Nick said. "There is reason to believe that a killer has been commissioned to murder you at some point in the next few days."

knew this was going to be a problem," Nick said. "I explained that to the man who asked me to deliver the message. His name is Luther Pell, by the way."

Vivian looked as if he had just handed her a live grenade. He didn't blame her. He had a few modest talents but they did not include a gift for delivering bad news in a tactful, nonthreatening manner. He wasn't a doctor or a member of the clergy or a funeral director. He was not very good at cloaking hard truths in soothing euphemisms. He was a private investigator. He dealt in facts. He viewed every case as a chaotic puzzle to be solved. When the pieces had been identified and put together properly, he went on to the next case.

One thing was certain—this job was getting complicated fast because Vivian was not the only one who was having a few problems coping with a sudden, unsettling turn of events. A blast of sensations had jolted his senses when she opened her door a moment ago. He had been made forcibly aware of the fact that he had been living what could only be described as a monastic life since Patricia had left.

Sure, part of it was the raw power of physical attraction. There was a hell of a lot of it, at least on his end, and it was easily explained by nearly a year of abstinence. But there was something else going on and he needed to figure it out fast because it was having a devastating effect on his sense of inner balance. He really needed the sense of control. He depended on it. Sometimes he worried that it was the only thing that anchored him in the world. Well, that and Rex.

Vivian Brazier was attractive but not in the traditional sense. Her features were too striking, too bold, too intriguing. Too compelling. The effect was definitely more than skin-deep. If she lived to be a hundred she would still be a fascinating woman.

Her high-waisted trousers and black silk shirt emphasized her slim, graceful frame. A couple of combs anchored her whiskey-brown hair behind her ears, framing mysterious, unreadable green eyes. She watched him in a way that warned him she saw things other people never noticed. They were the eyes of a woman who viewed the world from a different dimension.

The smile she had given him when she had answered the door, polite and professional though it was, had sent a thrill of delight across his senses. Now he was aware of a deep, prowling curiosity; a need to learn more about Vivian Brazier.

"I don't know this Luther Pell," Vivian said.

Rex leaned forward far enough to put his head in the vicinity of Vivian's right hand. She glanced down at him, frowning a little. Then she reluctantly gave him a couple of pats. Rex grinned a wolfish grin and inched a little closer to Vivian.

"If it makes you feel any better, I've never met Pell, either," Nick said. He paused and then decided there was no point keeping the truth from her. "He owns a nightclub in Burning Cove. There are rumors that he's got mob connections."

"That's not exactly a resounding testimonial."

"I know. But my uncle says Pell also has connections with the FBI and with a certain clandestine government agency. Evidently Pell used to run an intelligence operation during the Great War. All I can tell you is that Uncle Pete trusts him, and that's enough for me to take this threat seriously."

"Well, it's not nearly enough for me to believe what you're saying."

"You've got every reason to be cautious," he said. "But if you will call a homicide detective named Archer at the Adelina Beach police station, he will vouch for me."

"Detective Archer knows you?" Vivian asked warily.

"No, but he knows Luther Pell. They both served in the War. Why don't you go inside, Miss Brazier, and make the call? Lock your door. I'll wait out here until you're satisfied that I'm not dangerous."

Vivian eyed him with a considering look. "Does this have something to do with the Dagger Killer?"

He had already figured out that she was a very smart woman, he reminded himself.

"That," he said, "is a very interesting question. What makes you ask?"

"It's not as if I've got a long history of people trying to kill me. My only experience in that regard occurred about three weeks ago. Now here you are on my front step telling me that someone wants me dead. It strikes me that if there is no connection to the Dagger Killer, we're discussing an amazing coincidence."

He nodded, pleased that her reasoning paralleled his. "Strikes me that way, too. But I don't know the answer yet. Until I do, we should not leap to conclusions. Make the phone call, Miss Brazier. Then I'll tell you what I do know."

Another muscular young man, tanned, and with a mane of blond hair, appeared on the beach path walking toward Vivian's cottage. He was dressed for an exercise workout in a pair of swim trunks that looked about two sizes too small.

"Hi, Miss Brazier," he called. He glanced at Nick. "I know I'm a little early for my sitting but I don't mind waiting."

Vivian seized on the interruption. "You're right on time, Sam, but I have to make a phone call. It's a personal matter. Why don't you wait out here with Mr. Sundridge and his dog? As soon as I'm finished with the call we can get started on your portrait."

"Sure." Sam gave Nick an easygoing smile and extended one heavily muscled arm to shake hands. "I'm Sam Higgins. I'm a lifeguard."

"Nick Sundridge." Nick shook hands. "Traveling salesman."

It was, he decided, as good an explanation for his presence in Vivian's front yard as anything else.

Vivian bolted into the house and slammed the front door. Nick winced when he heard the muffled thud of the dead bolt sliding home.

Sam gave Nick another smile. "Salesman, huh? My pop was in sales up in Seattle. His company went under when the bad times hit so we moved down here to California. Pop's selling magazine subscriptions door-to-door now."

"I see. I hope he's making it."

"You know how it is, we all chip in. We're getting by. What's your line?"

"I'm not sure yet but I'm starting to think that sales might not be a good career path for me. I don't think I have the right personality for it."

"So, you're looking for work?"

"You could say that. I'm hoping to convince Miss Brazier that she needs an assistant."

That sounded good, Nick decided. Logical. Reasonable. A perfectly acceptable explanation for standing out here in Vivian's front yard.

Sam grinned. "You know, that's not a bad idea. Miss Brazier's a real popular photographer. All the guys who work out on Muscle Beach want her to take their pictures."

"Yes, I can see that."

"Personally, I'm a student of Charles Atlas." Sam got an evangelical glint in his eyes. "Are you familiar with his theory of Dynamic Tension?"

The problem with dealing with those who devoted themselves to developing the perfect body was that they tended to be obsessed with the subject.

"I've seen the ads in the magazines," Nick said.

"It's an amazing system," Sam said. "It utilizes the power of one's own muscles to develop strength and stamina. I'm here to tell you it has changed my life. Before I started the program I never could have gotten a job as a lifeguard. But in just seven days after starting the exercises I was on my way to becoming a new man."

"Is that right? What happened to the old one?"

The door opened abruptly. Nick exhaled a small sigh of relief. He and Sam and Rex all turned to look at Vivian. She no longer appeared as if she was going to run for the hills, but there was a new kind of subtle tension about her.

"You'd better come inside," she said to Nick. Her voice was cool and firm. "Sam, would you mind coming back a little later? Say an hour from now?"

"Sure, Miss Brazier," Sam said. "See you."

He waved and trotted back toward the path that led to the beach.

Vivian waited until he was gone. Then she retreated into the hallway and silently invited Nick and Rex to enter. They followed her into a dining room that had been converted into an office.

Nick understood. Vivian lived alone. She didn't need a dining room any more than he did.

There were matted photographs on every wall of the office. The subject matter varied. Moody landscapes, portraits that hinted at the sitters' most closely held secrets, and street scenes covered most of the available display space.

One picture stood out from the others because the style was quite different. It was an image of a gaudy carousel that had been manipulated in the printing process to make it look as if the horses were being ridden by wild-eyed ghosts. The result was eerie and macabre and, in some way he could not explain, humorous.

Something about the spectral riders caught his attention. He took a closer look and smiled to himself. Each of the ghosts had the same face, that of a man with sharp features and shoulder-length hair swept back from a dramatic widow's peak. Each ghost had a camera hanging from a strap around his neck. But the cameras appeared to be so large and heavy they acted as anchors. A carousel of the damned doomed to take endless photographs in hell.

"A year and a half ago I took a photography class from an instructor who favored the pictorial style," Vivian explained. "It's not my style but I wanted to learn the techniques. That picture was a class project."

Nick looked at her. "Did you pass the class?"

"Nope." She dropped into the chair behind the desk and gave him a chilly smile. "I quit. The instructor said my work was sentimental and that it lacked genuine artistic vision. He also said a few other things when he saw that picture."

"Because he realized it's a photographic joke featuring him?"

Vivian blinked, evidently surprised that he had noticed the humor in the image. He might be a poor excuse for a traveling salesman but he could see facts when they were right in front of him.

"Exactly," she said. "When he saw it, he understood that it was my way of telling him that he and his artistic vision could go to hell. That image is technically perfect, by the way. I will admit I learned a few things in the class. Forget my pictures. Evidently I have bigger problems than a failure of artistic vision."

Nick studied her in silence for a couple of beats, trying to figure out exactly how she was reacting to his bombshell. But it was hard to get a read on Vivian Brazier. She was a mystery. A lot of people, male or female, would have been in hysterics by now.

"What did Detective Archer tell you?" he said.

"Virtually nothing helpful. He said that no one seems to have any idea why I'm in danger but he was adamant that this Luther Pell person can be trusted. Pell told him the threat appears to be real and that you've got the qualifications needed to keep me safe while Pell and his consultant try to figure out who wants to kill me."

"Pell's consultant is my uncle Pete. He was a cipher expert, a code breaker during the War and for a few years afterward. I'm afraid it isn't just a matter of identifying and stopping the killer." Nick paused for emphasis. "We have to identify the individual who hired the assassin."

"I don't know what to think. This is all just so bizarre."

She sounded bewildered as well as unnerved.

Rex's ears pricked. He padded across the room, rested his head on her thigh, and looked up at her. Absently she put a hand on his head and stroked behind his ears. Rex got a blissful expression.

"I shouldn't have broken the news to you the way I did," Nick said. "In my own defense I'd just like to say that I'm not sure there is a good way to tell someone that her life is in danger."

"Detective Archer also assured me that you were indeed an investigator and that, although some people consider you rather odd and eccentric, you are neither crazy nor criminally insane."

"I cannot tell you how happy I am to hear that."

"I do not find this situation amusing," she said. "I simply cannot fathom why someone would want to have me murdered."

"If this threat is not connected to the Dagger Killer," he said carefully, "there is one other possibility that we should consider."

"What?" Vivian straightened in her chair and widened her hands in a gesture of futility. "Do you think one of my clients is unhappy with his or her portrait? That's ridiculous."

"I understand that you're an heiress. In my experience, money is frequently a motive for murder."

She looked even more stunned than she had when he had told her about the threat to her life. After a moment she pulled herself together and shook her head, conviction radiating from her.

"No," she said. "The only person who stands to gain financially if I were to die would be my sister. Trust me, it's absolutely inconceivable that Lyra would do anything to hurt me."

Nick considered briefly and then set the matter aside. He had learned early on that there was an astonishing amount of naïveté in the world.

"Are you and your sister the only heirs listed in the will?"

Her eyes widened. "I'm not sure. I've never seen my father's will."

The doorbell chimed.

"That's my next client," Vivian said.

"I'll let him in."

Vivian shot to her feet and flattened her palms on the desk. "Excuse me, this is my house and my place of business. I will greet the client."

"It occurs to me that it would be exceptionally easy for a killer to gain entry to your house and your place of business by simply making an appointment to have his picture taken."

"This is nonsense. I really don't think—"

The bell chimed again. Nick motioned to Rex. Together they left the office and went into the front hall.

Yet another exceedingly muscular and robust specimen of manhood stood on the front step. He looked to be about twenty years old. At least this one was partially dressed in a sports shirt, trousers, and sunglasses. The shirt was unbuttoned to the waist, displaying a lot of sculpted chest.

When Nick opened the door, the young man appeared startled but he quickly recovered.

"You must be the photographer's assistant," he said. "I'm Eric. I've got an appointment to pick up the photos that Miss Brazier took of me a few days ago."

"Wait here, please," Nick said. "I'll let Miss Brazier know that you've arrived."

Eric eyed Rex and retreated a couple of steps.

"Sure," he said. "I'll wait out here."

Nick closed the door and threw the bolt for good measure. Eric did not look dangerous but there was a long list of dead people who had made assumptions based on appearances.

He turned and found Vivian directly behind him. Her eyes narrowed.

"Eric is waiting on the front step," he said, trying to sound helpful. "He thinks I'm your assistant. I suggest we let him go on thinking that."

"Right." Vivian smiled a steely smile. She turned on her heel and stalked off down the hall. "Show him into my office, please. I'll get the prints."

Nick watched her disappear through the kitchen doorway. With a sigh he opened the door again.

"Miss Brazier will see you in her office. End of the hall on the right."

"Sure."

Eric moved through the doorway. Nick and Rex followed him.

A moment or two later Vivian appeared. She had a large envelope in her hand.

"I think the photos turned out very well," Vivian said. "I hope you'll be pleased."

Eric flushed and gave her a big grin. His eyes lit with excitement. "Can't wait to see them."

Vivian took three large prints out of the envelope and displayed them on the desk. Nick was standing close enough to see that the photos showed Eric in various dramatic poses. In one image he wore nothing but a pair of bathing trunks. In another he was in a swashbuckling stance, sword in hand, billowing white shirt open halfway down his chest in a scene that looked as if it had been inspired by an Errol Flynn film. The third shot showed him in a stylish jacket and trousers, the quintessential leading man. Cary Grant.

Eric was clearly elated. "You made me look like a real movie star, Miss Brazier."

"I know you have your heart set on becoming an actor, Eric," Vivian said gently. "I wish you all the luck in the world."

He looked up from the photos. "But I shouldn't give up my job at the garage, right?"

Vivian smiled. "Something along those lines. I do understand what it is to have a dream, believe me."

"Don't worry." Eric picked up the glossy photos and inserted them carefully back into the envelope. "If I don't make it in Hollywood I've got another plan."

"What's that?" Vivian asked.

"I've been talking to a friend of mine about opening a gym on the beach. You know, a place where guys can lift weights and really concentrate on building up their bodies."

Vivian was impressed. "That sounds like a very interesting idea. Let me know if you decide to do that. I could take some photos for you to use to market your gym."

"Yeah?" Eric brightened. "Thanks, Miss Brazier. I really appreciate it."

Eric headed toward the door, the envelope full of photos tucked safely under one arm. He did not seem to remember that Nick was in the room.

"I'll show you out," Nick said.

Eric glanced at him. "Oh, sure. Thanks."

Nick escorted him out the door and returned to the office. Vivian was sitting behind her desk, one hand resting absently on Rex's head, which was once again propped on her thigh. The dog appeared to be deeply in love.

"I've got more questions," Vivian said.

Nick went to the window and contemplated the small backyard and the beach beyond. "I'll answer the ones I can."

"How did Luther Pell and your uncle come to hear about the threat to my life?"

"A few days ago a journal of handwritten poems came into Pell's hands. The circumstances made him suspect that the verses might be written in code. He tracked down Uncle Pete, who succeeded in deciphering some of the most recent poems."

"Go on."

Nick turned away from the view and looked at Vivian. "Pell and my uncle are convinced that the poems are actually the private record of a professional killer for hire. Uncle Pete says each poem has a pattern. It starts with a date and certain personal details about the victim. There are also a couple of encrypted lines that identify the individual who commissioned the murder, how much that person paid, and the motive."

Vivian frowned. "Why would the killer put down so much information about the individual who hired him?"

Nick shrugged. "I think it's safe to say that at some point in the future the assassin will start blackmailing his clients."

Vivian shuddered. "Of course. He'll want to impress them with the details as a way of proving he knows their secret."

"The remainder of the verses in each poem describe the strategy and methods the assassin used to complete each commissioned murder. Uncle Pete told me that the killer apparently prides himself on creativity, but more importantly he has a strict pattern. He observes his victim for a month before he decides exactly how he will carry out the murder. Evidently he savors that part of the process."

"The murder?"

"That, too. But my uncle read a couple of the poems to me. I got the impression the killer enjoys stalking his victim. It gives him a sense of power. It's his cocaine."

"I can't believe I am the subject of one of those horrible poems. It makes no sense."

"To be clear, the last entry in the journal, the one that has your name in it, is not a completed poem. Uncle Pete said there are only a couple of lines. In addition to the date, they detail your name, the town where you live, and your profession."

Vivian rose and went to stand at the window. Rex followed, sat down beside her, and leaned heavily against her right leg.

"What about the name and address of the person who paid to have me murdered?" Vivian asked quietly.

"Luther Pell says apparently the journal was stolen before the killer recorded those details in the poem. The thief died in Burning Cove, which is how the volume fell into Pell's hands."

"If the killer lost his book of poems, perhaps he will abandon the commission."

"I don't think we can assume he'll stop. Judging by what my uncle read to me over the phone, I believe it is far more likely he will be obsessed with finishing what he started."

Vivian folded her arms very tightly and began to pace the small space, walking in circles. Rex accompanied her. Nick had to get out of the way when they went past him.

"Since the assassin began the project involving me about three weeks ago, time is running out fast, is that what you're trying to say?" Vivian asked.

"Assuming he sticks to his pattern of taking a month to complete each commission, yes."

Vivian frowned. "How can Pell be sure that the man who died with the poems in his possession wasn't the assassin?"

"Good question. The name of the thief was Jasper Calloway and Pell is certain he was not the hired killer."

"How can he possibly be sure?"

Nick paused and then decided he might as well tell her what Luther Pell had told him.

"Two reasons. Pell knows something about the thief. He says

Calloway was many things, but not a poet. Pell also said that Calloway was very . . . competent. He was thorough but he was careful not to be predictable."

"In other words, if Calloway had been the assassin, I would probably be dead by now, is that it?"

"That's Pell's theory and I'm inclined to agree with him. There's another reason to think that the assassin is still alive. Pell says he has been informed that someone in the underworld is trying to find the journal. That individual will pay any price. No questions asked."

Vivian turned quickly. "The assassin?"

"Maybe. Probably."

"How does Pell know such things?"

"I told you, he has mob connections. Someone from that world, a man known as the Broker, contacted Pell shortly after Calloway died. The Broker told him that someone is looking for the journal."

"There must be any number of people who would want to get their hands on that volume," Vivian said.

"Certainly. Any of the clients who paid for a murder, for starters. But he or she would have to know about the existence of the journal in the first place. It seems unlikely that any of the people who commissioned the murders would be aware of the volume, let alone that the poems were encrypted."

"Surely this Broker who contacted Pell knows the identity of whoever is willing to pay any amount to get hold of the volume."

"Not in this case," Nick said. "In the underworld there are ways to handle such things anonymously."

"Why did the Broker contact Pell?"

"He did it as a favor. He reasoned that the death of Calloway might be linked to the theft of the journal because of the timing and because he's not a great believer in coincidence."

Vivian stopped pacing and fixed her attention on a large photograph of a smiling, vivacious young woman.

Nick had never met the lady in the picture but there was so much personality radiating from the portrait he felt as if he knew something important about her.

Vivian glanced at him and followed his gaze.

"My sister, Lyra," she said.

"She looks . . . interesting. Like you."

Rex sat down beside Vivian and leaned his big furry body against her leg again. She reached down and patted him. He looked thrilled.

Vivian finally turned around. Her expression was resolute.

"Why you?" she asked. "Why did this Luther Pell choose you to protect me?"

"Probably because my uncle recommended me and Pell trusts my uncle's judgment. It's not as if he has a lot of choice."

"What do you mean? There must be any number of people who work as bodyguards here in the Los Angeles area. I'm sure some of the stars have personal guards."

"Luther Pell doesn't trust easily."

"How does this bodyguard business work?"

"Beats me," Nick said. "I've never done this sort of work before."

"You're serious, aren't you? What exactly do you do?"

"I investigate, Miss Brazier. I've never had a case that required me to stick close to the client night and day. Looks like we'll have to figure it out as we go along."

Vivian narrowed her eyes. "No offense, Mr. Sundridge, but that is not very reassuring."

"Try to look on the bright side," Nick said. "It's not as if I'm working alone. I've got Rex."

Rex's ears shot up at the sound of his name.

Vivian glanced at him, her gaze softening. "Rex looks like he can take care of himself."

"Definitely," Nick said. "And you, too. He was trained by a friend of my uncle's, a man who used to school war dogs. Actually, Harry trained both Rex and me. He told me on more than one occasion that of the two, I was the more difficult student. Rex is a very fast learner."

Vivian smiled. "Just like Rin-Tin-Tin. Growing up I saw every movie he ever made. I even wrote him a fan letter."

Nick kept his mouth shut. Rex was clearly his best asset at the moment.

"We'll need an explanation for your presence here in my house," Vivian said. "I suppose we could pretend that you're a distant relative visiting from back East."

"I've been thinking about that," Nick said. "It would be best if we left town."

Vivian stared at him, clearly flabbergasted. "I can't possibly do that. I've got two weeks' worth of bookings."

"We're talking a few days, a week at the outside. If we're right about the killer's obsession with sticking to his personal timeline, he'll make his move soon."

He saw the shock of what he did not say—that if she did not leave town she might end up dead within the week—flash in her eyes.

"How am I supposed to explain my sudden disappearance from Adelina Beach?" she said; the bleak expression in her eyes made it clear her heart was no longer in the argument.

"You can tell your clients that something personal has come up," he said. "A family situation. Leaving town will force the killer to take a few more risks because he will probably try to find you. With luck it will draw him out into the open where Pell and his people can spot him."

"What about my family? They'll be scared to death if I tell them what's going on."

He hesitated. "I don't want to tell you to lie to your family, but the truth is, it will be easier to deal with this situation if they aren't involved. It could put them in danger."

"I can't do that."

"Then I suggest you let everyone think you're taking a few days off to get some fresh creative inspiration."

"Right. Creative inspiration."

Vivian did not appear enthused by that plan. He cast about for a little inspiration of his own.

"How does a honeymoon at the Burning Cove Hotel sound?" he said.

He was rather pleased with the cleverness of the idea until he realized that Vivian was staring at him, horrified.

"Honeymoon?" she said. "Are you out of your mind?"

"It has been suggested on occasion," he admitted.

"Is that right? By whom?"

"The woman I married, among others."

Vivian's eyes widened. "Are you telling me you're married? After you suggested we have a fake honeymoon together at the Burning Cove Hotel? Your wife must be amazingly open-minded when it comes to your professional work."

"She's not my wife. According to the court, she never was."

"Now what are you talking about?"

"My marriage was annulled."

"Oh," Vivian said. She opened her mouth and shut it again.

Nick wasn't surprised. Over the course of the past year he had discovered that an announcement of an annulment had a way of terminating a conversation. It immediately raised questions that few people dared to ask aloud.

The doorbell chimed. Vivian turned toward the door of the office, clearly grateful for the interruption.

"That must be Sam," she said. "We'll have to continue this discussion later. I've got bills to pay."

"I thought your family was wealthy."

She shot him an annoyed look as she headed toward the doorway. "I'm on my own here in Adelina Beach. My parents don't approve of my desire to pursue a career as an art photographer. Father assumed that if he cut off my allowance I'd give up and go home to San Francisco."

"Why? What are the odds of making it as an art photographer?"

"About the same as the odds of getting discovered by a studio executive and becoming a red-hot movie star."

"That bad, huh?"

"Yep. Which is why I am only too happy to do bargain portraits for handsome, well-built men from Muscle Beach. They help pay the bills."

She went through the doorway. He followed, Rex at his heels.

"Your neighbors seem to have noticed the steady stream of Muscle Beach clients," he said.

"Hard not to notice them." Vivian glanced over her shoulder and gave him an icy smile. "I am the main source of entertainment on Beachfront Lane."

Chapter 12

et's say I agreed to go with you to Burning Cove for a few days," Vivian said. "How exactly is this fake honeymoon plan supposed to work?"

She had tried to focus on composing Sam's portrait but her mind kept leaping back to the unnerving fact that someone wanted her dead badly enough to hire an assassin. She had managed to get through the shoot with what she felt was a successful picture, but as soon as Sam had left, the anxiety had settled on her once again.

Someone wants to murder me. I may have less than a week to live. Who hates me so much?

She opened the door of the refrigerator and tried to concentrate on dinner. It was going on six o'clock. She had poured a couple of glasses of wine, one for herself and one for her new, unwanted houseguest. She had put a bowl of water on the floor for Rex.

There appeared to be little prospect of getting rid of Nick Sundridge and his dog even if she wanted to. The truth was it was comforting to have them with her. She really did not want to be alone tonight.

Dinner for three, however, was something of a challenge.

She was by no means an expert chef. She had grown up in a household that employed a housekeeper and a cook. But during the past few months her next-door neighbors had taught her some of the basics. She could do a halfway decent omelet and she could assemble a salad. She would need three omelets in all, she decided. Nick had produced a can of dog food from the trunk of the Packard, but Rex did not appear excited about it. Nick had explained that the dog usually ate whatever Nick ate.

"We'll keep a low profile," Nick said. "Pell says the best thing about the Burning Cove Hotel is that the security is excellent."

"Because so many wealthy celebrities stay there?"

"Its claim to fame is that it guarantees privacy. Pell assures me that you'll be safer on the grounds of the Burning Cove than you will be here in Adelina Beach."

"Who is going to pay for all this?"

"Pell. This is his case."

She took a carton of eggs, some cheddar cheese, and lettuce out of the refrigerator and set them on the counter.

"I can't stay there indefinitely," she warned. "I've got a life here in Adelina Beach. Clients. My art photography. You're sure this will be over in a week?"

"Pretty sure," Nick said. "One way or another."

She glared at him. He winced.

"Sorry," he said. "That didn't come out quite the way I intended. I can't say for certain that we'll get control of this situation within the week, but moving you to Burning Cove may give us the edge we need."

"What makes you so sure of that?"

"Burning Cove is a small town—a wealthy, exclusive small town, but nevertheless a small town," Nick said. "Very little goes on there that escapes the notice of the movers and shakers."

"Who are they?"

"Luther Pell and Oliver Ward. I mentioned that Pell owns a hot nightclub, the Paradise. Ward is the proprietor of the Burning Cove Hotel. Between the two of them they have eyes and ears everywhere in that town."

"Do you think the hired assassin will figure out we've gone to Burning Cove?"

"If he's following his usual pattern he'll be watching you."

She shuddered. "Stalking me."

"Yes."

Something about the way Nick said the single word made Vivian glance at him. Icy certainty shivered in the atmosphere around him. And suddenly she understood.

"You want him to follow us, don't you?" she said.

Nick gave her an approving look. "Here in Adelina Beach it's easy for him to fade into the shadows of Los Angeles. He's more likely to stand out in a small, isolated town like Burning Cove."

Vivian picked up her glass of wine, took a sip, and set the glass down on the counter. She started to crack eggs into a bowl. Rex observed the process with an intent expression. She glanced at him and decided to add a few more eggs. He was, after all, a large dog.

"For all we know the assassin could be a woman," she said.

"True."

His ready agreement amused her. "You don't have any illusions about the female of the species?"

"I know they can be just as deadly as the male," he said.

She smiled a little. "Obviously you are a man with modern attitudes when it comes to women. About this investigative work of yours—"

"What about it?"

"Judging by your clothes and that very nice custom Packard convertible parked out front I assume it pays well?"

"Occasionally. But if you're wondering how I can afford the clothes and the car, the answer is that after my parents were killed I went to live with my uncle. He's very good at investing. He taught me a lot. I've been . . . lucky."

"You've made money in the middle of the Depression?" She sniffed. "Something tells me more than luck is involved."

"Uncle Pete has a knack for spotting good investments. He taught me everything I know. I look for companies engaged in activities that are vital to an economic recovery. Mining. Oil. Steel. Firms involved in agriculture."

Vivian nodded. "The basics that the country needs to survive."

"That's the idea." He drank some coffee.

Vivian smiled. "My father would approve of your approach. So would my sister."

"Your sister?"

"Lyra got Father's talent for business. If he wasn't so old-fashioned he would have the sense to put her in charge of Brazier Pacific when he retires. He loves us very much but unfortunately he is not at all modern in his thinking. He wanted me to marry a man of his choosing, someone qualified to take charge of the company. I refused. Now that I'm gone he's putting pressure on Lyra to take my place. Same man, incidentally."

"Is she going to marry the man your father wants her to marry?"

"Looks like it." Vivian cracked the last egg into the bowl. "Next month she and Hamilton Merrick are planning to celebrate their engagement."

"Who is Merrick?"

"The man I was supposed to marry. My father and Hamilton's have been close friends and business associates for decades."

"So Merrick is set to take over your father's firm?"

The speculative edge on the question caught her attention.

"Don't go down that road," she said. "If Hamilton marries my sister, he's going to end up running Brazier Shipping. Why take the risk of having me murdered now? It would be more sensible to wait until he's safely married to Lyra."

"People are not always logical when it comes to large financial windfalls."

Vivian picked up a whisk and started thrashing the eggs. "I admit I can't say I trust Hamilton to be a faithful husband, but I refuse to believe he would hire a professional assassin." She paused, thinking about it. "How does one even go about finding someone who is in the murder-for-hire business? I doubt if they advertise in the telephone book."

"Good question."

Chapter 13

Nick dreamed the dream that had haunted him for the past year . . .

It is one o'clock in the morning. The rooftop of the hotel is cloaked in fog. Down below, the streetlamps infuse the mist with a ghostly light, but here on the roof visibility is limited to less than a yard.

The gunfire has finally ceased but he had been counting the shots. Six in all. Fulton Gage is out of ammunition.

"She's mine." Gage's voice came out of the fog. "She belongs to me. She betrayed me and she will pay for that. But you die first because you're the reason she left me."

"She left you because you hurt her."

"I punished her when she deserved it. She knows that."

"You're not only violent, you're insane," Nick says. He keeps his voice neutral. Clinical. Stating facts. That was how you manipulated a man like Fulton Gage.

"She made me lose my temper. She pushed and pushed until I snapped."

"I understand," Nick says. "You have no self-control."

"That's not the way it is. She made me hurt her."

"So she is more powerful than you? Interesting . . ."

There is a click. Nick knows that Gage has just discovered that there are no more bullets in his pistol. Now he will panic and make a run for the stairwell.

"You're out of ammunition, Gage," Nick says.

Suddenly Patricia is on the roof, too. She isn't supposed to be there. Gage has her.

"Looks like she dies first, after all," Gage says.

Now Nick understands the enormity of the miscalculation. Gage is going to throw Patricia off the roof . . .

Nick awoke from the dream on a sudden shock of acute awareness that told him something was wrong. He did not question the sensation. He had made that mistake a few times early on in his career and again in his nonmarriage. Things had not ended well on any of those previous occasions, so he took such warnings seriously.

It was not enough to be alarmed, however. He required more information.

For a few seconds he lay motionless on Vivian's sofa. He tried to open all of his senses for clues to the source of whatever it was that had awakened him. Rex had been curled up on the rug in front of the sofa but he was on his feet now, gazing into the deep shadows of the hall.

There were no telltale creaks of the floorboards. No click of a door lock or a draft of cold air indicating an intruder had pried open a window. But something had changed.

Rex whined softly. He glanced at Nick and then turned his attention back to the hallway.

Nick swung his legs over the edge of the sofa, pulled on his trousers, and got to his feet. He ignored the stiffness in his muscles—the sofa was not very large—and then he picked up the gun he had left on the coffee table.

Cautiously, using moonlight as his guide, he made his way through the jumble of equipment cases, cords, and other photography paraphernalia that littered the living room. He told himself he was probably lucky that Vivian had left the couch and the coffee table in the space. Otherwise he would have been sleeping on the floor.

He started down the hall. When he reached Vivian's door he paused and listened again. Silence.

Rex padded on ahead into the darkened kitchen. The dog was interested in the rear door of the house, not the front entrance. If there was someone out there he was in the backyard.

Nick flattened his back against the wall beside the kitchen window and twitched the shade aside. The porch light was on but the yellow glow of the bulb did not penetrate far into the darkness. The backyard lay in shadows.

Beyond the yard was the wide esplanade that bordered the beach. In the distance, strings of lights illuminated the pier.

Rex lowered his nose and sniffed at the threshold beneath the door. Nick was paying close attention, trying to read the dog's body language, when he heard the door of Vivian's room open. A moment later she appeared, a robe wrapped snugly around her. Her feet were clad in a pair of fluffy house slippers.

"What's wrong?" she whispered.

"Sorry," he said in equally low tones. "Didn't mean to wake you."

"I'm used to being awakened in the middle of the night."

"Yeah?"

"I pay the rent with my crime-and-fire-scene photos, remember? They mostly occur at night. Besides, I haven't slept well since that bastard Deverell tried to gut me with a very large knife."

"You live an adventurous life, Miss Brazier."

"So do you, Mr. Sundridge. Why are you prowling around my house in the middle of the night?"

"I'm up because Rex and I got a feeling that something had . . . changed."

"In what way?"

"Ever had the sensation that someone was watching you?"

"Funny you should ask. I've had the feeling a lot lately. Figured it was just nerves. Why?"

"In my experience, it's usually true," Nick said.

Vivian took a deep breath and let it out slowly. "Do you think someone is out there right now? Watching this house?"

"That's what it feels like. Rex seems to think so, too, and when it comes to this sort of thing, he's usually right."

"Well, there could be a logical explanation."

"Is that so?"

"It's after midnight and your car is parked in front of my place. I wouldn't be surprised if Miss Graham across the street is watching to see if you really are going to stay here all night. By tomorrow morning the whole neighborhood will be speculating about our relationship. Well, not exactly speculating. They'll be convinced we're having an affair."

"Are you worried?"

"No. Everyone around here has already concluded that I enjoy a rather unconventional lifestyle."

He nodded. "The Muscle Beach clients?"

"Right. So, what do we do now?"

"Rex and I are going to take a look outside. If someone is hanging around, Rex will flush him out."

Rex started barking furiously. He scratched at the door.

Nick hit the switch that doused the porch lights.

"Stay in the hallway," he said to Vivian. "Don't go near any windows."

"I really don't think it's a good idea for you to go outside—"

She was interrupted by the stunning sound of shattering glass in the living room.

Nick raced across the kitchen, Rex at his heels. By the time they reached the living room, the flames of the incendiary device were already leaping high, seizing on the swaths of gossamer drapery that Vivian used to control the studio lighting.

"My camera," Vivian yelped.

Frantically she tried to push past Nick.

The tripod and the big view camera were inches from the flames.

"Too late," Nick said. "This old cottage is all wood. It's going to come down fast. We need to get out. Now."

In the light of the rising tide of fire, Vivian's striking face was etched in anger and frustration. To his relief she did not argue.

"Yes," she said.

She turned on her heel and sprinted into the front hall. He followed hard behind her with Rex. At the door Vivian paused to yank open the coat closet. She grabbed a trench coat, slung the leather strap of a camera over her shoulder, and seized a metal lockbox and a portfolio case.

Nick took the portfolio case and got the front door open. Rex dashed outside, barking furiously. Vivian was right behind him. Nick raced after them, gun in hand.

Lights came on in the cottage across the street. The front door slammed open.

"Call the fire department," Nick ordered.

The figure on the front step ducked back inside. Other doors along Beachfront Lane opened.

"Mrs. Spalding," Vivian said. "She lives in the house next door. She's a little hard of hearing."

"I'll get her out," Nick said. "Rex. Stay."

Rex took up his post at Vivian's side. Nick loped up the walk to Mrs. Spalding's front door.

Sirens sounded in the distance. Rex had ceased barking but other dogs took up the chorus. Lights came on in the rest of the cottages. The night was in chaos.

Mrs. Spalding opened her door garbed in an aging bathrobe. By the time Nick got her out of the house a small crowd had gathered in the lane. Vivian's cottage was fully engulfed now.

Fire trucks arrived on the scene. Nick turned to make sure that Vivian was still safe.

A flashbulb exploded. He closed his eyes but not before he was partially dazzled by the glare.

"Damn it," he said. "What the hell do you think you're doing?"

"This is my night job, remember?"

He was dumbfounded. "It happens to be your house that is burning down."

"It's a fire. It will sell, provided I give the picture some context. Otherwise one burning building looks a lot like any other burning building. Context is the key to a fire photo."

As he watched, rendered momentarily speechless by her ice-cold nerve, she pressed the button that ejected the hot flashbulb. The used bulb hit the pavement near his feet and shattered. In a single, fluid motion, Vivian took a new bulb out of the bulging pocket of her trench coat, inserted it into the camera, and fired off another shot.

And another.

She loaded film and flashbulbs with the skill of a marksman firing a rifle.

A thought hit him, driving out his astonishment.

"Forget the fire," he said. "Get the crowd."

She did not look up from her work. "I always get a few crowd shots."

"We want lots of them. Try to get everyone you can."

She did pause briefly then.

"Why?" she asked.

"Because there's a chance he's here in this crowd. Firebugs like to watch."

"I've heard that," Vivian said. "But if he's after me, he's not a fire-bug, he's an assassin. Why would he risk sticking around?"

"I'll explain later. For now, just concentrate on the crowd shots."

"You bet. The expressions on the faces of the people watching a fire are always more interesting than the flames anyway."

Nick shook his head. "You're amazing."

She ignored him to slam a fresh film holder into the camera.

Chapter 14

Twenty minutes later she used the last film holder. She swung around to look at Nick.

"We need to get to the night editor at the office of the *Adelina Beach Courier*," she said. "My car was in the garage. It's a burned-out hulk by now. We'll take yours."

"You want to go to a newspaper office? At this hour?"

"With luck Eddy will let me use his darkroom."

Nick took one last look at the scene. The fire crew had the flames under control but it was clear there would be nothing left to salvage after things cooled down. The crowd was starting to dissipate. He had tried to get a look at every face but in the end there had been dozens of people milling around in the street. Several had arrived by car, drawn by the fiery light in the night sky. They had all watched, fascinated, as the beach cottage burned. The raw power of fire never failed to awe and fascinate.

"We'll have to give a statement to the fire chief first," he warned.

"I've barely got time to make the morning edition," Vivian began. She broke off when a man in a uniform strode determinedly toward her.

"Chief Bridges," he said by way of introduction. "I understand you were renting this place, Miss Brazier?"

"That's right," she said.

"Any idea what happened here tonight?"

"Isn't it obvious?" Vivian asked. "Someone tried to murder me."

The chief glanced at Nick.

"She's right," Nick said. "Someone lit a fuse, stuck it into a bottle of gas or some other flammable liquid, and tossed it through the living room window."

Bridges scowled. "You sure about that?"

"Positive," Vivian said.

"I hear you're a photographer," Bridges said. "That means you had a lot of film and chemicals around, right?"

"Yes," Vivian said, "but I assure you, I'm very careful. That fire did not start in my darkroom if that's what you're implying. Mr. Sundridge is right. Someone threw a homemade firebomb through my front window."

"We'll take a look in the morning," Bridges said. He sounded doubtful. "Nothing we can do tonight. How can I reach you? The cops will probably want to talk to you, too."

"We're going to find a hotel," Nick said. "Tomorrow I'll give you and the chief of police a call."

Vivian looked at Bridges. "I've got a great shot of you fighting that fire. It will be on the front page of the *Courier* if you let us leave now. But time is of the essence here."

"Me? On the front page?"

"It's a very powerful shot," Vivian promised. "You're going to look terrific."

"Huh. My wife will love that."

"It will also impress the mayor and the city council," Vivian said.

Bridges hesitated and then waved one hand. "All right, on your way. Don't forget to call headquarters tomorrow."

"Right," Nick said.

He took Vivian's arm and steered her through the crowd to where the customized Packard was parked at the curb. When he opened the door on the passenger side, Rex leaped into the front seat and took up his usual position.

"It's the back seat for you tonight, pal," Nick said.

He patted the small compartment behind the front seat that had been custom-made for Rex. The dog obligingly moved. When Vivian slipped into the passenger seat, he rested his head on her shoulder. She reached up to scratch his ears.

"The *Courier* office is on Park Street," Vivian said. "Hurry. It's late but with a little luck I can still make the morning edition."

Nick shook his head and got behind the wheel. He fired up the engine and put the Packard in gear. "Should I point out that you're wearing a nightgown and a pair of slippers?"

"I'm also wearing a trench coat. Don't worry about my modesty. All Eddy will care about is the photo."

He pulled away from the curb and took one last look around the street. The excitement was over. There were only a handful of people left. Whoever had thrown the firebomb through the window would have disappeared by now.

"Do you really think that we've got a chance of identifying the person who started that fire?" Vivian asked.

"Maybe," he said.

She glanced at him. "I won't be able to develop all of my pictures tonight. If Eddy does let me use his darkroom he'll only allow me to process a couple of photos, just the ones that will look good in the *Courier.* I'll have to wait until I can find a darkroom in Burning Cove to develop most of the crowd scenes."

"It's a long shot anyway."

"Got a piece of paper and a pencil?"

"Glove box. Why?"

She opened the glove box and took out the small notebook. "Photo editors are more likely to buy if you do the hard work of writing the headline and caption for them."

Ten minutes later Nick pulled up to the curb in front of a nondescript office building. A small, middle-aged man with shaggy hair and a pair of spectacles opened the door. He reeked of cigar smoke and alcohol.

"Vivian," he said. "What have you got for me?"

"House fire," Vivian said. "Here's your headline."

She handed him the slip of paper she had torn out of the notebook.

Eddy scowled at what she had written. "Mysterious Arson in Neighborhood Where Dagger Killer Was Captured. Coincidence?" Eddy looked up. "Damn. I'll buy a couple of shots. The Dagger Killer may be dead but he still sells papers. Let's see the prints."

"I need to develop my pictures first. My darkroom went up in flames tonight."

"Yeah, yeah, go on." Eddy waved her down the hall. "You know the way."

Vivian disappeared through a doorway. Eddy eyed Nick.

"Is she wearing a nightgown under that coat?" he said. "And slippers?"

Nick smiled. "Yes."

"Photographers," Eddy said. "Anything for a picture."

Chapter 15

I t was almost dawn before they got on the road to Burning Cove. Vivian's rush of nervy energy was starting to fade. In its place came a dose of reality. Someone really had tried to kill her tonight.

"Mind if I ask what's in that lockbox you grabbed on the way out of the house?" Nick asked. "Cash? Jewelry? Valuable papers?"

Vivian took her attention off the view of the highway that she had been contemplating through the Packard's windshield and glanced at Nick.

He was piloting the car with the ease and skill of a man who was accustomed to controlling a powerful vehicle; a man accustomed to controlling a lot of powerful things, she thought. A gun. A dangerous-looking dog. His secrets.

At the moment the dangerous dog did not appear fearsome. He was braced in the cramped back seat, savoring the scents carried on the breeze. It was obvious that he loved riding in the car. Vivian reached and gave him a couple of pats. He spared a moment to lick her hand.

It was going to be a long drive. She had never been to Burning

Cove but she knew that it was situated on the coast nearly a hundred miles north of Los Angeles. She had seen the newspaper photos of celebrities enjoying the pleasures of the exclusive seaside community. The town was far enough away from the city to have its own personality but close enough and glamorous enough to serve as a playground for movie stars, socialites, wealthy industrialists, politicians, and the occasional mobster.

The light, early-morning coastal fog was retreating rapidly, giving way to the golden warmth of the California sun. On any other morning, Vivian thought, she would have enjoyed the road trip with its spectacular views of rugged cliffs, inviting beaches, and the vast expanse of the dazzling Pacific Ocean. This was the magical, mythical California; the real-life fantasy that had induced so many people to find the start of Route 66 in Chicago and follow it all the way to the edge of the country. This was the California where anything was possible, the place where the future was being invented.

But this wasn't any ordinary morning. The beach cottage she had called home for nearly a year now lay in smoking ruins along with almost all of her photography equipment. She tried not to think about the expensive view camera that she used for portraits and her art work. It had been destroyed along with all of her props and lights. She had been lucky to save the sturdy Speed Graphic, her portfolio, and the contents of the lockbox.

And then there was her sweet little speedster—her very *expensive* little speedster. Her father had given it to her shortly before she announced her plans to become an art photographer. She could not afford to replace it. At best she might be able to buy a secondhand Ford or Hudson. She had to have a vehicle. She could not do her work without one.

"My future as an art photographer is in that lockbox," she said. "It's where I keep the negatives of my art photos."

Nick downshifted for a curve. "Are you going to continue doing the newspaper work while you build your art career?"

"If necessary. But it's stressful. I work freelance so I have to sleep with the radio tuned to the police band all night. And then, when I do get a salable shot, I have to develop it fast and get prints to editors who might buy them. That's not the worst part, however."

"What's the worst part?"

"Keeping that side of my work a secret from the people who run the galleries and museums. They make the rules when it comes to art photography. As far as they're concerned, an artist who dabbles in photojournalism is not a real artist."

"So you've been living a double life."

"Yep." Vivian shrugged. "It's always been hard to make a living as an artist."

Nick smiled fleetingly. "I don't think I'm ever going to forget the sight of you coming out of the *Courier* darkroom wearing a leather apron over your nightgown."

Luckily her nightgown was fashioned of cotton, not diaphanous silk or rayon, Vivian reflected. The gown, the trench coat, and slippers were the only clothes she had been able to salvage. She had removed the coat to develop the photos but she was wearing it again now. There was nothing else she could do until the stores opened.

Nick was in better shape because he had been wearing his trousers and a shirt when the firebomb exploded. In addition he'd had a spare pair of shoes in the trunk of his car. There was no getting around the fact that they both looked very much the worse for wear, however.

"The first thing we're going to do when we get to Burning Cove is find a darkroom so that you can develop the rest of those pictures that you took tonight," Nick said.

"I think the first item on our agenda had better be shopping for some clean, nonsmoky clothes."

"Good point," Nick said.

"Also, I need to telephone my sister and tell her about the fire. There's a chance the *Courier* story will go out on the wire because of the Dagger Killer connection. She may see it in a San Francisco paper later today. Thank goodness my parents are still out of the country. At least I don't have to explain things to them."

"What are you going to tell your sister?"

Vivian thought about that for moment. "For now, I'll just say the house fire was an accident and that I've decided to take a few days off to recover from the shock. I'll tell her I'm hoping to get some good landscape shots while I'm recuperating in Burning Cove."

"You don't want her to worry about you."

"No. She's got enough on her mind at the moment. There's a lot going on."

"Big society wedding?"

"Yes. It's amazing how much work is involved. So many decisions to be made. Between you and me, I'm hoping she calls the whole thing off."

Nick shot her a sharp glance. "Why?"

"She thinks Hamilton Merrick is Mr. Perfect but I've got my doubts."

"Why?"

"On the surface Hamilton does appear to be Mr. Perfect but he is not ready to settle down. Frankly, I don't think he'll ever be ready to make a commitment and keep it. I'm pretty sure he's being pressured by his family, just as I was pressured by mine. Just as Lyra is now feeling pressured."

Nick was silent for a moment. When he spoke again his tone was oddly neutral.

"Got a Mr. Perfect of your own I should know about?" he asked.

"Nope."

"Maybe someone who might wonder why you suddenly disappeared from Adelina Beach?"

"Just some clients. But when they find out that my studio was destroyed in a fire I think most of them will understand and reschedule. Forget my personal life. Do you really think we've got a shot at identifying the arsonist in the photos I took last night?"

"It's a possibility," Nick said. "In addition to watching the fire that he set he would have wanted to see if you died in the blaze."

"If he was hanging around he knows we both escaped."

"Yes. He must have been unnerved by the loss of his little black book of poems. And now he's bungled his last commission. Got a feeling that will rattle him."

"Now we wait to see if he gets desperate and reckless?"

"Right." Nick flexed his hands on the steering wheel. "It's Pell's job to identify the guy and catch him. My job is to keep you safe."

"You saved my life tonight. I'd say you're doing your job just fine."

"The job isn't finished yet."

"It strikes me that a bodyguard ought to cultivate a more positive, optimistic outlook. You know, so that the client doesn't get too scared."

"In my experience, scared clients tend to follow orders better than the carefree, never-take-anything-seriously kind."

Vivian glanced down at the hem of her nightgown peeking out from beneath her trench coat. Then she looked at Nick. His hard profile was shadowed with the stubble of a morning beard. His hair was tousled and his shirt was wrinkled and smudged with soot. They both smelled of smoke.

"The front desk staff at the Burning Cove Hotel is going to get a shock when we check in," she said. "We look like we spent the night in a sleazy nightclub and then wandered into a very bad alley. We don't even have any luggage."

"I think we can assume that the front desk staff at the Burning Cove is very well trained. Given the nature of their clientele, they've probably seen it all. I'll bet they won't even blink at the sight of us."

"But we're supposed to be posing as newlyweds, right?"

"So? We decided we couldn't wait to get to the honeymoon suite at the Burning Cove. We spent our wedding night at a convenient beach."

She wondered how he had spent his first wedding night. Depressed and mortified because he had been unable to consummate the marriage? Or was his bride the one who had been unable to deal with the physical side of things? Maybe he had discovered too late she was mentally unbalanced? There were not a lot of reasons for granting annulments. They ranged from humiliating to horrifying.

"Before you ask," Nick said in the same too-even tone he had used when he had asked her if there was a man in her life. "Technically speaking, my marriage that wasn't a marriage lasted about three weeks. The reality is that it ended on the wedding night."

"I see," she said gently. "I'm sure it was complicated."

"You have no idea."

Chapter 16

The failure was devastating. Inconceivable. First the loss of the journal and now a fumbled commission. A man could only take so much stress.

Jonathan Treyherne's fingers trembled so badly he could barely get the key into the lock of his front door. When he finally made it over the threshold he whirled around and slammed the door shut. He took several deep breaths, trying to come to grips with what had happened.

The gas bomb should have worked. If the hastily concocted plan had gone well it would have appeared as if Brazier and her lover had died in a house fire. An accident. People died in house fires all the time. In addition Brazier was a photographer. That meant there were bound to have been a lot of chemicals and film lying around. The chemicals were not highly combustible but most people, including most cops, didn't know that. As for the film, it was notoriously unstable and flammable.

Yes, the strategy had been put together without a lot of forethought. Nevertheless, it should have worked. But Brazier and the man had made it safely out of the house and now they were gone. Vanished. There was no way to know where they were at that moment; a hotel or an auto court most likely. He would find them eventually. He had to find them. There were only five days left to complete the commission. He had never missed his own, self-imposed deadlines.

He had been distracted by the theft of the journal. That was the problem.

He turned on the light and studied his reflection in the hall mirror. Nothing had changed. Good breeding, an elite education, and a handsome inheritance had endowed him with the perfect camouflage. He was every inch a member of the upper class, descended from an old, established East Coast family. No one suspected the hunter beneath the surface.

Under that charming façade, however, the hunter was howling. His book of encrypted poems had disappeared from the safe less than forty-eight hours after he had undertaken his most recent commission.

He was finding it increasingly difficult to suppress the rising panic. In his frantic effort to identify the thief he had wasted time spying on his elderly housekeeper and gardener. He had broken into their little cottage and torn the place apart. He had found nothing to indicate that they were anything but what they appeared to be—hardworking, respectable, and utterly oblivious to the true nature of their employer. In his frustration he had fired both of them.

He was equally certain that none of his former clients knew who or what he was.

It had dawned on him that since the police had not come knocking on his door he could probably assume that whoever had stolen the journal moved in the criminal underworld. He had a few connections there himself. In desperation he had placed a call to an anonymous telephone number. He had left a message. Within hours the unknown individual who called himself simply the Broker had returned his call. The Broker had said that, for a fee, he would put out the word that someone was willing to pay any amount of money for a certain book of poems. So far no one had signaled a willingness to sell.

Maybe the thief had been killed by a fellow criminal, one who had no interest in a notebook filled with poems. Maybe the volume had wound up in a city dump.

But he was afraid to let himself believe that the journal had been discarded or destroyed by someone who did not comprehend its value. He had to know exactly what had happened to it.

Again and again he told himself that the precautions he had taken by encrypting the commissions were sufficient to protect him. He had tried to convince himself that there was nothing in the journal that could be used to identify him. But he knew that was not entirely true. There was a great deal of information in the poems. Names, dates, addresses, methods. A smart cop or a savvy special agent at the Bureau might be able to put it all together in a way that pointed at him.

The man gazing out from the mirror realized that his sanity if not his life depended on balancing two equally critical tasks. He had to recover the poems before someone realized what they really were.

But he also had to complete the commission. This one was too important. It could not be ignored, set aside, or postponed.

Jonathan turned away from the looking glass and went into his study. He poured a stiff shot of brandy with a shaking hand and gulped down half the glass before he was satisfied that his nerves had begun to steady.

He lit a cigarette and went to stand at the window, looking out into the endless night. After a moment he began to think clearly once again. The Broker was his best hope for tracking down the journal. For now there was nothing more that could be done on that front.

It was time to get back to the business of completing the commission. The first step was to find Vivian Brazier.

Chapter 17

Burning Cove
The next day . . .

You're taking a vacation in Burning Cove?" Lyra asked, voice rising in astonishment. "After losing everything in that dreadful fire last night?"

"I didn't lose *everything*," Vivian said. "I've got one of my cameras and my handbag. Thankfully I was also able to save my art negatives and my portfolio. I went shopping as soon as the stores opened here in Burning Cove this morning. I picked up some clothes and other essentials. Trust me, I've got everything I need."

Including a very luxurious hideout, she thought. She was currently standing in the living room of one of the small guest villas scattered across the grounds of the Burning Cove Hotel. The French doors were open to the private patio and walled garden. Through the wrought iron gate at the far end of the patio she could see the sun-splashed Pacific.

Nick was lounging in the shade, reading a newspaper. Rex was stretched out beside him. It all looked serene and luxurious. *You'd never know there's a killer after me.*

Nick had been right about the impeccable discretion of the hotel staff. No one at the front desk had so much as blinked when the bedraggled, disreputable-looking honeymoon couple had checked in without luggage or wedding rings.

"You shouldn't be alone, not after what you went through last night," Lyra said. "I'll drive down to Burning Cove and keep you company."

Vivian tightened her grip on the receiver. The last thing she wanted to do was put Lyra in danger.

"We've already been over this," she said. "I'm fine, really. You have a big engagement party to plan, remember?"

Lyra was silent for a long moment. "All right, I can certainly see why you might need some time to recover. But you're okay, right? You weren't injured?"

"I'm fine."

"Thank goodness you were not asleep last night when the fire started," Lyra said.

"Mm."

"The press is reporting that the authorities think your chemicals and film may have been the cause of the fire," Lyra said.

"Yes, I know. But that was not the source, believe me."

"Maybe an electrical problem? It was an old house, after all."

"The authorities are conducting a thorough investigation," Vivian said. "I'm sure they'll figure it out."

That was a bit of a stretch. The police and the fire department in Adelina Beach were no doubt doing their best but their resources were limited.

"Doesn't it seem very strange that not long after you were attacked by the Dagger Killer your cottage is destroyed?" Lyra asked. "Talk about odd coincidences."

Vivian winced. Lyra was smart. She might be preoccupied with engagement party plans at the moment but that didn't mean she wasn't paying attention.

"It is weird," Vivian said.

"I don't like this. I still think I should be there with you."

"Trust me, if I were in danger, I couldn't be anyplace safer than the Burning Cove Hotel. There is a lot of security here. I promise I'll let you know if anything changes, Lyra. Meanwhile, don't worry about me. And whatever you do, don't wire Mother and Father. They would both be frantic."

Lyra sighed. "Sooner or later you're going to have to tell them everything."

"I know. I'm choosing later. I just don't want to deal with Father telling me he warned me that I wouldn't like living on my own."

"I understand, believe me."

"Your turn. How is the planning going for the engagement party?"

"Fine."

The sudden cool note in Lyra's voice aroused all of Vivian's sisterly intuition.

"What's wrong, Lyra?"

"Nothing."

"Don't give me that. This is Vivian you're talking to. Your sister."

"I'm fine, Viv, really. It's just that I'm feeling a little overwhelmed by all the details. Speaking of which, I'd better get off the phone. Got a meeting with the dressmaker today. Call me tomorrow even if you don't have any news, all right?"

"Lyra, do you want to talk?"

"Not just now. Bye, Viv. I love you."

"Love you, too. You know if you need to tell me something, anything—"

There was a click. Lyra was gone.

Vivian set the receiver down in the cradle. She went into the kitchen and poured herself a glass of iced tea. Nick looked up when she walked outside and sat down in a wicker chair.

"What's wrong?" he asked.

"You mean aside from the fact that my house was burned down last night and my name popped up in the private journal of a paid assassin?"

He raised his brows. "Aside from those issues, yes."

"It's my sister. I can't be certain because she's a pretty good actress, but I think she's upset and hiding something from me."

Nick folded the paper and set it aside. He picked up his tea. "Why would she hide anything from you?"

"For the same reason that I'm hiding things from her. Because she doesn't want me to worry. Her tone of voice changed when we talked about the engagement party coming up next month."

"So, something to do with the party?"

Vivian considered that. "More likely something to do with the fact that she's going to be married to the man of her dreams."

"Bridal jitters?"

"Maybe. Yes, I think so."

"She wouldn't be the first person to have second thoughts," Nick said.

Vivian raised her brows. "You sound like you've had personal experience."

Nick reached out and rested his hand on Rex's back. The dog immediately raised his head in response. Alert but not alarmed, not yet at any rate.

"Unfortunately," Nick said, "the bride did not pay attention to what her intuition was trying to tell her until it was too late."

"Too late?"

"Patricia had a nervous breakdown on what was supposed to be our wedding night. The marriage was never consummated."

The atmosphere on the patio suddenly became very still. Vivian held her breath, waiting for secrets to be revealed. She watched Nick with the same kind of focus that she used when she took photos. The energy around him was as strong and vital as ever but the shadows that she had sensed just beneath the surface grew more intense.

"What happened?" she asked, mesmerized.

"I told you, the marriage was annulled." Nick smiled a bleak smile. "According to the law it never existed."

"Were the grounds failure to consummate the relationship or mental instability?"

"No," Nick said. "The grounds were bigamy. The woman I married was already legally wed to another man. Patricia had done her best to assume another identity, but on our wedding night she lost her nerve because she felt guilty. We arranged for a quiet annulment."

"Did she go back to her real husband?"

"No. She was afraid of him. With good reason. He tracked her down and tried to kill her."

And suddenly Vivian could see the rest of the story as clearly as if she were looking at Nick through the lens of a camera.

"Patricia's husband is dead, isn't he?" she said.

She stopped there because she could not bring herself to probe any deeper. Nick had a right to his secrets. But he picked up where she had left off, answering the obvious follow-up question in a way that made her realize he was carefully choosing each word.

"His name was Fulton Gage," Nick said. "He fell from the rooftop of a hotel in San Francisco. Broke his neck."

She caught her breath. "Suicide?"

"Yes, according to the authorities."

"Hang on, did this happen about a year ago? I was still living in San Francisco at the time. I remember something in the papers. Two men were supposedly fighting over a woman. One of the men—the husband—jumped. The authorities said he was evidently distraught because his wife had run off with another man."

"There was a little more to the story," Nick said. "His plan was to shoot me first, but in the fog he ran out of ammunition. He couldn't see more than two or three feet. Unfortunately, he had Patricia. She was supposed to be hiding in a safe location but she knew that Gage would probably try to kill me. She felt guilty because she had put me in harm's way. She went to him. Pleaded with him not to hurt me. Offered to go back to him. He grabbed her and then he used her to draw me out onto the roof."

"So the press got it right. The fight was over a woman. One man wanted to murder her. The other saved her life."

"It sounds simple when you put it like that."

"I'm sure it was anything but simple," Vivian said. "How did you manage to save Patricia?"

"He was obsessed with the need to control her. I used that obsession to make him lose what little self-control he possessed. I pointed out that he was obviously so weak willed any woman could manipulate him. He had a gun. I figured he would either make a run for it when he ran out of ammunition or try to charge me. He came at me, following my voice in the fog. He had the knife that he had planned to use on Patricia. When he finally saw me, I'm sure that all he could make out was my silhouette. He didn't realize I was standing right at the edge of the roof. He lunged forward . . ."

Nick stopped talking.

"Obviously you got out of his way," Vivian finished quietly.

"At the last possible second. He went over the edge."

Vivian took a deep breath. "That was not your fault."

Nick was silent for a long moment. "Depends on how you look at it."

"Is this where you tell me you *knew* he would probably go over the edge if you managed to make him charge you?"

"I was a matador waving a red cape at a bull," Nick said, speaking very softly now.

"Wrong analogy," Vivian said. "One can and should feel sorry for the bull. It's just a beast that is following its instinct. I would hope you don't feel any sympathy for Fulton Gage."

"No. But like the matador I knew what I was doing. What does that make me?"

"A man who did what he had to do to save a woman's life. Sounds to me like you used words—the only weapons you had—to defeat a man who was armed with a pistol and a knife."

Nick did not respond. His hand rested on Rex's back.

"But a man died because of your words," Vivian continued.

"I still dream about it. And my dreams are . . . vivid."

"Nightmares."

"Yes."

"I can't get inside your nightmares to examine them, but do you think it's possible the reason they haunt you isn't because an evil, violent, obsessed man died but that you almost failed to save Patricia?"

Nick's jaw tightened. He watched her through slightly narrowed eyes. "I miscalculated. And because I miscalculated she nearly died."

"And what makes it even worse is that if she had died it would have been because she had been trying to save you."

Nick's smile was grim. "I told you it was complicated."

Vivian felt as if she were walking across a very narrow bridge above deep and treacherous currents.

She cleared her throat. "I can't help but notice that after Gage was dead, you and Patricia did not get married for real."

"No," Nick said. "We didn't get married for real."

It was obvious from the ice in his voice that the subject was closed. But Vivian suddenly understood.

"Whatever happened up on that roof scared the hell out of Patricia, didn't it?" she said before she could stop herself. "Afterward she was frightened of you."

Nick's mouth curved in a faint, cold smile. "Terrified."

"She married you because she sensed that you could protect her, but when you actually did save her life the violence unnerved her."

"Something like that, yes. She was—is—very fragile. Delicate."

"Got it. I'm not fragile or delicate. In the past month two people have tried to murder me. One is dead, which suits me just fine. And I can tell you right now that if you succeed in stopping the other guy, I'm not going to be the least bit frightened of you."

Nick's eyes warmed a little. "No?"

"No. In fact, I will buy you a drink."

"Deal."

She studied him for a long moment. "If it's any consolation, I don't think a marriage between the two of you would have been a happy union. At least, not for long."

That comment evidently caught him off guard. "What makes you say that?"

He did not seem offended or defensive. Simply interested.

"I have a feeling that, sooner or later, you both would have felt trapped in your roles. You would have become frustrated trying to keep your armor endlessly polished. Sooner or later the pressure to be the perfect princess, to always appear delicate and in need of being saved, would have made Patricia resentful. The parts you each chose to play would have made it difficult for the two of you to reveal your inner secrets to each other."

"You may be right. I hadn't considered things in that light. You are a rather frightening woman, Vivian."

She sighed. "You are not the first man to inform me of that, although most of the others have put it somewhat more diplomatically."

"Is that the real reason you've never married?" he asked.

"Apparently. My mother and my sister have both informed me on more than one occasion that I have a bad habit of scaring off any man who takes a serious personal interest in me. One of the reasons I liked dating Hamilton Merrick was because he wasn't terribly curious about me. We had fun together and that was enough for both of us. And then Hamilton had to go and spoil things by asking me to marry him."

"Maybe he cared more about you than you did about him."

"Nope."

Nick smiled. "Just to be clear, when I said you were a frightening woman I was making an objective observation. I was not stating my personal feelings."

"Are you sure of that?"

"You don't scare me, Vivian Brazier."

"Give me time."

Chapter 18

Last time I saw you, Uncle Pete, you were checking in to Dr. Presswood's Health Spa for another try at treating the insomnia and the fever dreams," Nick said. "How did it go?"

"About how you'd expect." Pete Sundridge snorted and settled deeper into one of the wicker chairs. "Dr. Presswood turned out to be another fraud."

"I told you that before you signed the check."

Pete glared. "Don't need you saying you told me so."

Peter Sundridge had shown up at the front door of the villa a few minutes earlier. He had been dressed as a hotel gardener and escorted to the room by a hotel security guard.

It was easy to mistake Pete Sundridge for a shady character. He could have played a gunfighter in a Hollywood Western. Lean and tough, even in middle age, he had the eyes of a man who did battle with demons on a nightly basis. Each new dawn was a small, personal victory.

Nick understood. He and Pete were both direct descendants of Arden Sundridge, who had headed west in the late eighteen hundreds seeking escape from the fever dreams that constituted the family curse. Arden had started out prospecting for gold but quickly realized that the real money lay in the business of supplying the miners with the provisions they required to chase their fantasies. His next insight had been the understanding that, in the West, water would always be infinitely more valuable than gold. He had begun buying land that could support crops and livestock.

The Sundridges had never had serious problems when it came to making money. They had a talent for it, a true gift for taking calculated risks.

It was the nightmares that caused trouble.

All of the Sundridges experienced startlingly vivid dreams occasionally but, according to family lore and Nick's own personal research, the curse of frequent, dramatic fever dreams struck hard only once or twice in each generation. He and Pete were the most recent examples.

Pete had chased quack cures for years. Nick had searched for answers in old books and the private journals of others who had suffered from similar afflictions.

The interesting thing, Nick concluded, was that it had been a long time since his uncle had appeared as cheerful and as enthusiastic as he did today. Going back to work for Luther Pell had been good for Pete.

"When it comes to frauds, it's not like you've got any room to talk," Pete continued. "Look at you, another fake marriage. That makes two in a row. You know, if you keep this up, it's going to be impossible to keep a lid on the rumors."

Nick glanced uneasily at the open doors of the villa. A short time ago Vivian had disappeared inside to get another pitcher of iced tea. She would return at any moment.

"What rumors?" he asked, careful to lower his voice.

"The ones about your annulment, of course." Pete snorted again. "You know damn well there was talk. People wondered if maybe you hadn't been able to be a real husband to Patricia. The fact that you haven't shown much interest in women in the past year hasn't helped matters."

"Uncle Pete, we've had this conversation. I told you to stop worrying about my personal life."

"What personal life? That's the problem. You haven't got one." Pete paused. A speculative gleam appeared in his eyes. "At least not until now."

"There was no wedding this time so there won't be any legalities to untangle when it's over. Miss Brazier and I are here under strictly false pretenses. Everything about our relationship is fake. In case you didn't notice, there are two bedrooms in this particular villa. We are using both of them. I'm on a job."

"Uh-huh." Pete studied the entrance of the villa. "An interesting woman, your Miss Brazier. Nothing like your last fake wife."

"She's not *my* Miss Brazier," Nick said. He was startled by the wistful sensation that whispered through him. "She's a client. You're the one who told Luther Pell that Vivian needs a bodyguard."

Pete's gunfighter eyes narrowed a little. "It's true. Someone's after her."

"Given that someone tried to kill her last night, I'm inclined to believe you. Have you made any more progress decoding those poems?"

"Some. Nothing that points to the identity of the assassin or the person who hired him to kill Miss Brazier, though."

"You're sure the killer is a man?"

Pete shook his head. "I can't even be certain of that." He opened the briefcase at his feet and took out a notebook. "Take a look at some of the unencrypted poems, compare them to the encrypted version, and see what you think. Far as I can tell, the victims were all standing in the way of something someone else wanted—money, an inheritance, control of a company. About the only other thing I noticed is that, in addition to taking a month for each of what he calls his *commissions*, the Poet usually takes a break between murders. About three months."

"The Poet?"

"That's what Luther and I are calling him until we get a proper name."

Nick opened the notebook and looked at the latest entries. "Huh."

"What?"

"He targeted Vivian almost immediately after he completed the previous commission. He didn't take the usual three months off."

"Right."

"So something made him change his pattern."

"Luther and I agree but we can't figure out what might have caused him to do that."

Nick thought for a moment. "If the murders are more than just a business for him, if he truly likes the process of stalking and killing another human being—"

"He does." Pete grunted. "Far as I can tell, he gets a real thrill out of his damned commissions. Gets depressed when they end."

"He's addicted to killing."

"Yep."

"In that case the change in the pattern may indicate that he's losing control of the addiction. He needs more and more of the drug. Or maybe he suffered some sort of psychotic break."

"He's already broken," Pete said. "Probably doesn't pay to try to analyze him."

"True." Nick closed the notebook. "I'll take a look at your transcript later and see if anything else stands out."

"You do that. I've got a talent for code breaking but I'm not nearly as insightful as you are when it comes to figuring out how the bad guys think."

Nick looked at him. "You're getting a kick out of working with Pell again, aren't you?"

"It's been a while since I got to do the one thing I do best. The encryption business hasn't been good since the government closed down the Black Chamber and then went after Luther Pell's department and fired his team. Idiots."

Nick raised a brow. "Pell's team?"

"'Course not. I was talking about those damn bureaucrats back in D.C. After the War they figured that they didn't need spies and encryption people anymore. What was it Henry Stimson said?"

"According to the legend it was something to the effect that gentlemen don't read each other's mail."

"What hogwash." Pete heaved a heavy sigh. "Well, those fools back in Washington will soon be scrambling to rebuild their spy apparatus. Everyone can see what's coming."

"War."

"Yep." Pete stretched out his legs and contemplated the tips of his shoes. "Pell tells me he's running his own private version of what he used to do when he handled the old Accounting Department. Calls it Failure Analysis, Incorporated. Does contract work."

"Is that right? Thought he owned a nightclub."

"Guess you could say Failure Analysis is a sideline of his. He doesn't advertise it, that's for damn sure."

"How does he get his clients?"

"Same way you do," Pete said. "Word of mouth. From what he told me it sounds like he's doing occasional consulting work for some of the same people who fired him and his team. He also does jobs for the FBI. He handles investigations that are too sensitive or too damn hot for a government agency or the Bureau. You know how it is. That sort don't like to get their hands dirty, especially if things go wrong and the cases blow up and land on the front pages."

Nick smiled. "Sounds like Mr. Pell has created a nice little market for himself. Smart."

Pete peered at him. "Pell appreciates people like us, Nick. People with certain talents."

"In our family we don't call what you and I have a talent. It's a curse, remember? That's why you're still wasting money on every fraud and charlatan who promises a quick fix for the nightmares."

"Haven't had any nightmares since I went back to work for Pell. Just the fever dreams that I can control. Feels good."

"About the fever dreams—" Nick paused and lowered his voice. "I may have found a book with some answers."

Pete's expression sharpened. "Yeah?"

"I came across it in an antiquarian bookshop. It's the journal of a man named Caleb Jones. It was written in the late eighteen hundreds. He was a private investigator who lived in London. He evidently took the existence of what he called psychical talents as a given."

"Psychical talents?"

"We'd call them paranormal abilities today."

"Damn it, we're not a couple of frauds pretending to have psychic powers."

"What I'm getting at here is that his way of solving a case sounds like a version of the Sundridge family curse. But he figured out how to control the visions, at least to some extent."

"Booze? Drugs?"

"No. Meditation."

"Bah. I tried that. Spent good money on a quack who promised to teach me how to meditate. Every time I tried it the nightmares got worse."

"I know—I've wasted some money that way, too. But this technique is a little different. Jones writes that our abilities are actually a kind of intuition. The trick is to control it."

There was cautious interest in Pete's eyes now. "You're sure this Jones character wasn't one of those charlatans who claims to be able to read minds and see the future?"

"All I can tell you is that it seems to be working for me."

"But you still get the fever dreams?"

"Yes. The difference is that I have fairly good control over them. I can go into one and out at will."

"Yeah?" Pete looked skeptical. "How's that work?"

"I line up the things I want to analyze and then I go into a self-induced trance."

"You hypnotize yourself?"

"Maybe. I think so. But I control the trance."

Pete squinted, still dubious. He snapped his fingers. "The answers pop up just like that?"

"No, what pops up, assuming I have enough information going into the trance, is the right question, the one I should be asking."

Pete nodded in a knowing way. "Ask the right question and the answer is a hell of a lot easier to figure out."

"Yes."

Pete studied the entrance of the villa. "How does Miss Brazier feel about your new way of dreaming?"

"She doesn't know exactly what I do or how I do it."

"Think she could handle it if she saw you coming out of a dream?"

"She's not Patricia."

"But you don't know how she would react?"

"No," Nick admitted.

"Best not put her to the test, then. Miss Brazier has reason enough to be worried at the moment. You don't want to scare her, leastways not until after we figure out who's trying to kill her."

Vivian walked out onto the patio. "I heard something about scaring me. I assume you're talking about the assassin?"

"Sort of," Pete said. "But don't you worry. Nick will take good care of you."

"I know," Vivian said. She sat down and crossed her legs. "When do I get to meet the mysterious Luther Pell?"

"Pell thinks it's better if he isn't seen with you and Nick until we have a better idea of what's going on," Pete said. "No one knows me. I'm just a gardener who came into the hotel through the service entrance."

"So we sit here in this very nice gilded cage and wait for the killer to come around and introduce himself?" Vivian asked.

"Doubt if we'll have to wait much longer," Pete said. "The Poet's on a tight schedule."

Vivian shuddered. "Thanks for the reminder. I think we should mess up his precious schedule. We need to do something to make him show his hand."

"We have done something to put him off balance," Nick said. "We moved to Burning Cove. Trust me, that will throw him for a while. It's going to take him a day or two to find us, assuming he knows what he's doing. Meanwhile, I need the time to study his poems and you need to get those fire scene photos developed."

"I'll require a darkroom," Vivian said. "The local newspaper will have one but I doubt if the editor would let me use it. I might be able to find a camera shop that would let me rent space and equipment."

Pete chuckled. "I don't think you'll have a problem using the *Herald*'s darkroom. All it will take is a phone call to the editor."

Vivian raised her brows. "Who makes the call?"

"Luther Pell or, more likely, the owner of this hotel, Oliver Ward," Pete said. "Ward's wife, Irene, is the local crime beat reporter."

"Why do I have the feeling this town is run by Luther Pell and Oliver Ward?" Vivian asked.

Pete shrugged. "Probably because that's pretty much the way it is. Every town is run by someone or some group. L.A. is run by the big movie studios. Burning Cove is run by a nightclub owner who used to be a government spy and the proprietor of a hotel who used to be a magician."

"California," Vivian said. "Land of opportunity."

Chapter 19

"Here you go, the *Herald's* darkroom." Irene Ward waved a hand at the partially open door. "Take your time. Don't forget the deal I made with my editor. The paper gets first crack at any photo that's worth a headline while you're visiting Burning Cove."

Vivian smiled. "And you get the story."

"Yep." Irene laughed. "It's always nice to work with another professional, someone who understands the news business."

Pete Sundridge had been right about one thing: All it had taken to obtain permission to use the *Herald's* darkroom was a phone call. But that call had been made by Irene Ward, not her husband. Irene was the *Herald's* star reporter. Her editor trusted her instincts and was willing to accommodate her because she had provided the paper with so many hot, front-page headlines.

Vivian had liked Irene Ward on sight when they had been introduced in Oliver Ward's private office. Vivian sensed a kindred spirit. They were both interested in the mystery beneath the surface.

"I'll wait out here in the hallway while you work your magic with the photos," Nick said.

"There are several films to be developed and printed," Vivian said. "I'm going to be in here most of the afternoon."

"Take your time," Nick said. He held up the briefcase that contained Pete's transcription of the poems. "I've got a little light reading to do."

Irene looked at Nick. "I'll get you some coffee."

﹡

It was nearly five before they finally got back to the hotel. They went out onto the villa's patio. Vivian opened the folder of large prints she had made. One by one she arranged them on the table. Nick examined each with an intense expression.

"These are excellent," he said. "Sharp focus. Fine grain."

"The Speed Graphic is a very good camera."

He smiled. "And you are a very good photographer."

"Thanks."

She moved to stand beside him and pointed out the people she could identify. "Some of these folks are my neighbors, of course. I know their names. Most of them have lived on Beachfront Lane for years."

"What about the others?"

Vivian used the magnifying glass, which had been magically produced by the hotel's front desk, to examine every unknown face in the scenes.

"The fire drew quite a crowd," she said. "There are a lot of people I don't recognize. Any one of them could be the firebug."

"We're looking for someone who will be hanging back, trying to stay in the shadows," Nick said, "trying to be invisible. By the time these photos were taken, everyone standing around in the street, including him, knew that we made it out of the house. He knew he failed."

Nick spoke in a cool, detached manner as if he were a calculating machine. But his eyes seemed to heat a little and she could have sworn she felt electricity shivering in the air around him.

"If he knows he failed, why would he stick around and take the risk of being noticed?" she asked.

"Wrong question," Nick said absently. "Why not stay to enjoy the show? He's not afraid of being recognized. He's been getting away with murder for years. He has confidence in his camouflage, whatever that is."

Vivian shuddered. "A real wolf in sheep's clothing."

"He's not afraid that he will be noticed but he is bound to be unnerved because he failed," Nick continued, very focused now. "He's not accustomed to failure. He'll be trying to put together another plan and he'll be in a hurry. Time is running out. He's going to have to improvise. He'll make mistakes because he's not used to changing his plans."

"You're getting all that from those poems?"

"Yes. He thinks of himself as a creative artist but he's actually obsessively rigid when it comes to murder." Nick took a close look at a figure dressed in a workman's dark jacket and trousers. A cap angled low over the eyes concealed most of the man's face. "Do you recognize him?"

Vivian scrutinized the figure. "No. He's dressed like a deliveryman or maybe a cabdriver."

"The clothes are right but there's something wrong with the way he's leaning against your neighbor's fence."

"What do you mean?"

"It's the pose. He's trying to imitate the casual slouch of a workingman but it's off somewhat. He's lounging against that fence in the manner of a man who is accustomed to lounging at the bar of his club. His shoes are wrong, too. They're not boots. They don't belong to someone who delivers fish or drives a cab. They look expensive. He was in a rush tonight. Didn't get the costume right. He just made his first mistake."

Vivian took a closer look.

"I see what you mean," she said. She shuffled through the photos, looking for other pictures that included the man in the cap. "He's in the first couple of photos but not in the last ones. He must have taken off when he saw me shooting the crowd."

"It would have been easy for him to slip away, especially after the fire department arrived. He probably had a car parked on a nearby side street."

Vivian crossed her arms. "So much for hoping these pictures would enable us to spot the guy."

Nick looked up. There was a lot of heat in his eyes now. The anticipation of the hunter, she thought.

"We don't have him yet," he said, "but we have a lot more information about him."

"We can't be sure of that. The man in the cap might be a perfectly innocent bystander."

Nick glanced at the photo and shook his head once. "Whatever else he is, he's not an innocent bystander. He was a man playing a part, I'm certain of it."

Vivian froze. "An actor?"

"A talent for acting is a job requirement for a man who has made a career of getting away with murder." Nick paused, eyeing her closely. "Why? What's wrong?"

"Probably nothing." She folded her arms. "But an actor showed up at the scene of the Clara Carstairs murder. He begged me not to take his picture. I didn't. There were no other photographers there so, in the end, no photos of him at the crime scene ever appeared in the papers."

"Did you recognize the actor?"

"Oh, yes. There was no mistaking that good-looking face. Ripley Fleming."

Chapter 20

Adelina Beach
That night . . .

Toby Flint adjusted the focus of his camera and peered through the lens. Much better. Now he had a detailed close-up of the woman's excellent breasts. He could see every detail of the nipples. It was as if he could reach out and touch them. Unfortunately touching the models was not allowed. That did not stop him from getting hard.

He was not the only man in the studio with a stiff cock. It was the weekly meeting of the Adelina Beach Photography Club. Tonight's theme was Women of the Ancient World. The room was packed, mostly with men. They had formed a circle around the nude model who was stretched out in a languid position on a cheap bedsheet that was supposed to be exotic silk drapery.

The sweat on the brows of the male photographers could have been explained by the hot lights that illuminated the tableau but the bulges in their trousers told the real story. They were here for the same reason that Toby had decided to show up for the meeting tonight. It gave them a legitimate reason to get close to a real, live naked woman and take pictures for their personal collection.

Toby was pretty sure that every man in the club had turned up for the event because it was understood that Cleopatra would be posing nude or nearly so. After all, you couldn't do serious, artistic photography without nude models.

The truth, Toby thought, was that taking pictures of naked young women was about as close as he could get to sex these days. He couldn't afford the kind of classy lady who insisted on being taken out to dinner and a show before falling into bed with a guy. Couldn't afford the type who worked in brothels, either. He was almost broke. Again.

He'd made a few bucks with his shots of the Clara Carstairs murder—enough to buy some film and flashbulbs—but that was it. He didn't have nearly enough cash to pay off his gambling debts and he could not see any way to obtain the amount that he needed.

He probably should have been down at the police station, hovering over the teletype machine in hopes of getting early word of a nice little murder or car wreck or fire, but what was the point? He was in too deep. He could not possibly make enough with a few crime-and-fire shots to get free of the very dangerous man who had loaned him the money for the last, ruinous night on board the offshore gambling ship.

He had attended the photography club meeting tonight in a desperate effort to distract himself from the hopelessness of his financial situation.

The model's name was Millie Crosley, and under other circumstances he would have been very distracted. She was a real looker, another aspiring actress who was doing photography modeling to pay the rent while she waited to be discovered by Hollywood.

She was good, Toby decided. There was a lot of sensuality in her pose. Her dark hair tumbled in waves across her rounded shoulders. One long leg was drawn up in a seemingly casual manner that revealed the luscious curves of her thigh and hip. Her heavily made-up eyes were half-closed in a way that was meant to project sultry, seductive heat. A gossamer-thin scarf was draped in a coy fashion across the dark triangle of hair between her thighs. Aside from that, her only attire consisted of a lot of cheap dime-store necklaces that fell artfully across her bare breasts.

Several shutters snapped. The model smiled, reached down, and removed the scarf that had veiled her privates. She separated her thighs just enough to reveal a little more forbidden territory. It was the moment everyone had been waiting for. The temperature in the room shot up several degrees. There was a lot of commotion as most of the men frantically tried to get the close-up.

Toby reached into the pocket of his coat and discovered that he had used his last film holder. Briefly he considered trying to talk one of the other *artists* into loaning him some spare film but he saw at once it was hopeless. Every man around him was lost in the hot excitement of the moment.

No one noticed when Toby left the circle of photographers and headed for the door.

He went outside into the night. A light fog partially obscured the quiet street. He opened the door of his battered Ford sedan and got behind the wheel. For a moment he sat quietly staring into the mist-shrouded darkness while he considered his options. There was only one left. Time to head for Mexico. If he hung around Adelina Beach he was a dead man. He had forty-eight hours to come up with the cash. That was simply not going to happen.

It wouldn't be a quick, clean death. The loan shark would make an example of him.

A rustling sound in the back seat warned him he was not alone in the sedan. He froze, terrified. The shark had sent his enforcers after him before the deadline.

He lurched out of his paralysis and grabbed the door handle in the vain hope of escaping from the car. But it was too late. He heard the snick of a gun being cocked.

He had waited too long to make a run for the border. He was out of time.

※

Fifteen minutes later he discovered somewhat to his amazement that he was still alive.

He was alone in the Ford now. There was a thousand dollars in fresh, crisp bills in his wallet and the promise of another thousand if he carried out his end of the deal. It would be more than enough to pay off his gambling debts. He would be free of the shark. He would give up the gambling and concentrate on his photography. Maybe go back to his art work or come up with a proposal for a *Life* magazine piece. A bright new future glittered on the horizon.

All he had to do was find Vivian Brazier and make a phone call. He did not want to think about what might happen after he made that call. It was none of his business.

Chapter 21

Burning Cove
The next day . . .

Nick spent most of the day on the villa's patio, immersed in the poems. From time to time he was aware that Vivian was growing restless. Irene Ward came by at noon and invited her to lunch in the hotel dining room. Nick ordered room service. He took a couple of breaks to walk Rex and clear his mind, but for the most part he concentrated on the killer's words.

The details the FBI and the cops would need to close at least some of the murders were in the lines that Pete had succeeded in deciphering. Names. Dates. Addresses. Motives. Amounts paid.

But the killer's secrets were buried in the encrypted verses.

. . . The tide of night rolls in consuming the glorious moments of
transcendence.
Once again the hunter is lost in the devouring mist, drowning in it.
The path back to the brilliant, dazzling clarity of dawn
appears . . .

"Nick."

Vivian's voice pulled him out of the harrowing poem. He looked up and saw her standing in front of him. She was holding a newspaper in her hands.

"What's wrong?" he asked.

"Sorry to interrupt you but I thought you should see this. It's the afternoon edition of the *Burning Cove Herald*. Take a look at the photo on page two."

She handed him the paper. He turned to the second page. The photo showed a well-dressed man emerging from the rear of a limo in front of the grand entrance of the Burning Cove Hotel.

"That's Ripley Fleming," Vivian said. "According to the *Herald* he checked in earlier today."

Chapter 22

I t was an eerie stillness that awakened her that night. Not silence, not exactly, Vivian decided. More like a sudden, bone-deep awareness.

Nick.

She did not understand how she could be so sure that the feeling was connected to him but she did not question it. Linked to that certainty was a sense of urgency. She did not question that, either.

She opened her eyes to the moonlit shadows of the bedroom and listened closely. The strange sensation of stillness that had aroused her was something of an illusion. If she concentrated she could hear the music of the hotel's lounge trio. Laughter and voices drifted from the vicinity of the bar. Nothing had changed since she and Nick had gone into their separate bedrooms a couple of hours earlier.

And yet . . .

Just my imagination. You've been under a lot of stress lately. Don't worry, nothing's wrong.

Rex would be barking a warning if someone had somehow managed to get through the multilayered rings of hotel security protecting the villa.

On the other hand, she was being hunted by a professional killer, an assassin skilled in the art of making it look as if his victims had all died in accidents and of natural causes.

The edgy restlessness became more intense. She had always believed she possessed strong nerves but there were limits to what anyone could handle. In the past year her night work as a freelance photojournalist had exposed her to some grisly, deeply disturbing sights. Not long ago someone had tried to murder her in her own darkroom. Then someone had firebombed her cottage. She was the target of a paid killer.

A woman could take only so much. Given the circumstances it would have been astonishing if her nerves *hadn't* been affected.

She needed to get up, to move. A medicinal shot of whiskey might help. She remembered seeing a bottle in the liquor cabinet.

Pushing the covers aside, she rose, slipped her feet into a pair of slippers, and reached for her robe. The door of her room was slightly ajar. She had opened it just before getting into bed because she found it comforting to know that Nick was right next door. He had told her that he would leave his door partially open, too, so that Rex could patrol the villa.

She slipped through the doorway. In the dim glow of the wall sconce she saw that Nick's door was no longer ajar; it stood wide open. The bed was revealed in a shaft of moonlight. Nick was not in it.

She sensed movement and turned to look into the living room. Rex loomed in the shadows. He padded forward to greet her. He did not appear concerned. She took that as a good omen. She gave him a couple of pats and then moved on across the room.

There was no sign of Nick but the French doors were open to the night. She went to the threshold and studied the enclosed patio and garden. Nick stood quietly in the moonlight, gazing through the wrought iron gate at the silvered ocean.

"Nick?"

He turned slowly to face her, but in the dense shadows she could not make out his expression.

"It's all right," he said. "There's nothing wrong. I just came out here to do some thinking."

She walked across the patio to join him. When she got close she was aware of a little heat in his eyes. As if he was running a low-grade fever, she thought. He had a towel draped around his neck.

"Are you all right?" she asked.

"Yes."

The fever heat in his eyes was just a trick of the moonlight, she decided. It was already fading. But as she watched he used the towel to dash sweat off his forehead.

"You're not feeling ill?" she asked.

"No, damn it, I am not ill. There's nothing wrong. You can go back to bed."

Understanding whispered through her.

"You came out here to think about the killer's poems and the man you noticed in the photos, didn't you?" she said. "You're working. I'm sorry I disturbed you."

She started to turn back toward the shadowed front room of the villa.

"You asked me why I did not marry Patricia after she was . . . widowed," he said. "I told you it was because the violence that took place on the hotel rooftop frightened her. That was true but it wasn't the whole truth. There's more to the story."

She stopped and faced him. "I'm listening."

"For generations the men of the Sundridge line have had a tendency to experience odd dreams."

"Everyone has strange dreams from time to time."

"Not like the Sundridge curse dreams," Nick said. Grim certainty resonated in the words. "Not like my dreams."

"How are they different?"

"The kind of dreams I'm talking about feel more like visions. Sometimes they seem like premonitions. I get the sense that if I don't do something—if I don't act—someone will die."

"Okay, that kind of dreaming definitely sounds unnerving."

"The visions used to strike randomly, day or night. But I've developed some control over them. Most of my ancestors found some way to cope with the curse, too. But it's very easy for those who witness a man in a fever dream to conclude that he is . . . unbalanced. That kind of dreaming makes intimate relationships—marriage—highly problematic. Disturbing."

"Your dreams made Patricia think you might be insane?"

"We never shared a bed but at one point during the short time that we were together she walked in on me one night when I was dreaming."

"Like I did just now?"

"You thought I was ill."

"It looked like you were running a fever. I didn't think you were crazy."

"You might change your mind if I told you what I just saw in my vision," Nick said.

"Try me."

Once again he fell silent. Once again she thought he might not respond.

"I saw a man moving through gray fog," he said. "Now and then he comes across someone else in the mist. He kills the other person and for a while the fog clears. It's as if he has performed a sacrifice. He finds himself on top of a mountain. He can see for miles. But the fog always returns. When it does he realizes that another sacrifice is required. Sacrifices are not performed randomly. They require a ritual."

"We're talking about the Poet, I assume."

"Yes."

"What does your vision tell you about him?"

"He's not simply a cold-blooded businessman who kills for money. I think he murders people because on some level he believes that is the only thing that keeps him sane."

"And he doesn't comprehend that murdering people in a ritual sacrifice is exactly what makes him *insane*?"

"That is the one thing he can never admit or acknowledge."

"Which means you've figured out his deepest, most closely held secret, his vulnerable point."

Nick watched her in silence for a very long time.

"You understand, don't you?" he said finally.

"Your fever dreaming sounds a lot like what I do when I focus my camera. I open my senses, my inner eye, and try to see beneath the surface. I try to ask the right question, the one that unlocks a few secrets." She smiled. "It's called intuition, Nick. Neither one of us is crazy."

"That's what Jones wrote in his personal journal."

"Who is Jones?"

"Never mind. That's how I work, too. Patricia married me because she hoped I could protect her. When she opened the door that night and saw me emerging from a trance, she was convinced that she had chosen a mentally unbalanced eccentric who was as dangerous as the man she was hiding from. Later, on that rooftop, the violence overwhelmed her."

"She was already terrified, unnerved, and feeling guilty for having deceived you. She had run from one man because he threatened her with physical harm only to find herself with another man who might be deranged."

"Yes."

"Why do you do what you do, Nick? Why did you become a private investigator?"

"I'm not sure. It's the only work that feels right for me."

"I think you are drawn to that work because it allows you to use your talent, your keen intuition," Vivian said. "Do you realize how fortunate you are? You've found a purpose in life and you have the ability to fulfill that purpose. Be grateful."

"Do you think it's really that simple?" he asked.

"Yes, I do. Obviously your kind of intuition is powerful and it has complicated your life. I'm sure it will continue to do so. But I think you would have far greater problems if you tried to ignore or suppress it."

"You've known me for less than three days but you know more about me than Patricia did in the weeks that we were together. More than anyone does, except for Uncle Pete."

"You and Patricia were a mistake. It's over. Let it go." Vivian started to turn away. "I think that's enough personal history for now. I'm going to get a shot of whiskey to help me get back to sleep."

"That sounds like an excellent idea."

She paused. "What about your visions?"

"I'm through for now. I don't have enough information yet to ask the right questions."

"I understand."

Once again she started across the patio, heading toward the darkened living room.

"Vivian."

She went very still, everything inside her tense with anticipation. She knew then that on some level this was what she had been waiting for since the moment she had opened her door at the beach house and found him on the front step.

Her name. Spoken in the intimate shadows of a moonlit garden.

When she turned back to face him, she found him standing less than a foot away.

"Yes," she said.

He did not speak. Instead, he held out his hand. She took it.

He pulled her gently toward him and covered her mouth with his own.

Chapter 23

Toby Flint lit another cigarette with shaking fingers, dug some change out of the pocket of his overcoat, and stepped into the phone booth. What he was about to do scared the hell out of him but he had no choice. He shouldn't have followed Vivian to Burning Cove. He should have just taken the blood money, paid off the loan shark, and left town. He would never let himself get in so deep again.

But even as he made the vow he knew he was doomed. The gambling gave him a thrill he couldn't get any other way. And once in a while he won . . .

Toby dialed the operator.

"Burning Cove Hotel," he said.

He braced one hand against the wall of the booth and gazed out into the night-darkened street. It was after midnight and that particular section of downtown Burning Cove was drenched in silence. The stylish shops and sidewalk cafés were closed. During the day the palm-shaded plazas were crowded with fashionable people on vacation in the glamorous seaside town. But at this hour the neighborhood was deserted. Visitors were spending the evening in the local nightclubs and hotel lounges hoping to see and be seen with celebrities and stars.

The shopping district seemed peaceful but he couldn't shake the sense that he was being watched.

"Burning Cove Hotel," a polished male voice said. "How may I assist you?"

"I want to talk to Vivian Brazier."

"I'm sorry, sir, there is no one here by that name."

"Look, I know she's staying there."

"There is no one registered under that name. I'm afraid you have the wrong hotel."

"Wait, don't hang up. Damn it, I know she's there." Toby tried to think. "She may have checked in under another name. She probably has a camera with her. She's a photographer."

"That's not a helpful description. Several of our guests have cameras. I strongly urge you to try one of the other local hotels."

"If you won't put me through at least take a message. This is important."

"We don't take messages for people who are not registered."

"Tell her Toby Flint called. Tell her it's a matter of life and death. I need to talk to her. Now. Tonight. I'm in a phone booth on Olive Street near a shop named the Elegant Lady. Tell her I've got some important information to sell her. I'll wait thirty minutes. After that I'm going to disappear."

"We don't—"

"Just give her the damned message. Be sure she knows to bring some cash."

Toby slammed the receiver into the cradle. That was it. He'd done what he could to make up for his betrayal. He'd give Cinderella thirty minutes, no more.

After a couple of minutes he realized he didn't like standing in the phone booth under the glare of the streetlight. It made him feel vulnerable. A target. His sedan was parked across the street. The money he had received up front was in a briefcase in the trunk of his car. He would add whatever cash Vivian brought with her tonight and then he would head for Mexico.

The plan to collect from both the killer and from Vivian and then hightail it to the border had come to him that morning. The shark would not be able to follow him into Mexico. Neither would the killer.

He moved out of the phone booth and started across the street to his Ford. Halfway to his goal he heard a vehicle engine roar to life. A car pulled out of the shadows of a nearby alley and came toward him, accelerating rapidly. He was pinned in the blinding glare of the headlights.

He hesitated, frantically trying to calculate whether he should run toward his car or try to retreat.

The second or two that it took to overcome the panic and make a decision turned out to be two seconds too long. He lurched toward his sedan but it was too late.

The car slammed into him. He was thrown onto the hood of the vehicle. Pain exploded through him. He was vaguely aware of glass shattering. An instant later he was flung to the side like so much garbage.

He was still conscious when he heard the vehicle brake to a halt. The driver got out from behind the wheel and took a quick look around the Ford. Toby was vaguely aware of the trunk being opened and closed. He knew the briefcase containing the thousand dollars had been found.

A moment later the killer bent over him and went through his pockets. The small notebook he used for recording crime scene details was removed. The last entry in it was the name of the killer.

The killer got back in the car and drove away.

Toby realized in some detached way that he had been a fool to try to warn Vivian and maybe make a few extra bucks in the process. It was the gambler in him. He'd taken one last big chance and it had cost him his life.

Chapter 24

The kiss was meant to be tender, tempting, exploratory. But when Vivian wrapped her arms around his neck, abandoning herself to the embrace, Nick felt as if he had been struck by lightning. An exhilarating rush of energy swept through him. The world fell away and he was flying.

This was the kiss he had been anticipating ever since she had opened her front door and looked at him with her mesmerizing gaze. He had told her about the fever dreams, the violence that had taken place on the hotel rooftop, his annulled marriage. He had allowed her to see his secrets.

Vivian had never blinked.

A very modern woman. An exciting woman. A woman who was not afraid to take chances. Maybe she thought they could tumble into bed together with no lasting consequences. Could be she believed she was safe from the dangers of desire. And maybe that was the truth— for her.

He was very certain things would never be the same for him. But in that moment the future was not important. All that mattered was the woman in his arms.

Vivian gave a soft murmur of surprise. He got the sense her response to the kiss had caught her off guard. He knew then that he was not the only one heading into uncharted waters.

She leaned into him, her soft breasts crushed against his chest. Her scent thrilled him. When she trailed her fingertips across the back of his neck he thought he would come apart.

He found the sash of her robe and slipped it free of the simple knot. The garment fell open, revealing the pale nightgown. It was not the serviceable cotton gown she had worn the night of the fire. This was the one she had purchased at a shop in Burning Cove. It was fashioned of some gossamer fabric that looked as if it had been woven with moonlight.

He rested his palm lightly over the firm peak of one breast. Vivian gasped as if she had been burned.

Reluctantly he started to pull away.

"No," she said. She trapped his hand with one of her own. "No. I want you to touch me."

She sounded dazed by her own desire. She pulled his shirt free of the waistband of his trousers.

"Vivian," he whispered.

"This is probably not a good idea," she said against the side of his throat.

"Probably not," he agreed. It was one of the hardest things he had ever said. "Too soon."

He lied. It wasn't too soon, not for him. He had been waiting a lifetime for this kiss.

"Sometimes you don't get a second chance to compose the picture," Vivian whispered. "You have to take advantage of whatever light you've got."

He groaned and moved his hands to the curve of her hips. "Which one of us are you trying to talk into bed? Me or yourself? Because if it's me, you don't have to bring out the logic and reasoning. I was ready the moment you opened your front door in Adelina Beach."

She gave a soft, shaky laugh and buried her face against his chest. "I knew you were a romantic at heart."

He caught her face between his hands and looked down into her moon-shadowed eyes.

"Whatever is going on here, it's not romantic," he said. "It's not about hearts and flowers. It's about something a lot more elemental."

Rex left his post in front of the wrought iron gate and trotted briskly back across the patio and into the living room. He gave a sharp, warning bark from the interior of the villa.

Nick released Vivian instantly. "There's someone here."

The doorbell chimed. Rex barked again. Nick went into the villa, turned on a lamp, and checked the peephole in the front door. A young man dressed in the uniform of the hotel staff stood on the step.

"It's all right, Rex," Nick said.

He opened the door.

"I'm Hank, sir. Front desk. The night operator just took a phone call from a man asking for Miss Vivian Brazier. The caller was, of course, informed that no one by that name was in residence. The manager, however, instructed me to inform you immediately of the message."

Chapter 25

He's gone," Nick said. He brought the Packard to a stop at the curb and studied the empty phone booth in the glare of the headlights. "He told the front desk he would wait for you in front of that shop, the Elegant Lady, but there's no one around."

"He's here," Vivian said. "I recognize that Ford parked at the curb. It belongs to Toby."

"You're sure?"

"Yes. Toby shows up at the same crime-and-fire scenes that I cover. Trust me, I'd know that beat-up sedan anywhere."

She started to open her door.

"Wait." Nick wrapped one hand around her wrist, stopping her. "He's not in the car. Take a look. There's no one sitting behind the wheel."

Vivian reluctantly settled back into the seat. "He must be here somewhere. Maybe he's hiding in a doorway. He might be scared. Don't you see? There's only one reason he would track me down and tell me he's got information to sell. He knows something about the fire that burned down my cottage. This is the break we've been hoping for."

"Maybe." Nick took the gun out of the holster he wore under his jacket and cracked open his door. "This is where Rex and I get to earn our keep. We'll take a look around."

"I'll come with you."

"No, you will stay in the car until I tell you it's safe to get out." He reached for the flashlight he had stowed under the seat. "Understand?"

She eyed him thoughtfully. "That sounds a lot like an order."

"It is."

"I don't take orders well."

"You will as long as I'm in charge of keeping you alive. Stay in the car."

He did not wait to see if she was going to argue. He opened his door and got out. Rex followed, bounding nimbly out of the compartment behind the front seat and down onto the pavement.

"Search," Nick said quietly.

Rex immediately trotted toward the shadowed vestibule of a nearby store. He sniffed a few times, sat down, and looked back at Nick.

Nick moved forward cautiously. When he got closer he aimed the flashlight into the vestibule.

A man was sprawled facedown in the doorway. Not a transient bunking down for the night. Not a drunk who had passed out in the nearest convenient location. In the beam of the flashlight the blood on the sidewalk appeared almost black.

Nick patted Rex. "Good job. Anyone else around?"

Rex appeared unconcerned. His work was done. Nick concluded they were probably alone. He crouched to feel for a pulse. He did not expect to find one. He was right.

"Bad news," he said to Rex. "I need information and Toby Flint obviously had some."

He went through the dead man's pockets.

In the stillness of the night the sound of the Packard's door opening seemed unnaturally loud. Nick looked around and saw Vivian standing on the curb next to the vehicle.

"Is it Toby?" she asked, anxiety and sorrow mingling in her words.

"Probably," Nick said. "I think someone must have gone through his pockets. They're empty."

"I can tell you for certain if it's him," she said.

"You're not going to want to take a close look. He's pretty cut up and . . . broken. There's some glass. Must have been hit by a car."

"I've done a lot of crime scene photography, remember? I've seen bodies before."

"I doubt if they were bodies of people you knew," Nick said. "It's different."

"I have to be sure it's him because if it is—"

"Stop right there. Whatever happened here, it's not your fault that this man is dead. The person who murdered him is the one responsible."

Vivian did not respond. She walked toward the doorway. Nick could tell that she was having to make herself go through the ordeal. When she got close, he leaned down and tugged on the deadweight of one shoulder, turning the body just far enough to give Vivian a view of the victim's face.

"Yes." Vivian wrapped her arms around her midsection and quickly turned away. "It's Toby. And you're right—it's different when it's someone you know. Dear heaven. So much blood."

"Hood ornaments will do that," Nick said. "One of these days they'll probably outlaw them. I'll call the police from the phone booth. And then I'll call Luther Pell."

"At this hour?"

"He operates a hot nightclub. Trust me, he'll be awake."

Chapter 26

can't imagine how Toby managed to find me," Vivian said. "My sister is the only one who knows I'm here in Burning Cove. I called her shortly after we arrived because I knew she would worry if she saw the reports of the fire that burned down the cottage I was renting in Adelina Beach."

It was nearly three o'clock in the morning. She and Nick were back in the living room of the villa but this time they were not alone. Luther Pell and Raina Kirk, the sophisticated, enigmatic woman who was obviously much more than a friend, had joined them.

Nick had mentioned that Pell had served in the Great War, which meant he was probably in his late thirties or early forties. There was some silver in his dark hair and a host of secrets in his eyes. It was obvious he had come directly from his nightclub. He wore an elegantly cut evening jacket, a crisp white shirt, and a black bow tie. His trousers were perfectly creased and broke at the precise angle over his gleaming shoes. There was a gold watch on his left wrist.

Raina Kirk was an equally intriguing mystery. Pell had introduced her as a private investigator but she did not fit the Hollywood image of someone in that business. She was cool and poised in a midnight-blue evening gown that swirled around her ankles when she walked. Her hair was pinned up in an elegant chignon. When she spoke, there was a polished East Coast gloss on each word.

"Did Toby Flint know you have a sister in San Francisco?" Nick asked.

Vivian realized that Luther and Raina were waiting expectantly for her response. She got a queasy feeling. *Should have thought of that myself.* She sighed and looked at Nick.

"You know," she said, "sometimes your habit of leaping to the worst possible conclusion is a little depressing."

"Sorry," he said. "I can't help it. Character flaw, I'm afraid."

Luther snorted softly, evidently amused.

"If it's any consolation, it appears to be a family trait, Miss Brazier," he said. "It's why his uncle was so useful to me in the old days."

"I see," Vivian said. "The answer is yes, Toby Flint did know that I have a sister and that she lives in San Francisco. He showed up at my place on the beach one weekend when Lyra was visiting me. I introduced them."

"Did Flint visit you often?" Raina asked.

"No," Vivian said. "Only when he wanted to try to talk me into giving him some film or flashbulbs or when he was desperate for gas money. He was always going to pay me back, of course, but he never did. His finances were precarious, to say the least. He is . . . was . . . a good news photographer. His pictures sold well. Editors liked them. But he was a gambler. The kind that loses."

"Which means he was probably in deep with some very rough people," Luther said. "I should be able to verify that with a few phone calls, but for now I think we can assume he had a financial motive to track you down here in Burning Cove, Miss Brazier."

She narrowed her eyes. "You mean the killer may have paid him to find me?"

It was Nick who answered. "That sounds logical."

"But that means the killer knew Toby had some knowledge of my personal life," she said.

Nick exchanged a glance with Luther.

"Yes," he said. "It does."

"The only people who might have been aware that Toby and I knew each other would be a couple of Adelina Beach freelance photographers and Eddy, the night editor of the *Courier*," Vivian said. She shook her head. "I just can't see any of them as paid assassins."

Raina raised her brows. "Why not?"

Vivian turned both hands over, palms up. "For one thing the assassin keeps his memoirs in the form of encrypted poetry. In addition he charges a lot of money for his so-called commissions. Trust me when I tell you that if any of the freelancers I know has a lot of money, he's keeping it very well hidden. Finances aside, I've spent enough time with my late-night colleagues to be quite certain none of them has any interest in poetry. I suppose it's *possible* one of them is working as a hired killer on the side but I really doubt it."

"Maybe one of them is the client," Raina suggested, "the person who paid to have you murdered."

Vivian looked at her. "I'm quite sure none of the freelancers I know could afford the assassin's fees. And there's no viable motive. I was probably the least successful photographer in the group. None of them had anything to fear from me. I certainly wasn't a threat to their livelihoods."

There was a short silence while they all considered those simple facts.

Nick looked at her. "We need to find out exactly how Flint discovered you were not only in Burning Cove but that you were staying at this hotel."

"I'll call my sister first thing in the morning," Vivian said. "I'll ask her if someone contacted her to inquire about my whereabouts. I didn't tell her to keep the information a secret because I knew it would make her worry. The last thing I wanted to do was give her the impression I was in danger. She would have jumped into her car immediately and driven here."

"You made a reasonable decision," Raina said gently. "In your shoes I would have done the same thing."

Vivian tightened her hands around the arms of the chair. She thought about the bloodied and broken body lying in the dark shadows of a doorway.

"Poor Toby," she said. "He must have been desperate. If he did take money to locate me, he probably felt guilty about it."

Nick gazed at her as if she had started speaking in tongues. "What the hell makes you think that?"

"Well, it's obvious, isn't it? He came to Burning Cove to warn me. His message was that he had to see me tonight, remember? It was a matter of life and death."

Luther and Nick exchanged unreadable looks. Raina smiled a sad smile.

Vivian glared at all of them. "You don't think Toby made that call to warn me, do you?"

"Until proven otherwise," Nick said with great precision, "we will operate on the assumption that Flint took money not just to locate you but to lure you out of the safety of the hotel grounds. Keep in mind his instructions were for you to show up alone in a deserted neighborhood tonight."

"Instead, you and Rex accompanied me." Vivian hesitated. "Do you suppose the killer was watching us when we found Toby's body and took off when he realized I wasn't alone?"

"I don't know," Nick said. "I didn't hear any other cars in the vicinity and Rex did not seem to be concerned, but that doesn't mean no one was watching, possibly from inside one of the shops. But I am certain of one thing: The car that killed Flint sustained a considerable amount of damage. There was a lot of glass at the scene. Looked like one head-light was shattered. There will probably be some bent chrome and blood on the fender."

"Detective Brandon is in charge of the investigation," Luther said. "He's a good man. He'll notify all of the local garages and repair shops to watch for a car that looks like it has been involved in a collision of some kind. He'll keep me informed."

"I seriously doubt that whoever was driving that car tonight will take it to a local garage for repairs," Nick said. "It's more likely the killer will dump it over the side of a cliff. If it winds up underwater, it may never be found."

Vivian thought about that. "If the killer does dump the car, he'll have to find another vehicle."

"Or steal one," Raina suggested.

Nick tapped one finger lightly against the chair arm. "In fact, it's possible he used a stolen car to kill Toby Flint. In which case, even if Brandon does locate the vehicle, it will be a dead end as far as the in-vestigation goes."

Vivian looked at him. "There you go with the unquenchable op-timism."

"What can I tell you?" he said. He gave her a thin, cold smile. "You're seeing me in one of my more upbeat moments."

The phone rang. Vivian flinched. Phone calls at three in the morn-ing rarely brought good news. Nick leaned over and picked up the re-ceiver.

"I see," he said. "Thanks. I appreciate the information."

He hung up and looked at the others.

"That was Oliver Ward," he said. "He checked with the front desk. Ripley Fleming never left the grounds this evening. He dined in the hotel and went directly to the bar. He's still there."

Chapter 27

The following morning they ate breakfast on the patio, bacon and eggs for the humans, chopped-up steak and eggs for Rex.

The morning fog was rapidly dissipating and the air was fresh and invigorating. Nick watched Vivian spread butter on a slice of toast and decided the day was almost perfect: a California fantasy day.

But, as was invariably the case with fantasies, there was a dark side.

Vivian put down the butter knife and paused before she took a bite of the toast.

"What are you thinking?" she asked.

He picked up his fork and went to work on the mound of fluffy scrambled eggs.

"I'm thinking that Toby Flint died the same way Morris Deverell, the Dagger Killer, did," he said. "Both were run down by a car."

He ate the eggs. They tasted good. Some of the best, if not *the* best scrambled eggs he had ever eaten. It was the woman on the other side of the table that made the meal such a gratifying experience. He could get accustomed to having Vivian sitting across from him at breakfast every morning.

She stared at him and then, very carefully, set the uneaten toast back on her plate.

"Do you really think there's some connection between Toby Flint and Morris Deverell?" she asked.

"Back at the start of this thing it was at least possible to argue it was a coincidence that you've been attacked twice within a month. Now that two individuals with connections to you have been run down by vehicles, I'm ready to throw the coincidence theory out the window."

Vivian fed Rex some bacon under the table and looked thoughtful.

"You told me that coming to Burning Cove might be a way to lure the killer out of hiding," she said finally. "I don't think we're going to make any progress in that regard if we hang around the hotel all day and all night. We need to take action and we both know that means we will have to leave the grounds again."

Nick started to argue but he stopped and drank some coffee instead. He didn't like it but he knew she was right. He replaced the cup in the saucer with great precision, eased the plate aside, and folded his arms on the table.

"First, make the call to your sister," he said. "Find out if Flint used her to locate you. We need to confirm that theory."

"All right."

Vivian crumpled her napkin, put it beside her plate, and went into the villa to place the call.

Nick started to reach for his coffee. He noticed that Rex was watching him with a very fixed gaze.

"You got Vivian's bacon," Nick said. "You don't get mine, too."

Rex was almost vibrating with anticipation. His gaze did not waver.

"I should never have let you take that correspondence course in hypnosis," Nick said.

He picked up the last strip of bacon on his plate and tossed it to Rex.

Chapter 28

Vivian picked up the telephone receiver, asked for long distance, and gave the operator the San Francisco number.

The housekeeper answered on the third ring.

"Brazier residence."

"Good morning, Dorothy. It's Vivian. I'm calling for Lyra."

"How nice to hear your voice, dear. I'm afraid you missed Lyra. She was gone by the time I arrived this morning."

"An early-morning tennis game?"

"Why, no. She must have packed her suitcases late last night. Looks like she took half her wardrobe with her. She left a note saying she needed some time to herself."

Vivian tightened her grip on the phone. *Don't borrow trouble. There will be a reasonable explanation for Lyra's absence.* "Did Lyra's note say where she was headed?"

"No, dear. Between you and me, I'm afraid your sister has a raging case of bridal jitters."

"Lyra?"

The old Lyra might have done something unpredictable like take off without letting anyone know where she was going, but the new Lyra was never unpredictable.

"Any woman can have some second thoughts when it comes to marriage," Dorothy said. "It's a very big step, after all."

"Yes." Vivian tried to clear her head. She did not want Dorothy to know she was alarmed.

"You're worried about your sister, aren't you? I can hear it in your voice."

"You know me too well, Dorothy."

"I should after all these years. I really don't think you need to be concerned. Miss Lyra and Mr. Merrick are a perfect couple. We all know she's had a crush on him forever."

"Yes," Vivian said. "The man of her dreams. Mr. Perfect."

"But if your sister is having some serious second thoughts—"

"Yes?"

"Well, then, maybe she should listen to her intuition," Dorothy said.

"I agree with you," Vivian said.

She hung up the phone and went back out to the sunlit patio. Nick got to his feet.

"What's wrong?" he asked.

"I'm not sure," Vivian said. "Dorothy, the housekeeper, said that Lyra packed her bags last night and left sometime early this morning. There was a note but Lyra did not say where she was headed. Dorothy thinks my sister is having a case of bridal jitters."

"What do you think?"

"I have a feeling Lyra found out that the man she thought was the perfect match for her isn't quite so perfect."

"Well, that makes life here a little more interesting."

Vivian frowned. "Why?"

"Mr. Perfect was on our rather vague list of suspects, remember?"

"He was on your list, not mine."

"He was on one of our lists. That's all that matters. If Hamilton Merrick is the one who hired a killer to get rid of you so that your sister would inherit your share of your father's estate, it will be fascinating to see what he does now that he's in danger of having his second chance at a Brazier bride canceled."

Chapter 29

"You're worried about your sister, aren't you?" Nick asked.

It was midafternoon. He and Vivian were standing in front of the Ashwood Gallery in the center of Burning Cove's fashionable shopping district. Vivian had brought her portfolio with her. *You never know,* she had said.

Rex was with them, ambling along at the end of a leash, investigating interesting scents.

Vivian was contemplating a large, matted photograph displayed in the window. Nick was examining the reflections in the glass. There was no indication they were being followed by Ripley Fleming or anyone else. He reminded himself that, even in Burning Cove, where celebrity sightings were common, it would be impossible for a movie star of Fleming's stature to venture out in public without causing heads to turn—not unless he was very, very good when it came to the art of disguise.

At first glance the movements of the individuals strolling on the wide sidewalks appeared random. Some sauntered, relaxed and unconcerned. Most were enjoying the warm sunshine and the ambience of the glamorous town. Those who wanted to see and be seen were sprinkled about like confetti. Here and there acquaintances recognized each other and stopped to chat. Others were intent on getting to an appointment on time.

And then there were the lovers; all sorts of lovers. They ranged from the secretive type, who pretended not to notice each other in public, to the dreamy-eyed couples, who did not give a damn if the whole world knew they were in the grip of transcendent passion.

Nick reminded himself that he was not interested in transcendent passion—at least not at that particular moment. Thinking of transcendent passion had a way of disrupting his focus.

The trick was to spot the one person in the crowd who did not fit into the pattern, an actor in disguise who was wearing the wrong shoes, for example.

"It's not like Lyra to take off without telling anyone where she was going," Vivian said. "I don't think this is a case of bridal jitters. Hamilton must have said or done something to break her heart. Damn it. I knew this would happen. To be honest, I hoped it would. But I wanted to be there for her when she finally realized that Hamilton was not Mr. Perfect. I don't know where she is so I can't even call her."

"Take it from me," Nick said, "she's a whole lot better off finding out the truth about him now rather than after the wedding."

Vivian shot him a quick, irritated glance.

"I'm aware of that," she said.

"Sorry. Voice of experience."

"I know." Vivian took a deep breath. "But she's my sister."

"And you think you should have protected her. I understand. But sometimes a person has to run headfirst into the brick wall in order to see it."

"Voice of experience again?"

"Yep."

Vivian turned back to study the large photograph.

"I've had some experience in bad choices myself," she said. "Thankfully I never got as far as the altar but things ended badly. There was a ghastly scandal. My parents were mortified. It was one of the reasons why I left San Francisco a year ago."

"Married man?" Nick asked.

"Nope." Vivian made a face. "He was an artist. I took a class in pictorialism from him."

"Right. The *Carousel of the Damned* photograph that I saw hanging in your office?"

"If you took a close look at the specters riding the horses, you probably noticed they all had the same face."

"I noticed. That's the face of the man who took advantage of you?"

Vivian looked surprised. "He didn't take advantage of me. I knew exactly what I was doing. I got what I expected—lots of drama. Lots of fascinating conversations about the future of photography. I also recall a great many discussions about how artists had to be free. We could not be bound by social conventions, et cetera, et cetera. Things went splendidly for a while. But I made the mistake of falling for his line."

"He told you that he loved you?"

"No." Vivian narrowed her eyes. "The bastard told me that he admired my art."

"Ah." Nick tried to process that. "He lied?"

"Yes. And I caught him red-handed. I overheard him talking to the owner of a very prestigious San Francisco gallery. He went on and on about how female photographers would never be able to produce high art. Their work is too sentimental. Too emotional. It lacks artistic vision. It's suitable only for greeting cards. He didn't break my heart. He made me furious. There was a huge scene, of course."

"Because that's what artists do?"

"Absolutely. Things got rather personal. Observations about each other's inadequacies in bed were exchanged."

"In front of the gallery owner?"

"Yep. Word of the scene spread like wildfire. Needless to say, I got a reputation for being fast. The gossip got worse when I turned down Hamilton Merrick's proposal and left town to pursue my art in Adelina Beach."

"What about the reputation of the artist?"

Vivian waved that off. "His reputation didn't suffer a bit. He's an artist, after all. And male."

"Right. Double standard and all that."

Vivian studied him for a long moment. "Your romance disaster was a lot rougher than mine. You nearly got killed. Think you'll ever take another chance on love and marriage?"

The question stopped him cold. A couple of days ago he wouldn't have hesitated. His answer would have been a flat no. He was not so sure now. The kiss in the garden last night had changed some crucial element in the equation. He needed to recalculate.

When in doubt, dodge the question.

"I don't know about love and marriage," he said, going for a lighter note, "but I've got nothing against passion."

She nodded, deeply serious. "People say that passion is a reckless, potentially destructive force, and I'm sure that is frequently the case. But I think love is infinitely more dangerous. Passion blazes hot and fierce and then it burns out. You'll get scorched but you'll probably survive. Love is more complicated. More mysterious."

They were like a couple of gamblers playing high-stakes poker, he thought.

"In other words, you don't have anything against passion, either?" he asked.

"Not as long as the only people who are put in harm's way are the two who decide to light the fire. It's not right to burn innocent third parties, though."

"Agreed," he said.

Okay, that sounded like progress, he decided. He tried to think positive. There were no innocent third parties involved here, just a hired killer and the client who had paid him to murder Vivian. No relationship was perfect.

Vivian went back to examining the photograph in the window. The small sign in front of the picture read, FEATURING NEW IMAGES BY WINSTON BANCROFT. The scene was an artfully posed close-up of a female nude framed by a window and set against a backdrop of a vast, abstract desert. Considering the subject matter, it struck Nick as oddly lacking in genuine sensuality.

"What was the name of the artist?" he asked. "The one with whom you had the scandalous affair?"

Vivian flashed him a sly, amused smile. "Winston Bancroft."

"I was afraid that would be your answer. If you ask me, Bancroft doesn't just disapprove of female photographers. He doesn't like women."

Vivian turned quickly, eyes tightening a little at the corners. "What makes you say that?"

Nick shrugged. "Something about that picture. It's cold. Lifeless. He might as well have been photographing a robot."

Vivian gave him a brilliant smile. "It strikes me the same way. It's as if Bancroft deliberately composed the pictures to make the viewer regard the subject as an object, not a human being."

"Your pictures are a lot more interesting because you make your subjects appear mysterious, as if they're hiding secrets."

"Thanks," Vivian said. "I appreciate the kind words, believe me. But I have to face facts. Bancroft is the one who has his photograph in the gallery window."

"Your photographs will be in the window one of these days. Go on in and say hello to the gallery owner. Show her your portfolio."

Vivian tightened her grip on the portfolio case and gave him another determined smile. "Wish me luck."

"You don't need luck. You've got talent."

She looked surprised by the comment.

"Thank you," she said.

She opened the door. A bell chimed somewhere inside. Nick watched through the window as Vivian walked briskly toward the desk at the far end of the room. A middle-aged woman in a severe black business suit got to her feet to greet her.

After a moment he returned to the reflections in the window, watching for anyone who did not fit into the patterns. Rex got bored with a nearby palm tree and settled down on the sidewalk below the window.

Nick leaned down to give him an affectionate pat. When he straightened he saw what he had been looking for all along, the one person who did not fit into the rhythms of the street.

A figure dressed as a deliveryman, cap pulled down low over his eyes, lounged in the shadows of a narrow walkway on the far side of the busy plaza. He turned and disappeared down the flagstone path but not before Nick had marked the air of elegant ennui that did not belong to a man who made his living with his hands.

"Got you," Nick said softly.

Rex looked up at him and grinned.

Chapter 30

O f course I remember you, Miss Brazier." Joan Ashwood smiled. "We met at the Kempton Gallery exhibition in Adelina Beach several months ago. You had two excellent landscapes on display. They both had sold tags on them."

Joan was middle-aged with the patrician demeanor of a woman who had been born to sell art to those who could afford the best but didn't trust their own judgment. She had been surprised when Vivian had walked through the door but her welcome had been gracious.

She probably thinks I'm going to try to talk her into displaying some of my pictures. Which is exactly what I'm hoping to do.

"Yes, that's right." Vivian relaxed a little. "A hotel in Adelina Beach picked them up to display in the lobby. They were my first two art sales."

And so far, my only two art sales. But she did not say that aloud.

"Are you on vacation or did you come to Burning Cove to take photos?" Joan asked.

"I'm here to relax but I've got my camera with me. I'm hoping to get some good landscapes. The coastline is very scenic."

"If you want my advice, forget the landscapes. Ansel Adams has the corner on that market."

Vivian sighed. "You aren't the first gallery owner to give me that advice."

"Anyone with a camera and some luck with the weather can get a good landscape shot," Joan said. "You know the famous Eastman Kodak slogan."

"*You press the button, we do the rest.*'"

"I fear that will become increasingly true in the future."

"Landscape photos are not my favorite genre but I thought it was a good place to start." Vivian tightened her grip on her portfolio. "Lately I've been working on a new series, however. Something quite different."

Joan glanced at the leather portfolio. "I assume you brought some examples with you?"

"Ever had an artist walk into your gallery without some samples of his or her work?"

Joan chuckled. "No, and that's fine by me. I'm always interested. Let me see what you've been doing."

Vivian opened the portfolio and removed two pictures, both male nudes. She placed them on the counter.

"I'm calling the series Men," she said. "Eventually there will be twelve photographs. Each will focus on a different aspect of how men are perceived in our modern world. I want the viewer to question their own assumptions about what it means to be perceived as male. To re-think the very meaning of manhood."

She stepped back and held her breath, waiting for a reaction.

Joan reached for her glasses, slipped them on, and studied the photographs with a sharp gaze. She looked at them for a very long time. Vivian's heart sank. She braced herself for a lecture on the difference between pornography and art.

Joan finally removed her glasses and set them aside. Intense satisfaction glittered in her eyes.

"Oh, yes," she said softly. "I can sell these. They are riveting. You invite the viewer to question assumptions and roles but at the same time there is a startling intimacy and sensuality in these figures. Amazing."

Vivian managed to breathe again. Euphoria sparked through her.

"I'm glad you like them," she said, trying to sound cool and casual.

"I'll need limited editions. Let's say sixteen of each. Large size. Thirty inches by forty inches would be ideal. The bigger pictures make more of an impression. Usual contract terms. Oh, and I'll want an exclusive on these images for the duration of the contract."

"Certainly." Vivian struggled to conceal her excitement. "I'll print and mat the pictures for you as soon as I can set up a new darkroom."

"How long will that take? I would very much like to have them for my show next week."

Vivian's euphoria died in an instant. It would take time to put a new darkroom together. She could not ask to use the *Herald*'s facilities again, not for the purpose of printing pictures intended for a gallery show. She would find a way to print the pictures. She had to find a way.

"I've, uh, lost the cottage I was renting in Adelina Beach," she said. "But I expect to find new lodgings soon. I will get another darkroom set up right away."

"You're welcome to use mine while you're here in town," Joan said. "It's in the back of the shop."

Vivian nearly collapsed with relief. "Are you a photographer?"

"I was a hobbyist for a few years. I don't do much photography these days, but I'm still a member of the Burning Cove Photography Club, hence the darkroom. I don't have much use for it myself, but I make it available to other members of the club. It's fully equipped with a commercial enlarger and an extra-large easel."

"That sounds perfect. What time would be convenient for me to use it?"

"Would tomorrow work for you? I'd like to get a couple of your pictures on the wall as soon as possible."

"Absolutely," Vivian said. "I really appreciate this." She slipped the prints back into the portfolio and turned to leave. But two steps toward the front door she stopped and turned back. "Do you mind if I ask you a question?"

"What is it?"

"You looked surprised to see me when I walked through your front door a few minutes ago."

"Well, yes, I admit I was rather startled. It was the portfolio, you see."

"What about it?"

"I had heard that you had given up trying to make it as a serious photographer."

Vivian's mouth went dry. "I beg your pardon?"

"I was under the impression that you were pursuing a career in, well, to put it politely, photojournalism. Crime scenes. Fires. Famous actors caught in scandalous situations. That sort of thing."

Vivian clutched her portfolio very tightly. "Where did you hear that?"

"You know how it is in the art world. There are always wild rumors circulating. I believe that an associate of mine, the proprietor of the Kempton Gallery in Adelina Beach, mentioned that none of the more exclusive galleries there were hanging your work these days because of your association with the press."

Vivian recalled her last depressing encounter with the owner of the Kempton Gallery. He had treated her latest photographs as if they were beneath contempt.

"Richard Kempton told you that?" she said.

"Yes. He said it was all over town that you were no longer serious about your art."

A wave of fury swept through Vivian. She took a deep breath. "That explains a few things."

"I'm sorry," Joan said. "But everyone knows the art world can be very cruel to an artist who is believed to have dipped her toe into commercial photography."

"Given the rumors, why are you willing to hang my pictures?"

Joan winked. "Let's just say I know what it's like to try to balance on the very fine line between the commercial world and the art world. Before I opened this gallery I sold hats at Bullocks Wilshire in L.A."

"Really?"

"Nobody pays much attention to a woman who sells hats, even very expensive hats. But things are different now that I sell art. People who move in the most exclusive circles are terrified of being accused of having acquired bad art. Here in Burning Cove my wealthy clients will buy whatever I tell them to buy."

"What's the difference between selling hats and selling art?"

"As far as the business end of things goes, there is no difference. It's all just smoke and mirrors."

"What about artistic vision? Doesn't that matter?"

"Absolutely. But whether or not the works of an artist with a great vision actually *sell* is very much up to dealers like me."

Chapter 31

W hat the hell just happened in there?" Nick asked. He glanced through the window and saw the dealer sitting down behind her desk. He turned back to a flushed and seething Vivian. "Did that gallery owner insult you?"

"What?" Vivian looked startled. "Oh. No, not at all. She wants to hang two of my prints and she's offered me the use of a fully equipped darkroom that she maintains in her back room. I've got an appointment to develop my pictures tomorrow."

"That's great." Nick took her arm and steered her toward a sidewalk café. "So why did you come out of the gallery with fire in your eyes?"

Vivian's jaw tightened. "Because she enlightened me about why my career had stalled in Adelina Beach."

"Did she?" Nick asked softly. "And what exactly did she have to say about it?"

"Evidently there are rumors going around to the effect that I have debased my artistic vision by dabbling in scandal sheet photography."

"Debased, huh?"

"None of the reputable galleries in Adelina Beach will hang my work for fear of making it look as if the proprietors can't tell the difference between real art and cheap, freelance photography. Apparently the owner of the Kempton Gallery started the rumors. So much for keeping my newspaper work a secret."

"But the proprietor of the Ashwood Gallery here in Burning Cove is willing to display a couple of your photos in spite of those rumors?"

Vivian clutched the portfolio to her breast. "She saw what I was trying to do with my series, Nick. But in addition she said there was intimacy and sensuality in my work."

Nick reflected on the parade of muscular young men who had displayed their very fit bodies in Vivian's studio.

"Hard to miss the intimacy and sensuality in your pictures," he said.

Vivian shot him a suspicious glance. "What's that supposed to mean?"

"I was just confirming the gallery owner's opinion. If she's willing to hang your photos in spite of the rumors of your newspaper work, it's obvious she has a lot of confidence in her own taste."

Vivian looked a little more cheerful. "Yes, it is."

"Huh."

She gave him another wary look. "Now what?"

"I was just wondering when the rumors about your descent into the world of scandal sheet photography got started."

"I'm not sure. After I moved to Adelina Beach I did some work in the old-fashioned pictorial style. But my heart wasn't really in it. I found it interesting from a technical point of view but not compelling, if you know what I mean."

"I think so."

"It was when I moved into the new, modernist style that I found my feet as an artist, so to speak. The first couple of pictures, both landscapes, got some attention. Kempton actually took both and sold them. But shortly after that the rejections started."

"Interesting."

Vivian shot him a quick, searching look. "Something happened out here while I was inside the gallery, didn't it?"

"How can you tell?" he asked, intrigued.

She waved a hand. "Let's just say I can feel it. Something about your energy." She glanced down. "And Rex's energy, too. Both of you look—I don't know—as if you were a couple of hunters who had picked up a trail."

He smiled, cold satisfaction moving through his veins. "That's exactly what happened. You're good at this kind of thing."

"Well? What happened?"

He took her arm. "Let's have coffee. I'll tell you all about it."

He waited until they were seated at a small table in a sidewalk café, two cups of coffee in front of them, Rex stretched out under a chair.

"I saw the man with the cap and the wrong posture," Nick said quietly.

Vivian had been about to take a sip of coffee. She went very still.

"Where?"

"He was watching us from an alley on the other side of the plaza. No, don't look around. He's gone now anyway."

"You're sure it was the same man that we saw in the photos I took at the fire?"

"Same slouch, same build, same cap. Too far away to be sure about the shoes, but it was the same man. Even if the clothes had been wrong I would have noticed him."

"Why? Is he that unusual?"

"No, that's just it. He's very, very good at making himself unnoticeable. Which is, of course, why I caught him watching us."

"I don't . . . oh, wait. I get it. He stood out simply because he was trying hard not to stand out."

"Right," Nick said, pleased that she understood. "But there was something else, too. You know what it's like when you get the sensation someone is watching you? You turn around and, sure enough, the person is looking at you and you know it's not an accident, because just as you're about to lock eyes, he turns away a little too quickly."

"Of course. Most people have had that experience. Is that the feeling you got?"

"Yes." Nick picked up his cup and swallowed some coffee. Enjoying the whisper of knowing. The certainty.

Rex's ears twitched. He raised his head, silently asking if it was time to hunt. Nick reached down and gave him a pat.

"Not yet, pal," he said.

Vivian looked at him over the rim of her cup. "What do we do now?"

"We return to the hotel and act like nothing happened. I will call Luther Pell and let him know our guy is here in Burning Cove and watching us. The time has come for Pell to call the Broker and put the word out that a certain journal of handwritten poems is for sale at a very high price."

Chapter 32

Jonathan Treyherne dropped the receiver of the pay phone back into the cradle and stood quietly for a moment, trying to get his nerves under control. His heart was pounding and he was sweating hard.

His offer had been accepted. The Broker had just informed him the journal was in the hands of an anonymous individual who was willing to sell at an absurd price. The Broker had advised him against going through with the deal. No book of poetry was worth the huge sum the seller was demanding. But Jonathan had insisted the handwritten poems were the work of a famous, long-dead poet and that the volume was worth a fortune to collectors.

The Broker had gone on to explain it would take time to work out the logistics of the transaction. The arrangements had to be acceptable to both buyer and seller. There were a number of ways to carry out such business deals, according to the Broker. The safest method was to use a trusted, professional go-between. Jonathan had refused that approach. He did not want to take the risk of allowing someone else to get hold of the journal, not even for the length of time it took to complete the transaction.

There was another reason why he did not want anyone else involved. He needed to get close to the seller; close enough to kill him.

The phone booth was located at a gas station. Jonathan had parked behind the garage. He got into his car and drove back to the isolated cottage he had rented on a bluff overlooking the cove. He had chosen the house and the location because it afforded ample privacy but the amenities were limited. Among other things there was no phone so he had been obliged to use pay phones to stay in touch with the Broker.

When he got back to the cottage he let himself inside, poured a stiff shot of whiskey, and lit a cigarette. He went outside onto the porch and looked down at the rough surf crashing on the rocks. The sky had been cloudless all day but he had lived by oceans all his life, first on the East Coast and now here in California. He had learned to sail when he was a boy. He knew how to read the sea as well as surfers and yachtsmen did. There might not be any clouds in sight but the waves were thrashing too roughly in the cove and there was a subtle swell lifting the incoming tide. The breeze off the sea was picking up. A storm was approaching. It would probably make landfall in the next twenty-four to forty-eight hours.

He liked storms. They provided both a distraction and a cover. It was easy to remain hidden in a good storm. The subject never saw you coming.

He forced himself to think in his customary strategic manner. The problem of the journal was on the way to being resolved. He would set it aside for now. It was time to focus once again on the commission.

Today he had begun to suspect that the man who accompanied Vivian Brazier everywhere was not a lover, after all. That meant he was more of a problem than he had appeared to be at first glance.

Something about the manner in which Sundridge had contemplated the window of the Ashwood Gallery while he waited for Brazier to reappear had seemed off.

As Jonathan had watched from the shadows of the narrow walkway it had dawned on him he might be visible as a reflection in the glass. The more he considered the possibility that he was the one under surveillance, the more unnerved he had become. He had been forced to abandon the scene.

He told himself it didn't matter. Sooner or later Brazier would return to the Burning Cove Hotel. He would be able to find her again when he was ready to complete the commission. The hotel had excellent security but that security was not designed to keep out people like him, people who looked like they belonged in such exclusive, expensive surroundings.

What concerned him now was the possibility that the man's arrival in Brazier's life was not simply an inconvenient coincidence. The more Jonathan considered the matter, the more he wondered if the stranger was a bodyguard. That raised a host of unnerving questions. What had made Brazier conclude she needed protection?

A chill crackled through him as the obvious answer struck with the force of a bolt of lightning. The anonymous individual who was now in possession of the journal had managed to decipher the last entry, the one that named Vivian Brazier as the next commission.

Jonathan suddenly felt queasy. Light-headed.

He downed the last of the whiskey in an attempt to regain his nerve.

It took him a few minutes before he began to realize he could make the new development work in his favor. If his assumptions about the stranger were correct—if he was a bodyguard—then he had to be taken out first.

Jonathan went back into the cottage, poured another glass of whiskey, and began to pace. He had to come up with a plan. He had a lot to work with. Burning Cove was a small town and it was isolated on the coast. It didn't have the resources of a big city. There was a lot of dark, empty land around the glittering core of the town.

He went into the kitchen and started rummaging through the cupboards and drawers.

He found the ice pick in the liquor cabinet. It would do nicely.

Chapter 33

Vivian saw the mountain of expensive pink leather suitcases and hatboxes piled on the tiled floor of the Burning Cove's large lobby and stopped in her tracks.

"Oh, dear," she said.

Nick halted, too. So did Rex.

They both looked at Vivian.

"What's wrong?" Nick said.

She took a deep breath. "I recognize those suitcases."

He glanced at the pink leather cases. "You do?"

"I'm afraid so."

"Vivian." Lyra appeared from behind the row of potted palms that shielded the front desk. She rushed across the lobby and threw her arms around Vivian. "Thank goodness. These people keep insisting that you are not registered here. I told them I was your sister but they still refused to admit you were on the premises. I think they were getting ready to chuck me out into the street."

"What on earth are you doing here in Burning Cove?" Vivian

asked. She returned the hug and then stepped back. "Are you all right? I called home this morning. Dorothy told me you had packed up and left town without letting anyone know where you were headed. I've been worried about you."

"I'm here because you're here. Where else would I go?" Lyra gave Nick a bright, vivacious smile. "Are you going to introduce me to your friend, Viv?"

"Nick Sundridge, my sister, Lyra Brazier," Vivian said quietly. "And before you say another word, Lyra, let's get you registered at the front desk. We'll talk later. In private."

"Good plan," Nick said. He looked grim. "We definitely need a little privacy."

⁂

"I can't believe it," Lyra said. She sounded awed as well as deeply impressed. "You and Mr. Sundridge are registered here as a couple on their *honeymoon*? You had better hope our parents don't find out. Mother would probably faint. I can't even imagine Father's reaction. He might go so far as to strike Mr. Sundridge."

"Mr. Sundridge will keep that possibility in mind if he happens to meet Mr. Brazier," Nick said. "Thanks for the warning. It may give me time to duck."

Vivian ignored him. She focused on Lyra.

"Our parents are accustomed to me doing unpredictable things," she said.

"Here's a news flash," Lyra said. "A scandalous affair with an artist, turning down a respectable marriage proposal, and leaving town to pursue a photography career qualify as *unpredictable*. Posing as someone's wife in order to check into one of the most exclusive hotels in California is far beyond *unpredictable*. I do believe you have topped your own record, Viv. You are no longer just a fast woman. You are downright wild. I'm proud to be your sister."

She reached for one of the small, elegant sandwiches, which had been delivered to the villa a short time earlier, and took a large bite.

There was something very different in her sister's demeanor, Vivian thought. It wasn't a new trait, rather a return of the bold, adventurous spirit that had vanished years ago when Lyra had stepped into the role of the good daughter. The new old Lyra was a welcome sight but she had chosen an unfortunate time to rediscover her youthful daring and recklessness.

Satisfied that Lyra was, indeed, a member of the family, the hotel's front desk had moved smoothly and efficiently to find a room in the main building overlooking the pool for the new guest. Lyra had directed the bellhops to transport the heap of pink luggage to Number 24. She had taken a few minutes to freshen up and change into a pair of fashionable trousers, stacked heel sandals, and a silk blouse. Then she had hurried to join Vivian and Nick at the villa.

By the time she arrived, Vivian had ordered afternoon tea with all the trimmings. Between the two of them, Lyra and Nick were making serious inroads on the sandwiches. Rex had managed to snag a couple, too.

"If Mother faints, it won't be because of me," Vivian said. "It will be because you returned Hamilton's ring and called off the marriage. I still can't believe you did that. Okay, I *can* believe it, but I'm still stunned. What on earth happened?"

"What do you think happened?" Lyra lounged back into a wicker chair and propped her heels on a hassock. "I discovered you were right. Hamilton is a lying, cheating rat. He would have made a dreadful husband."

"You were so sure he was perfect for you."

"I changed my mind when I found out he was having an affair."

"Damn," Vivian said. "I was afraid of that."

Lyra held up a hand, palm out. "Please don't say it."

"Don't worry, I wouldn't dream of saying I told you so, because I never actually said that. I just tried to drop a few veiled hints to the effect that Hamilton might not be quite as perfect as he appeared."

Lyra raised her eyes heavenward and sighed. "Yes, you did. But I ignored them."

"Did you confront him with your suspicions?" Vivian asked. "It's only fair to give the man a chance to explain."

Lyra gave her a steely-eyed look. "There wasn't any explaining to do. I found them in bed together."

"Ah." Vivian winced. "I'm so sorry. I know you cared for him."

"Not anymore. In hindsight, I don't think I ever felt any genuine passion for him. I just kept telling myself that he was the right man. Mother and Father approved of him. And he is so handsome. Great dancer. Great kisser, too. We had fun together. Enjoyed the same things." Lyra heaved a tragic sigh. "It was all just too good to be true. Perfect."

"I understand," Vivian said gently. "What did he say when you found him with another woman?"

Lyra looked very fierce. "The other woman was Emily Parker."

"You're joking. Your best friend? The woman who was going to be one of your bridesmaids?"

"For the record, Emily and I are no longer best friends." Lyra sniffed. "Hamilton actually had the nerve to try to tell me she meant nothing to him. He claimed he had not wanted to pressure me into intimacy until our wedding night but that he had to find some physical relief in the meantime. He explained in great detail that it was very unhealthy for a man to be *congested*."

There was a hoarse cough from the other side of the patio. Vivian and Lyra turned to glare at Nick. He cleared his throat.

"Sorry," he said. "Cucumber sandwich went down the wrong way." He grabbed his teacup.

Lyra turned back to Vivian. "Hamilton claims his doctor told him that regular sexual exercise is good for the health, at least it is if you're male."

There was another rusty cough from the other side of the patio. Vivian and Lyra turned toward Nick again. He assumed a somber expression.

"It's a good thing you discovered the truth about Merrick before you married him," he said. "Much less messy this way."

Lyra ignored him.

"You should have seen poor Emily," she continued. "She was standing there next to the bed, in her robe, listening to Hamilton tell me he had just been using her to satisfy his physical needs. She was furious. She grabbed a heavy crystal perfume bottle off the dressing table and hurled it straight at him. I swear, I was positively inspired. I saw his trousers hanging over a chair. I threw them out the window into the street."

"Brilliant," Vivian exclaimed. "I'm proud of you."

"Emily refused to lend him a pair of pants from her father's closet," Lyra continued. "Hamilton had to run out onto the sidewalk in his underwear. It was very entertaining."

Nick looked impressed. "You two are a couple of extremely dangerous women."

"I may not have been dangerous before," Lyra said, "but I am now. I am a changed woman. I'm going to follow in your footsteps, Vivian. From now on I am a free spirit. I will never again be bound by the boring conventions of society. I shall never marry."

"It's probably best to never say never," Vivian cautioned. "Regardless, I am very glad you discovered the truth about Hamilton in time to call off the wedding."

"Consider it a stroke of luck," Nick offered.

Lyra studied him, deep interest sparking in her eyes. "You sound like you've been through a divorce, Mr. Sundridge."

"Annulment." Nick tossed a small sandwich to Rex, who caught it neatly in midair.

Shock flickered in Lyra's eyes. She recovered quickly. "I see."

The phone rang inside the villa.

Nick grabbed another sandwich and stood. "I'll get it. That will probably be Luther Pell."

He disappeared inside the villa.

Lyra turned back to Vivian, eyes wide.

"An annulment?" she whispered. "Dare I ask about the grounds?"

"It's not my story to tell."

"I see," Lyra said. She nodded in a commiserating way. "You must have felt sorry for him. That is very kind of you, but pretending to be married to him is probably not the best way to cure Mr. Sundridge. Impotence is a serious affliction for a man. He ought to see a doctor."

"Hold on, I think you misunderstand—"

"Mother has assured me a woman can always fake things in bed if necessary. But a man, well, a man must perform or be labeled *incapacitated* or something. You are a very capable woman, Viv, but you don't have any medical training. Mr. Sundridge should seek help from a physician."

"For pity's sake, Lyra, you have got this all wrong. Mr. Sundridge is not impotent—"

She broke off because she realized Lyra was looking past her.

"Don't let me interrupt," Nick said. "The conversation just keeps getting more interesting by the minute."

Vivian pulled herself together. "Was that Mr. Pell on the phone?"

"Yes," Nick said. Satisfaction heated his eyes. "He said the Broker called to inform him the buyer who is eager to acquire the journal has agreed to Pell's price."

"No negotiation?" Vivian asked.

"None."

Lyra glanced from Nick to Vivian. "What are you two talking about?"

"I'll explain in a minute," Vivian said. She looked at Nick.

"The buyer must want that journal very badly," she said.

"Evidently, but he's not going to get it tonight," Nick said. "Luther and I agree that we need to drag things out a bit to make sure the buyer is hungry enough to meet us on territory we control."

Lyra was following the conversation very intently but she did not interrupt again.

"Is Mr. Pell coming here to help put this strategy together?" Vivian asked.

Nick shook his head. "No. If the buyer is watching, and we must assume that he is, another visit to the hotel by Pell might make him skittish."

"What do we do now?" Vivian asked. "Sit around and wait?"

Nick smiled at Lyra. "I thought we might show your sister the nightlife scene here in Burning Cove. We're going to the Paradise Club tonight."

"Wonderful," Lyra said. "Do you think there will be some movie stars in the crowd?"

"Possibly," Nick said.

Vivian drummed her fingers on the arm of her chair while she mentally cataloged what remained of her very small wardrobe. "I did a little shopping when we arrived in Burning Cove but I just picked up the essentials. I certainly didn't see any need to purchase an evening gown and all the accessories."

"Don't worry," Lyra said. "I realized you must have lost most of your clothes in the fire so I brought several things from your closet with me. Just the items that are still in fashion, of course."

Vivian stared at her, nonplussed. "That was very thoughtful of you."

"Why do you think I arrived with so many suitcases?" Lyra said.

Nick smiled appreciatively. "Clearly the Brazier women are not only dangerous, they are very smart."

Vivian shot him what she hoped was a stern look. "I think it's time we told Lyra exactly why we're holed up here at the Burning Cove."

"Right," Nick said. The amusement warming his eyes vanished as swiftly as it had come. "We should probably do that. One question first, though. Lyra, did you tell anyone that Vivian was staying here at the Burning Cove?"

Lyra's brows rose. "Yes, as a matter of fact. One of her freelance photographer friends telephoned me to see if I knew where she was."

"Toby Flint?" Vivian asked.

"Yes," Lyra said. "He said it was important he get in touch with you right away. Something about teaming up with you to do a special photographic essay for *Life*. It sounded like a wonderful opportunity. Why? Is there a problem?"

"I'm afraid so," Vivian said. "A big problem."

Lyra got a knowing expression. "I was sure there was more going on here than the obvious."

"The obvious?" Vivian asked.

"The two of you running off to Burning Cove to see if you could cure Mr. Sundridge's little impotence prob—" Lyra stopped herself mid-word. She cleared her throat. "Never mind. Explain."

Chapter 34

've been in some very exclusive nightclubs in San Francisco," Lyra announced, "but none were as much fun as this one. The Paradise looks like a movie set. I can picture Claudette Colbert or Clark Gable or Greta Garbo walking down that red carpet to one of those star tables at the edge of the dance floor."

Vivian picked up her cocktail glass and surveyed the glamorous room. "You're right. The Paradise looks as if it was designed by a decorator who set out to create a Hollywood fantasy version of a nightclub."

She and Lyra and Nick occupied a booth that had a clear view of the orchestra and the dance floor. It was almost eleven o'clock but the night was young as far as the crowd was concerned. The orchestra was playing a slow, sultry piece while women in shimmering beaded gowns floated on the arms of men dressed in elegant evening jackets. The dance floor was illuminated in an endless cascade of sparkling lights from the mirror ball overhead.

The only member of the group who wasn't present to enjoy the show was Rex. He had been left at the villa. No killer would take the risk of trying to break in to set a trap with the dog on guard.

Vivian took a tiny sip of her sidecar. Thanks to Lyra's foresightedness, she was wearing a sleek gown of garnet-red satin. She had purchased it shortly before leaving home. It had been left behind in San Francisco along with the other clothes she had not expected to wear in her new life.

Now, bathed in the romantic glow of candlelight, she decided it was perfect for an evening at the Paradise with Nick. The lustrous fabric had been cut on the bias so that it clung lightly to her body and flared out below the hips. The front was styled with a high, deceptively demure neckline. Fluttery sleeves revealed her arms. The back plunged to the waist. Black fishnet gloves veiled her hands.

Lyra looked even more at home in the club. Her natural flair for style lent her an aura of glamour that would have suited a star. Her bronze satin gown was cut to display her excellent figure to full advantage. Matching elbow-length gloves and a gossamer wrap finished the look.

"Stick around and you will probably see a few stars," Nick said. "If they're in town, they'll show up here sooner or later."

"Burning Cove is so much more exciting than San Francisco," Lyra said. She picked up her pink lady. "We should have visited Burning Cove months ago, Viv. Look what we've been missing."

"Under other circumstances I would probably enjoy it more," Vivian said.

Lyra's glow faded into genuine concern. "I still can't believe someone wants you dead, and before you say anything, Nick, I agree with Vivian. Hamilton is a lying, cheating rat but I can't imagine him sinking so low that he would actually hire someone to murder Viv. For one thing, I doubt that he would even know how to locate a paid assassin."

"Good point," Vivian said. "We've been wondering about that aspect of things. It's not as if murder-for-hire businesses advertise in the phone book."

"No," Nick said. He picked up his glass and gently swirled the whiskey so that it caught the light of the candle flame. "The problem raises some interesting questions but not the most important one."

"Which is?" Lyra said.

"Motive," Nick said. "You and Vivian seem to be convinced that Merrick is innocent. I agree that if he is guilty he would be an anomaly."

"Why?" Vivian asked.

"Judging by what my uncle has managed to decipher so far, all of the killer's commissions in the past couple of years appear to have originated in the Los Angeles area. Before that he was murdering people in New York. There's no indication any of his clients or his victims lived in San Francisco. The assassin evidently prefers to work on territory he knows well."

"I am no longer a fan of Hamilton Merrick but I think I can give you one more reason why he wouldn't take the risk of hiring someone to murder me," Vivian said. "He simply isn't that ambitious."

Lyra had been about to take another sip of her pink lady. She paused. "You're right, Viv. Hamilton was born to attend parties and sail his yacht. He has no real interest in business. He isn't obsessed with making money because he knows he's going to inherit plenty of it."

"If you're both right," Nick said, "if money is not the motive, then we are left with only one other likely possibility."

Lyra's eyes lost their sparkle. "You think the motive is somehow connected to Viv's photography."

"Yes," Nick said. "I do. It's felt that way right from the start."

"I just can't see any way there could be a connection," Vivian said, "not now that the Dagger Killer is dead. He was the only one who had a reason to murder me."

She stopped talking because a familiar figure was approaching the table.

"Forgive me for interrupting," Ripley Fleming said. He smiled at Vivian. "I thought I recognized you in the lobby of the Burning Cove

Hotel this afternoon. We met briefly a few weeks ago. You may not remember me."

He must have known that he was not the kind of man a woman would forget, Vivian thought, but the humility was charming. She smiled.

"Of course I remember you, Mr. Fleming," she said.

"I'm afraid I did not catch your name at the time," Ripley said.

"Vivian—" She stopped because Nick was giving her foot a less than subtle nudge under the table.

"I see you know my wife," he said smoothly. "The name's Sundridge, by the way. Mrs. Vivian Sundridge. I'm Nick Sundridge."

He got to his feet and shook hands with an easy manner, as if he was accustomed to making the acquaintance of famous film stars. But Vivian got a shiver of awareness across the back of her neck. She glanced at him. In the flickering candlelight his expression was cool, controlled, polite. But she was certain he viewed Ripley with deep suspicion.

"A pleasure," Ripley said, evidently unaware he was being assessed, analyzed, and cataloged as a potential threat.

"Mr. Fleming, allow me to introduce my sister, Lyra Brazier," Vivian said.

Lyra was glowing with excitement. She extended one gloved hand.

"I'm thrilled to meet you, Mr. Fleming," she said. "I'm a fan. You were absolutely amazing in *Shock*."

Ripley smiled. "Thank you, Miss Brazier. Please call me Ripley."

Lyra was beyond glowing now. Vivian could have sworn she was sparkling.

"And you must call me Lyra," Lyra said.

Ripley did not release her hand and Lyra showed no great urgency to retrieve it.

"Would you care to dance?" he said.

"Love to," Lyra said.

She was out of the booth and on her feet in seconds. Ripley took her arm but he paused long enough to smile at Vivian.

"You did me a great favor, Mrs. Sundridge. I wanted you to know that I haven't forgotten and that I meant what I said at the time. I'm in your debt."

"There is no debt, so please don't worry about it," Vivian said. "And you must call me Vivian."

"Thank you, Vivian," he said.

He swept Lyra down a carpeted aisle to the dance floor.

"Don't say it," Vivian said.

Nick did not take his eyes off Ripley and Lyra. "Don't say what?"

"Don't say something along the lines of what are the odds the famous actor whose reputation I protected when I declined to photograph him at the scene of the Carstairs murder would make it a point to stop at this table tonight."

"That's a rather long and convoluted sentence so I won't say it. I'll shorten it. What are the odds?"

"Probably not all that bad when you think about it," Vivian said. "Burning Cove is an obvious destination for an actor of Fleming's stature."

"He's staying at the same hotel."

"So? He's Hollywood royalty. The Burning Cove Hotel is where people like Fleming stay when they're in town."

"Any way you slice this it comes up looking a lot like a very striking coincidence."

"There are such things as coincidence, you know."

"Not when we're in the process of trying to catch a killer—" Nick broke off because a waiter was approaching the booth.

"A message from Mr. Pell." The waiter put a small envelope down on the table.

"Thank you," Nick said. He opened the envelope. There was a card inside.

"Is something wrong?" Vivian asked.

"No," Nick said. He slipped the envelope inside his jacket. "It looks like something has finally gone right for a change. Pell is upstairs in his private quarters. He just got a call from the Broker. The individual who wants to buy the journal has agreed to our arrangements. The transaction takes place tomorrow night."

Vivian tensed. "I know you and Luther believe you have things under control but there is no such thing as a foolproof plan."

Nick smiled. "Careful. You're starting to sound like me. Always looking for all the possible ways things can go wrong."

"Maybe your pessimistic view of the world has started to rub off on me."

"There's a fix for that."

"What?"

"Why do you think they invented dancing?"

Nick got to his feet and reached out to take her hand.

When they walked onto the dance floor he took her into his arms.

"You're right," she whispered. "Dancing is an excellent remedy for dark thoughts."

His warm palm slid down the bare skin of her back.

"I can think of something that works even better," he said.

He said the words very softly in his midnight voice. A thrilling shiver of anticipation electrified Vivian's senses.

Probably the wrong time but definitely the right man.

Chapter 35

can hardly believe it," Lyra said. "My first night in Burning Cove and I danced with a famous movie star at the hottest nightclub in town. And then I danced with lots of other men. This is the best night of my entire life. No wonder you left home, Viv. Partying in Burning Cove is so much more fun than going to all those boring society affairs back in San Francisco."

Vivian smiled ruefully. "I think you've had a few too many pink ladies."

It was shortly after two in the morning. She and Nick and Lyra were standing outside Lyra's room at the Burning Cove Hotel.

"Who cares?" Lyra did a giddy pirouette in the hallway, her skirts swirling around her ankles. "I'll tell you one thing. I am never, ever going back to San Francisco."

When she stopped spinning she staggered a little. Vivian caught her by one arm to steady her. Nick took Lyra's other arm.

"She's going to feel a little different in the morning," he said to Vivian.

"I think you're right," Vivian said.

Lyra gave that observation a few seconds of close consideration. Then she giggled.

"You may be right," she said. "But you know what? I don't care if I have a hangover. It will be worth it. *I danced with Ripley Fleming.* And then I danced some more. I danced the whole night."

"Yes, you did," Vivian said. "Now give me your room key."

"Sure." Lyra fumbled with the catch of her small crystal-beaded handbag. When she got it open she handed the key to Vivian.

Vivian opened the door. "Need any help getting ready for bed?"

"Nope." Lyra sailed past her and flipped the light switch. She turned around with a laughing smile. "You two can run along now. I'll be just fine."

"Lock the door," Nick said.

"You bet," Lyra said.

She smiled and closed the door. There was a loud snick as the bolt slid home.

"Have fun, you two," she called through the heavy wood paneling.

Nick took Vivian's arm. They walked out into the softly lit gardens, following the path that led to their villa.

"You're worried, aren't you?" Nick said.

"It's been a long time since I've seen Lyra in such a carefree mood," Vivian said. "It's a little unnerving."

"You're used to being the wild sister," Nick said. He sounded amused.

"Well, yes, I suppose so."

"Looks like you now have some competition."

"Evidently. Don't misunderstand me—I'm very glad Lyra discovered the truth about Hamilton before the wedding and I'm relieved she gave him back his ring. But now I'm afraid that in this new mood she'll do something rash."

"Such as?"

"I don't know," Vivian said. "That's the problem. There are so many ways an attractive, vivacious woman with a lot of money and a reckless, devil-may-care attitude can get into trouble in places like Burning Cove."

"There you go, thinking dark and depressing thoughts again. I believe I mentioned I have a remedy for that."

A fizzy little wave of anticipation shivered through her, heightening her awareness. It was as if some part of her was suddenly attuned to the invisible energy of the night, the lush gardens, and most of all to the man who stirred her senses as no other man ever had.

"Yes," she said. "You did tell me that."

Nick brought her gently to a halt in the shadow of a grape arbor and took her into his arms. When his mouth closed over hers, the effervescent tide of anticipation was transformed into a hot wave of desire. She melted against his hard, lean body.

"Vivian," he said against her mouth, "I want you so damn bad."

"I'm glad," she managed in a throaty voice. "Because I want you, too."

"Enough to do something reckless and maybe a little dangerous?"

"Such as?"

"Come to bed with me and we will find out together."

Somewhere inside she thought she heard a voice whisper words of caution. *It's too soon. He's still a stranger in so many ways.*

But the voice was thin and faint; easily ignored. The alluring whispers demanding she seize the moment were far more compelling. They called to her, challenging her to take what might be a once-in-a-lifetime chance to discover the truth about the strength of her own passions.

"Whether or not I accept your invitation depends on the answer to a question I need to ask," she said against his warm throat.

"Now you've got me terrified. What's the question?"

She pulled away from him, just far enough to meet his eyes. "Will I be the only one taking chances tonight?"

"Don't worry, I've got a tin of pros."

It took her a beat to realize he was talking about prophylactics—condoms. She felt the heat rise in her cheeks and was suddenly very glad of the shadows. She did not know whether to be pleased or infuriated. Had he been *expecting* her to simply fall into bed with him?

"You came prepared?" she asked, trying to keep her tone neutral.

"That's a trick question, isn't it?" He cradled her face in his hands and traced the lines of her jaw with his thumbs. "If I answer yes, I'm in trouble because it will look like I've been planning to get you into bed from the start. If I say no, you'll wonder why I just happen to have the pros with me when I'm supposed to be doing my job, keeping you safe."

"You're right. It was a trick question. Don't bother answering."

"Too late. The answer is the hotel bellman. When he delivered the dinner jacket I ordered this afternoon there was a tin in the pocket."

"Was it there because you requested it?"

"I'm afraid so. Does knowing that ruin the moment?"

"Nope. It means that your intuition really is very good. But just to be clear. When I asked you if I was the only one taking chances tonight, I wasn't talking about prophylactics."

"Ah. You meant that going to bed with me is risky because neither of us knows how it will end."

"Something like that."

He moved one hand through her hair as if he was threading strands of silk through his fingers.

"No," he said, "you are not the only one taking a chance tonight."

She threw her arms around his neck. "In that case, my answer is yes."

"Vivian."

He spoke her name as if it held a kind of magic; a name to conjure with in the darkness of night.

He scooped her up in his arms and carried her through the scented garden to the front door of the villa.

Chapter 36

Vivian wasn't entirely sure how he got her through the door and into the shadowed hall. She was vaguely aware of Rex. The dog showed up briefly to greet them. When he discovered he was not going to get the usual amount of attention, he disappeared into the living room.

The next thing she knew, she was in Nick's room. He set her on her feet beside the bed, reached down, and ripped the quilt and sheet aside. Breathless, she fumbled with the fasteners at the waist of the gown.

"Let me do it," Nick said.

He put his hands on her shoulders, turned her gently around, and undid the hooks and eyes. The garnet satin cascaded into a pool at her feet, leaving her in a pair of dainty panties, a silky bra, garter belt, stockings, and red evening sandals.

"You are so lovely," he said.

There was wonder in each word.

He touched her breasts as if they were delicate works of art. Then he moved his hands to her waist and lifted her out of the crumpled gown. He sat her on the edge of the bed.

When he went down on one knee in front of her she almost stopped breathing. *Don't do this. Don't ask me to marry you. It's too soon. It's crazy. I don't want to have to think about anything else except tonight. I don't want to have to think at all. I just want to be with you.*

But of course he didn't stun her with an out-of-the-blue proposal. What had made her think he would do such a thing? He had made his thoughts on intimate relationships clear earlier that day when they had been standing in front of the gallery. *I don't know about love and marriage but I've got nothing against passion.*

She allowed herself to breathe again. There was no need to panic. Nick had experienced one disastrous runaway marriage. He would be wary of making another serious commitment. And hadn't she decided she was a modern woman who was not bound by society's rules and conventions? She planned to devote herself to her art.

Unaware of her tumultuous thoughts, Nick cradled first her right foot and then her left in his strong hands and undid the straps of her sandals.

The important thing was that both of them understood that a single night of passion meant nothing more or less than what it was—a single night of passion.

She watched Nick, wondering if he had any idea of just how sensual the act of removing her shoes was.

"The other freelancers called me Cinderella," she said. "Every time I showed up at midnight at a crime scene they said I must be looking for Prince Charming. Tonight I feel like I found him. Except you should be putting on my glass slippers, not taking them off."

He stroked her stocking-clad leg and then got to his feet.

"I'm not Prince Charming," he said, "so I don't have to follow the script."

"Thank goodness."

She undid the fasteners on the dainty garter belt, rolled her stockings down, and slipped them off her feet. He watched, seemingly mesmerized, as she took off the belt.

At that point she was chagrined to discover that she did not have the extra ounce of boldness it took to remove her silk panties.

"Your turn," she said softly.

He peeled off the evening jacket and tossed it over a chair. Then unbuckled the holster and set it on the table beside the bed.

He sat down and started to remove his shoes.

"Let me," she said.

She knelt in front of him and took off his shoes and socks.

"You have very nice feet," she said. "Strong. Well made."

"Vivian, you are going to drive me right out of my mind."

He stood and started to loosen the black bow tie. He never took his eyes off her. The energy in the room excited her senses in ways she had never experienced.

She rose and took over the task of untying the length of black silk. It wasn't easy because her fingers trembled. She finally got the tie undone. Nick stripped it off and draped it around her neck. He tugged on the ends, pulling her close for another deep kiss.

When he finally raised his head his eyes were fever hot. Everything inside her tightened in anticipation. He deliberately removed her panties.

She sat down before she collapsed and watched, fascinated, as Nick took off his crisp white shirt and undershirt. He reached into the pocket of his trousers and took out a small tin. She watched him walk around the end of the bed. He set the condoms on the nightstand next to the gun without saying a word. Then he finished undressing.

She had sensed the fierceness of his erection when he had held her close in the garden but the sight of his aroused body was both thrilling and shocking. She'd had the one ridiculous affair with Winston Bancroft and she had photographed a great many nude or nearly nude men, but this was different.

This was really different. Nick was different.

Nick started toward the bed. "You had better not be thinking of grabbing your camera and taking a photograph."

He surprised a nervous laugh from her. "I didn't mean to stare." She scrambled into bed, pulling the sheet up to cover herself. "It's just that I wasn't expecting you to have such an, ah, impressive physique."

He looked as if he wasn't sure what to do or where to go with that observation. She thought he turned a little red. But before she could decide if she had embarrassed him, he switched off the lamp and got into bed.

He stretched out under the sheet and propped himself up on his elbow to look down at her.

"You've seen a lot of naked men," he said.

"Yes, I have, as a matter of fact." She turned on her side and drew her fingertips down his chest. "I believe that I am exceptionally well qualified to judge the male form." She drew her palm lower, across his firm belly, and lower still. She closed her fingers around him. "Trust me, when I say impressive, I mean impressive."

He gave a short, hoarse groan that was half laugh and half raw desire and leaned over her, caging her with his arms. His mouth came down on hers.

The kiss was long and hot and wet. When it ended she was clawing at the bare skin of his back. He paused long enough to open the tin and sheath himself. When he was ready he turned back to her and began a long, leisurely journey of exploration. He used his mouth, his tongue, and his fingers to arouse and ignite until she was desperate for him. She had never before been so close to the edge.

Her climax rose up out of nowhere, taking her by surprise. At first she did not comprehend what was happening. In the next moment wave after wave of sensation rippled through her.

"Yes," she said. She grasped a fistful of sheet in one hand and sank the nails of her other hand deep into the sleek muscles of Nick's shoulders. "Yes. Yes. *Yes.*"

And then it was over. She was thrilled, exultant, amazed. It was as if she had just found the secret to the best photograph of her life. When she finally caught her breath she started to giggle. The giggle became laughter.

Nick sat up and watched her, bemused.

"That's not quite the reaction I was hoping for," he said.

Horrified that she had accidentally offended him, she pushed him onto his back and sprawled on top of him.

"I've got news for you," she said. "It was exactly what I was hoping for."

He caught hold of her shoulders and smiled another of his rare, wicked smiles. His eyes got a little hotter.

"Is that right?" he said.

"It's never happened to me, you see." She brushed her mouth across his and smiled what she knew was a very smug sort of smile. "I had almost convinced myself that I would never know what it felt like. Don't you understand what just happened?"

"Well, biologically speaking—"

"Forget biology. You just proved that I'm not frigid."

He raised his brows. "The possibility that you might be frigid never once crossed my mind."

She smiled. "When you told me that your marriage had been annulled, it never once crossed *my* mind that the problem might have been your inability to carry out your husbandly duties in the bedroom."

"You're sure?"

"Okay, I admit it was on the list of possibilities but it was at the very bottom."

"I am prepared to offer further proof that I am not incapacitated."

She reached down and wrapped her fingers around him. "Yes, I can see that."

She stroked him, her grasp increasingly tight. He sucked in a deep breath.

"I can't take this much longer," he warned.

"No waiting necessary."

She sat up, straddled him, and slowly lowered herself until he was filling her completely. His eyes half closed. He gripped her thighs. When she began to move, he thrust into her again and again. She was still so sensitized from her release that the experience of having him deep inside her was almost unbearable. She was balanced on the exquisite edge between pain and pleasure. She knew from his sweat-soaked body and the fierce expression on his face that he was there on the same edge.

When his release struck with the force of a storm, they both went over together.

Chapter 37

Nick emerged from the bathroom smiling a decidedly satisfied smile.

"What's so funny?" Vivian asked.

"You. Sorry." He climbed back into bed. "Where in hell did you get the notion that you were frigid? Been reading Dr. Freud or one of his followers?"

"Winston Bancroft."

"Oh, right. The art photographer who insulted your talent. You said things ended with a major scene."

"Yes. There was a bit more to the story than the insult to my talent. That was reason enough to end things, of course. But I also discovered the reason he lied to me and said glowing things about my art was because he wanted to get his hands on my family's money."

"Talk about adding insult to injury." Nick paused. "Huh."

"It's hard to make a living as a photographer, even for someone of Winston's stature. In his defense, he has his dreams, just as I have mine. Winston's goal was, and probably still is, to establish his own art school, an academy, and a gallery that will focus on elevating photography into the fine arts."

"What, exactly, got said in the course of the big breakup scene?"

"Well, first I told him that I'd had to fake every orgasm I'd ever claimed to have had with him, all three of them."

"You said that in front of the gallery owner?"

"Yep. That made Winston furious, of course. That's when he called me frigid. He said I obviously had a deep-seated neurosis that prevented me from achieving orgasm."

"That must have been some scene."

"I'm afraid so. When I told Winston that I didn't think there was anything wrong with me and that he was the one with the problem, he was even more outraged. He turned a very interesting shade of purple. I stormed out of the office and out of his life. Haven't spoken to him since."

"Huh."

"That's the second time you've said that in the past couple of minutes."

"Well, damn."

"Damn?"

"Looks like we have to add another suspect to our list."

"Winston?" Vivian was floored. "Forget it. He was angry when I walked out but not that angry."

"Is he still living in San Francisco?"

Vivian hesitated. "Well, no. Last I heard he had joined an artist's colony on the coast."

"Where on the coast?"

Vivian groaned. "About twenty miles south of here. That's why he's been able to get his work installed at galleries in places such as Burning Cove and Adelina Beach. Curators and gallery owners love him. He can be very charming."

"That puts him squarely in the Los Angeles area. If we're right that the killer finds his clients in and around L.A.—"

"I just can't see Winston wanting to murder me. There wouldn't be any point. The only way he could have gotten his hands on my father's money is if he had married me. That option is definitely off the table."

Nick rolled onto his side and looked at her. A low-grade fever burned in his eyes.

"Money isn't the only motive for murder," he said. "The desire for revenge is an acid that destroys everything it touches."

"We can't just keep adding names to your suspect list."

"You're right." Nick eased the covers aside and sat up on the edge of the bed. "It's time to edit our list."

"How?"

"By going back to the issue that has been bothering us from the start."

"What is that?"

"The fact that an unknown photographer who is trying to make her mark in the art world was the target of not just one but two attacks within the span of slightly less than a month."

Vivian smiled at the energy around him. "Do you always go right back to work after making love?"

She winced at her own words. *Should have said, Do you always go right back to work after going to bed with someone?* She shouldn't have used the word *love*.

But Nick was apparently too preoccupied with his thoughts to pay attention to nuances. He got to his feet and went to the door. He paused to look back at her.

"No," he said. "Usually I just go to sleep afterward. Something about being with you seems to have cleared my head."

He was serious.

Well, at least she was proving to be useful, she thought.

Chapter 38

They got a couple of hours of sleep before room service delivered breakfast. They ate the grapefruit, eggs, and toast at the small table on the patio. Rex wolfed down the steak and eggs the kitchen had sent to the villa in a large bowl.

Nick discovered that he was ravenous. It was not an unusual state of affairs. He was always hungry when he started making progress on a case.

Vivian picked up the silver pot and poured two cups of coffee. Nick polished off the last slice of toast, sat back, and picked up his notebook.

"All right, here's what we've got," he said. "Our list of suspects includes Hamilton Merrick, Lyra's fiancé. His motive is the Brazier family fortune."

"Hamilton no longer has a motive," Vivian pointed out. "He's now an ex-fiancé."

Nick looked up from his notes. "That doesn't mean he can or will call off the assassin. He may think he can convince Lyra to forgive him.

Or he may simply want revenge now. It's also quite possible that he has no way to contact the killer to stop the process."

"Okay, he stays on your list but I still can't imagine him commissioning a murder."

"In that same category, we also have Winston Bancroft. Motive: revenge." Nick tapped the pencil against the notebook. "They say that revenge is a dish that is best served cold but the truth is, people usually prefer to serve it blazing hot."

"I think Winston would go the blazing-hot route. I told you, he's inclined toward heavy drama. I can't see him waiting this long to exact revenge. What's more, if you think about it, he's already been avenged. He's the one who has work hanging in prestigious galleries, not me."

"If you're reading him right—"

"Pretty sure I am."

"It means he goes to the bottom of the list." Nick put a check mark beside Bancroft's name. "I will also admit I'm inclined to agree with you about Hamilton Merrick. Not because he isn't the type to hire a killer but because it would have made more sense for him to wait until he was safely married to Lyra before he got rid of you."

"And why would he take the risk of having an affair with one of Lyra's friends before the wedding? He had to know that if Lyra found out she would end the engagement. In fact, given what I know about Hamilton, I wouldn't be surprised if he unconsciously wanted to be discovered in bed with Lyra's friend. It got him out of a marriage he probably does not want."

Nick studied his notes again. "People rarely use a lot of logic or common sense when they indulge in an affair."

There was an acute silence from the other side of the table. Nick looked up. Vivian was very busy feeding bacon to Rex under the table. It occurred to him she was probably thinking about their own newly minted affair and the possibility that logic and common sense had not been involved.

"I'm not an expert on this sort of thing but it sounds like you've just ruled out our two prime client suspects," she said. "What about Ripley Fleming?"

"I can't see him as a client," Nick said. "There's no connection between the two of you. But he makes a very good assassin. Perfect cover. Perfect camouflage. Talented actor. We know he showed up at the scene of the Carstairs murder and now he's here in Burning Cove."

Vivian shook her head. "The thing is, he seems genuinely grateful to me for not taking his photo that night."

"If he is the killer, he had every reason to be grateful. Doesn't mean he doesn't plan to kill you."

"We know he didn't leave the hotel grounds the other night, so he couldn't have murdered Toby Flint."

"I'm not so sure he didn't leave. According to Oliver Ward there were plenty of sightings of Fleming throughout the evening but it's impossible to know where someone is every single minute. If Fleming is our man in the work clothes and cap, he could have used that disguise long enough to slip out of the hotel through a service entrance, murder Flint, and then return to the bar."

"Still, he seems so nice."

Nick raised his brows. "You'd be amazed how often people say exactly that after a killer is arrested."

Vivian made a face.

"There is, however, one other possibility," Nick continued. "An unknown figure. We'll call him Mr. X for now."

"We don't know anything about him."

"You're wrong. We know a lot about him because of the timeline. Morris Deverell, the Dagger Killer, attacked you about a month ago because he realized you were the one who told the cops the killer was probably a photographer working in the pictorial tradition."

"That turned out to be the truth. Remember, the police found an expensive camera and a collection of daggers in Deverell's house."

"And then he was mysteriously run down by a car immediately after he escaped from the hospital." Nick paused. "*Before* he could talk to the cops."

Vivian went very still. "You're convinced someone murdered him after he escaped from the hospital, aren't you?"

"Yes. Probably the same someone who helped him escape. Now Toby Flint is dead by the same means. There has to be a connection."

"Mr. X murdered both of them. Motive?"

"Both men knew too much. Mr. X has the answers we need. With a little luck he'll walk into the trap that Luther and I have set for tonight."

Vivian's brows rose. "Since when do you believe in luck?"

"Since I met you."

She smiled a dazzling smile. "It's so nice to know I am contributing to this investigation."

"I wouldn't be this far along without you."

"Do we have any special plans for today?"

"No. Today is all about waiting and looking as if we aren't the least bit concerned that a killer is watching you."

"In that case, is there any reason why I can't use Joan Ashwood's darkroom to develop a couple of prints for her to hang in her gallery?"

Nick thought about it. "No, not as long as Lyra and I accompany you. I don't want you to be alone today."

Chapter 39

The storm struck in full fury shortly before midnight. Vivian was sitting in a booth in the Burning Cove Hotel's elegant bar. She was not alone. Lyra was with her. So were Raina Kirk and Irene Ward. Rex was under the table, enjoying occasional pats from the women.

The glamorously shadowed lounge was packed because most of the hotel guests who otherwise might have chosen to spend the evening at one of the local nightclubs had decided to stay on the grounds. It was not as if the hotel did not offer plenty of first-class entertainment. A jazz trio was playing on the small stage and the cocktails were served up by skilled bartenders who put on a show every time they crafted a drink.

Security was tight but the beefy men wearing extra-large tuxes remained mostly in the shadows.

Raina took a sip of her cocktail and set the glass on the table.

"Don't worry, Vivian," she said. "Everything will be fine. Luther has had a lot of experience setting traps for bad guys and he assures me

Nick knows what he's doing, too. Mr. Sundridge is an investigator, after all."

"I know." Vivian swirled her drink in an absentminded way.

She reached under the table to touch Rex. He licked her hand as if he understood she needed reassurance. She had given up trying to shake the sense of impending disaster that had been plaguing her since Nick had left the hotel an hour ago. She would not be able to relax until it was over and Nick walked through the door of the lounge.

"It's not as if there are only the two of them involved in this thing," Irene pointed out. "Oliver is with them tonight, and so is Detective Brandon from the Burning Cove Police. Brandon has officers watching the road in and out of the rendezvous point. When the assassin picks up the journal, they'll move in and grab him."

"You make it sound so simple," Lyra said.

"Simple plans are usually the best, according to Luther," Raina said.

"Oliver agrees," Irene said. "He says that even the most complicated magic trick has a fairly simple explanation. It's all about distracting the audience with a good story."

"Exactly," Raina said. "Tonight the assassin is the audience. The story is that he is finally within reach of something he wants desperately."

"The journal of poems," Irene said.

"Right," Raina said. "He'll believe he's safe because the deal was set up by an underworld figure, the Broker."

Lyra was fascinated. "Does Mr. Pell really have underworld connections?"

Raina's smile was difficult to interpret. "Luther is a complicated man with a complicated past. Let's leave it at that, shall we?"

Something in her tone sent a tiny chill of awareness across the back of Vivian's neck. She looked at Raina, trying to read her eyes, but the flickering candlelight made it difficult. The only thing she could be certain of was that Raina's past was complicated, too. Everyone had secrets.

Curious, she decided to try a little careful probing.

"How long have you been here in Burning Cove?" she asked in what she hoped was a casual manner.

"Not long," Raina said. "I used to live in New York."

That explained the East Coast accent, Vivian thought.

"I've never met a female private investigator," Lyra said. "It sounds very exciting. How do you go about getting a job like that?"

"I don't know how other people do it," Raina said. "But in my case I just rented an office, put out a sign, and advertised in the local phone book."

"Do you carry a gun?" Lyra asked.

Raina was starting to look amused. "I own a gun, if that's what you want to know. But I rarely carry it. The cases I handle are seldom dangerous. For example, I run background investigations on people this hotel and the Paradise Club are considering for employment. I do some missing persons work. I'm also trying to market my services to women who are considering marriage."

Lyra was fascinated. "What services do you offer them?"

Irene smiled. "She means she's available to take a close look at the past behavior of the man the client is planning to marry."

Lyra's eyes widened. "What a fantastic idea. I wish I'd hired you to look into my ex-fiancé's history, Raina. I mean, I knew Hamilton had a certain reputation as a ladies' man but I thought that was all in the past. I never dreamed he was actually cheating on me with one of my best friends."

Vivian glanced at the rather large handbag Raina had with her. "You brought your gun with you tonight, didn't you?"

Raina nodded, saying nothing.

"Raina had a rather nasty experience recently," Irene said. "She and several other people were taken hostage at the Paradise Club."

Vivian looked at Raina. "I read about that in the papers. Luckily none of the hostages was hurt."

"Luck," Raina said, "had nothing to do with it."

Lyra started to ask another question but she stopped and smiled at the familiar figure making his way toward the booth.

"Look," she said, "here comes Ripley Fleming."

Chapter 40

The storm was a complication they could have done without, Nick thought. He was behind the wheel of the Packard, making his way along Cliff Road, a narrow, winding, two-lane strip of pavement that followed the bluffs above the ocean. The rain was coming down hard now, severely limiting visibility, even for someone with his excellent night vision.

He was alone in the sedan. Luther and the others were waiting at the old pier. The trap had been set. It remained to be seen if the killer would take the bait.

How badly do you want that journal, Mr. X? How desperately do you want to complete the commission?

The first hint of engine trouble came when he tried to accelerate out of a sharp turn. The car did not respond with its usual surge of power. The steam appeared when he went into the next curve. It wafted up from the front of the vehicle.

The engine was overheating. That should not be happening. He took very, very good care of the Packard. The radiator hose was in excellent shape.

He eased the car to the side of the road before the big eight-cylinder engine died and he sat quietly for a moment, running through possibilities and probabilities.

He left the headlights on to warn other motorists there was a vehicle parked on the edge of the pavement although it was unlikely there would be much traffic on such a stormy night.

He found the flashlight in the glove box, opened the door, and got out from behind the wheel. He left his hat behind. He was going to get drenched. There was no point ruining the fedora as well as his jacket and trousers.

He walked around to the front of the car and raised the hood. Hot steam hissed from the nearly empty radiator. He crouched and aimed the flashlight under the car. The perfectly good radiator hose had burst in at least three places. The water meant to cool the engine had drained out somewhere along Cliff Road.

He straightened and used the flashlight to check his watch. It was going to be a long walk to the pier where Luther and the cops were waiting. The deal for the journal was due to take place in an hour.

The low growl of a car engine rumbled in the distance. He looked back down the road and saw the twin beams of a pair of headlights. They flashed briefly and then disappeared when the vehicle went into a curve.

He opened the driver's side door, reached inside, and doused the headlights. Then he closed the door again. The rainy darkness closed in hard and fast. He switched on the flashlight and surveyed the rocky, weather-beaten landscape on the far side of the road, away from the bluff. It offered few places of concealment. He decided his best option was a cluster of boulders.

He crossed the pavement, moved behind the largest rock, and turned off the flashlight. Moments later a car cruised slowly out of a curve, windshield wipers slashing. The headlights picked up the darkened Packard.

The driver pulled to the side and came to a halt directly behind the Packard. The headlights illuminated the vehicle but the rain reduced visibility. The motorist could probably tell there was no one sitting behind the wheel but that was about all that he would be able to see.

After a moment the driver got out of the front seat. He left the lights on and the engine running. A familiar cap was pulled down low over his eyes in an attempt to ward off some of the rain. He held a flashlight in his left hand but his right arm was stiff and straight at his side.

Nick could not see the gun but he was sure it was in the driver's right hand.

"Hello," the driver shouted. "Anyone around? Looks like you had some car trouble. I'd be happy to give you a lift into town."

Nick waited.

After a moment the driver walked to the passenger side window of the Packard and aimed the flashlight into the front and rear seats. Satisfied that there was no one inside he immediately moved to the back of the car and opened the trunk.

"So you're the Poet," Nick said.

The driver gave a violent start of surprise and dove for the shadows on the far side of the Packard, putting the vehicle between himself and Nick.

"Who the fuck *are* you?" the Poet shouted. "How did you get hold of my journal? How did you break the code?"

"It's a long story. Let's just say breaking the code was the easy part."

"You're not law enforcement."

"No. Just someone who knows your poems are records of your so-called commissions. Names, dates, clients. The techniques you used to make the murders look like natural causes, suicides, or accidents."

"Did you really think I was dumb enough to walk into the trap you set up at that old pier tonight?" the Poet said.

"The possibility occurred to me, yes. I know you're desperate to recover the journal."

"I knew you had it figured out when you grabbed the photographer. Why are you protecting her?"

"Isn't it obvious?" Nick said. "Miss Brazier is the bait I needed to trap you."

"You failed. I never had any intention of showing up at the pier tonight. In case you're wondering, I got to your car in the hotel parking lot last night."

"Out of curiosity, what did you use on the radiator hose? A knife?"

"Ice pick." Hot satisfaction seethed in the Poet's voice for a few seconds. "The same thing I'm going to use on the photographer. Here's the part I know you'll appreciate. It's going to look like you killed her. Newly wed husband discovers that his bride isn't the woman he believed her to be. Grabs the ice pick. Act of passion."

"Oddly enough, I've already lived out a very similar script. But in that case, the woman survived. Someone else died instead."

"What are you talking about?"

"Your lack of originality."

"Where's the journal?" Rage and frustration crept into the Poet's voice.

"You haven't given me much of an incentive to answer that question."

"Here's the deal. We're going to do a trade. You give me the journal, you get to live."

"Fair enough, but it won't work because I can't hold up my end of the bargain."

"What the fuck are you talking about?"

"I don't have the journal. Not on me. It's not in the car, either."

"*Where is it?*"

The Poet's voice was rapidly becoming shrill.

"You're almost at the breaking point, aren't you?" Nick said. "That kind of mental instability is a real problem for someone in your line of work."

"Tell me where the journal is."

"It's exactly where the Broker told you it would be," Nick said quietly. "At the pier."

"I don't believe you. You wouldn't let it out of your sight. It's too valuable. It's hidden inside the car."

Nick did not respond.

"Who are you?" the Poet asked. He sounded calmer now. Back in control. Barely.

"Haven't you figured it out yet?" Nick said. "I'm your competition."

"What the hell—? You think you can take my place? You're out of your mind."

"You're losing your edge. Your skills are no longer sharp. Take the disguise you used the night you firebombed Miss Brazier's cottage. You wore the wrong shoes. A rich man's shoes."

"You don't know what you're talking about."

"I realize you've been working under a time constraint and that you were feeling the pressure. But, seriously, talk about amateurish techniques. In the end you couldn't even safeguard your journal, the one thing that could send you to death row. Face it. Time to retire."

There was a shock wave of silence from the far side of the Packard.

"One thing I'd really like to know," the Poet said finally. "How did you steal my journal?"

"I didn't steal it," Nick said. "Someone else did. I just picked up the rumors about it and followed them to the source."

"What rumors?"

"The minute you notified the Broker that you were interested in buying a certain book of handwritten poems at any price, no questions asked, the rumors began circulating."

"So much for the Broker's promise of anonymity," the Poet said. "You can't trust anyone these days."

"The Broker kept his word. That's why he has survived as long as he has. But when something extremely valuable comes on the market there are always rumors."

"Who stole my journal?" the Poet screamed.

His pistol roared in the night, punctuating the words.

One down, five shots to go, Nick thought. Unless the Poet was carrying extra ammunition. Probably not. Judging by the accounts in the journal he was not accustomed to using a gun for his kills. He preferred more subtle methods.

"You like to think of yourself as a poet," Nick said. "I was inclined to agree after I read your early works. I was impressed by your originality. Back at the start of your career you were brilliant. But obviously your glory days are behind you."

"Shut your fucking mouth."

Nick sensed the hysteria in the words and aimed for it.

"Maybe you should have gone into psychotherapy instead of taking this last commission," he said. "Dr. Freud would probably have some interesting theories about your case."

Another shot cracked in the night.

Two down. Four to go.

"I will admit I've got a question for you," Nick said. "Who's your client? The one paying you to murder Vivian Brazier."

"You really think I'm going to tell you?"

"The information would have been helpful but it's not necessary. You're a spider who likes to sit at the center of a web. Now that you're finished it won't be hard to follow the strands to get all the answers. There are just so many details in those poems."

"You have no idea who you're dealing with."

"Does insanity run in your family?"

"*You fucking bastard.*"

Another shot cracked in the night. Three down. Three to go.

"I've analyzed several of your poems," Nick continued. "Figured out how you work. You lure your clients with veiled offers to make their problems go away. For a hefty fee, of course. Make it look like an accident or natural causes. The client probably tells himself or herself that is exactly what happened. An accident. Natural causes. Suicide. But one of these days you'll start blackmailing your clients, won't you? It's a clever business model but it's got one flaw."

"What are you talking about? There is no flaw."

"It's the money," Nick said. "It always leaves a trail."

"You're crazy."

"I'm not the one who gets excited about murdering people and then falls into a deep depression after the kill. We both know you belong in an asylum."

"No." The Poet's voice rose to a shrill scream. *"That's a fucking lie. I escaped the curse. I'm in control."*

Fury and panic shivered through each word.

Interesting, Nick thought.

"Your mental state is deteriorating, isn't it?" he said. "You're losing your grip on sanity. It's all there in the poems, you know. The euphoria of the kills used to last you for weeks, months even. But not now. You need to kill more often and you are no longer doing it carefully. It was just a matter of time before you got caught."

"That's not true. Not true. I'm in control."

The low rumble of a powerful engine sounded in the distance.

"Hear that car?" Nick said. "My associates are about to arrive."

"Now what are you talking about?"

"That car is bringing the people who were waiting for you at the pier, just in case my calculations were wrong. You were right about one thing. I did set up a trap to catch you tonight—two of them. The first one, the trap with the highest probability of working, was this one. I was almost certain you would find a way to stop me before I got to the pier. But if for some reason you didn't fall into this trap, my friends would have caught you in the second one."

"You crazy son of a bitch."

The Poet exploded from behind the shelter of the Packard. He ran for his car, firing again and again in rapid succession.

Nick counted off the shots. Four, five, six.

The Poet yanked open the door of the vehicle. Nick broke from the cover of the rock pile and lunged across the road.

The Poet whirled around and pulled the trigger.

Shit, Nick thought. *Miscounted.*

The bullet caught him in the upper right shoulder but momentum and grim determination propelled him forward.

He collided with the Poet, slamming him hard against the side of the car.

The Poet grunted, dropped the empty gun, and yanked a long, slender object out from under his jacket. Nick wrapped both hands around the Poet's arm and twisted sharply.

The Poet screamed. The ice pick fell from his nerveless fingers.

The approaching car braked sharply. The headlights speared Nick and the Poet. Luther emerged from behind the wheel. Another man climbed out of the passenger's seat. He had a gun in his hand.

"Brandon, Burning Cove Police," he growled. "Nobody moves."

Nick stepped back, sucking in air. The Poet slumped against the fender of the car, cradling his wrist and moaning softly.

"Brandon, this is Sundridge, the private investigator who set this up tonight," Luther said.

Brandon grunted. "Cut this a little close, didn't you?"

"I could come up with only an estimate on the timing," Nick said. He realized that his upper shoulder was on fire. The pain grew steadily. "Damn."

Luther aimed the flashlight at him. "What the hell? You're bleeding."

"I noticed," Nick said.

Brandon pulled a pair of handcuffs out of his pocket and moved forward to take charge of the Poet.

"You're under arrest," he said. "Who the hell are you?"

The Poet screamed, howling his fury and despair into the teeth of the storm. He flung himself forward with such speed and ferocity that Brandon, caught off guard, instinctively stepped out of the way.

As the Poet rushed past him in a mindless effort to escape, Brandon brought up his pistol and took aim.

"No, don't kill him," Nick said. "We need him alive."

"Nick's right," Luther said. "Don't worry, he won't get far on foot, not in this storm. The roads are blocked in both directions."

The Poet was silhouetted briefly in the glare of Luther's headlights. Nick registered the trajectory and broke into a run.

"Stop him," he shouted.

But it was too late. With a final scream the Poet threw himself off the cliff.

The shriek ended a second later.

Luther and Brandon raced forward and aimed their flashlights down at the thrashing surf. Nick found his own flashlight and joined them.

"I don't see him," Luther said.

"Must have been swept out to sea on a wave," Brandon said. "With luck the body will wash up onshore."

"He didn't have enough speed to land in the water," Nick said. He swept the beam back and forth across the rocks at the bottom of the cliff. "There he is."

The Poet was sprawled on an outcropping. He did not move.

"Well, damn," Brandon said. "That's gonna be a problem."

A siren wailed. A heavy engine rumbled in the night. Nick turned to watch a patrol car and a speedster arrive. Oliver Ward got out of the sleek speedster, bracing himself on a cane. Two uniformed officers jumped out of the patrol car and ran forward.

"Get on the radio," Brandon said to one of the officers. "We're gonna need some help recovering a body."

Nick headed toward the nearest car, Luther's coupe, and leaned against it. The pain in his shoulder was making it difficult to think. Luther yanked open the door. "Sit down before you fall down. We need to get you out of that coat."

Nick half fell into the front seat.

Luther went to work, quickly stripping off Nick's jacket and shirt. He fashioned a thick bandage out of the shirt and secured it in place with his necktie.

"You've done this before," Nick said.

"More often than I want to remember."

"The War?"

"Yeah."

Luther finished the first aid work, propped Nick up in the passenger seat, and got behind the wheel.

"I'm taking Sundridge to Dr. Skipton's clinic," he said to Brandon and Oliver Ward.

"Bad?" Oliver asked.

"Not as bad as it could have been," Luther said. He fired up the engine. "But he's lost some blood."

"Go on," Brandon said. "We'll catch up with you later."

Luther pulled out onto the road.

"Lucky for you that bastard was using a twenty-two," he said, shifting gears. "Not much stopping power."

"Could have fooled me," Nick said. He knew his words were starting to slur. "I was trying to count the rounds. Thought he'd fired all six."

"Hard to keep track when the lead starts flying."

"It's depressing, you know."

"Getting shot?"

"That, too. But mostly it's depressing to know that I almost got myself killed because of poor math skills."

"Look on the bright side." Luther drove faster. "Vivian Brazier is safe now. If the Poet isn't dead, he's headed for that gas chamber they're installing in San Quentin."

Nick tried to shake off the fog that was invading his senses. He forced himself to focus for a moment longer.

"Vivian won't be safe until we find out who hired the assassin," he said.

Chapter 41

Nick was sitting on the exam table in the clinic when Vivian came through the door, riding an invisible storm of energy. She was not alone. Uncle Pete was right behind her. He looked worried, too, but mostly he appeared relieved.

"What went wrong?" he asked.

"A small miscalculation," Nick said.

"I told you your plan had a couple of weak points."

"Yes, you did mention that," Nick said.

Vivian halted directly in front of him and examined the bandage on his upper right shoulder.

"Are you all right?" she asked. "Did you lose a lot of blood? You should be lying down. Are they going to admit you to the hospital?"

"I'm okay," he said. "According to Dr. Skipton I have no business taking up space at the local hospital."

The doctor stuffed some bloody clothing into a trash bin and looked at Vivian. "He'll be fine, although he's going to be sore for a few days. Got the bullet out. Wound is clean. Fortunately the other guy was only using a twenty-two. Not a lot of stopping power."

"People keep telling me that," Nick said. "I would just like to say it still hurts."

Skipton shrugged. "Next time do a better job of counting off the shots fired."

Nick groaned. "Easy for you to say."

Pete's brows shot up. "That was the miscalculation?"

"Yes," Nick said. "Could we just leave it at that?"

An officer appeared at the door. "Excuse me, Doc, but if you're finished in here, Detective Brandon would like you to examine the body of the guy who shot Mr. Sundridge."

"This is turning into a busy night," Skipton said. He picked up a black leather medical satchel and paused to nod at Vivian. "See to it Mr. Sundridge doesn't do anything too energetic for a while. I don't want him to ruin my sewing work."

Vivian flushed. Nick realized the doctor had concluded it was her job to take care of him.

"I understand, Doctor," she said.

Nick got a giddy little rush of pleasure. She hadn't argued; hadn't tried to push the responsibility off on Uncle Pete. Surely that was a good omen. Or maybe he was just delirious.

Skipton went out the door.

Nick concentrated on Vivian.

"Luther called you?" he said.

"Yes," she said. "Lyra and Raina and Irene and I were in the lounge at the hotel. Ripley Fleming was dancing with Lyra. Luther gave us the address of Dr. Skipton's clinic, but Lyra and I don't know our way around town. Neither does Mr. Fleming. Raina knew exactly where the clinic was located, though. She drove me here."

"Fleming was with you tonight at the hotel?"

"Yes." Vivian narrowed her eyes. "Why?"

"Never mind," Nick said. He caught Pete's eye. "We'll talk about it later."

Luther strolled into the room. "The Poet is dead but there was identification on the body. The name is Jonathan Treyherne. The address is an expensive neighborhood in Los Angeles. Raina is going to make some phone calls to her contacts in L.A. I'll let you know what she finds out."

"I need to get inside Treyherne's house before the police tear it up," Nick said.

"Brandon agreed to hold off contacting the L.A. police for a day or two."

"It's nearly dawn," Pete said. "You heard the doctor, Nick. You need to rest up before you go tearing out those stitches."

"Your uncle is right," Vivian said.

"I agree," Luther said. "You need some rest before you make the drive back to L.A."

Nick gave up. He looked at Vivian.

"We'll spend what's left of tonight here," he said. "Tomorrow we'll find out what Raina learns from her contacts. The next day we'll drive to L.A."

"You are not driving anywhere," Vivian said. "The doctor put me in charge, remember?"

"We have to get the name of Treyherne's client," Nick said.

Luther glanced at Vivian. "I think you're safe, at least for now, Miss Brazier. We know Treyherne's clients are not aware of his identity. That means whoever paid him to murder you has no way of knowing that he's dead."

Chapter 42

Nick stood in the middle of Treyherne's living room and asked the questions that had been the most important ones all along.

"Why didn't you encrypt the name of the client when you took your last commission, Jonathan Treyherne? And what about the motive? Did you intend to add that information later? Or was there some other reason for not identifying the client or the motive?"

He asked the questions aloud but there was no one around to hear him except Rex. They had found the big house closed up when they arrived a short time ago but it had been no problem to get in through the rear entrance.

Treyherne had come from New York. That much was clear from the older poems in the journal. His accent had been upper-class, educated. His bearing had been that of a gentleman who was comfortable in a rich man's world. Old money usually meant old and valuable furnishings, silver, and art. Yet everything in the mansion looked new and modern—including the art on the walls.

When Jonathan Treyherne moved out to California he had evidently done what so many others did when they moved West—he'd left his old life behind.

Raina had exhausted her contacts in Los Angeles. In the process she had turned up little more than what they already knew or surmised about Treyherne. He had appeared on the scene a few years earlier and slipped seamlessly into the most exclusive social circles. It appeared he had no family, just money.

If not for the earliest poems recording his kills back East, one could almost conclude that Treyherne had no past.

But every man, even a wealthy professional assassin who wrote harrowing poetry, had some personal history. Nick's intuition told him he had to find it. He needed answers.

He began the way he always did when he was on the hunt for information. He walked through every room in the house, taking his time, absorbing the feel of the place. He opened drawers, locked and otherwise. Men as wealthy as Treyherne always had a private safe. He found it behind a sensuous Tamara de Lempicka painting of two female nudes. He took out the stethoscope he had brought with him and went to work.

It did not take long to get the safe open. The only thing inside was a small financial ledger. A rush of anticipation flashed through him. He loved financial records.

He slipped the ledger inside his jacket and continued his prowl through the house. There were more financial records in the desk in the study. Nick flipped through them quickly and concluded they were the usual mundane transactions of a wealthy man's life—payments to a tailor, dues at various clubs, wages for a housekeeper and a gardener, the fees paid to the decorator who had furnished the mansion.

The accounts did not appear to be important but you never knew. Nick helped himself to the volume and a slim folder filled with what looked like Treyherne's personal correspondence.

He and Rex finished the tour and left the mansion via the same door they had used to enter it. They made their way through the quiet neighborhood to where the Packard was parked and drove to an isolated location overlooking the ocean.

He spent an hour with Treyherne's financial records. There was only one routine quarterly payment that did not have an obvious explanation. For some years Treyherne had sent checks to Maple Tree Farm. The address was in Maine. He had not missed a single quarter right up until the last check. That one was dated a year and a half earlier.

Shortly after the final check to Maple Tree Farm had been sent there was a transfer of a large sum of money from Jonathan Treyherne's Los Angeles bank to an account at an Adelina Beach bank.

The money had been deposited into the account of Morris Deverell.

"We just struck gold, Rex."

Rex had been leaning out the window, inhaling the salty breeze. He turned at the sound of his name and gave Nick an inquiring look.

Nick opened the folder that held Treyherne's correspondence. There was a letter from a New York law firm addressed to Jonathan Feathergill. The first letter dealt with the transfer of a large sum of money from the Feathergill Trust to the account of Jonathan Treyherne at a Los Angeles bank. The date coincided with Treyherne's move to the West Coast.

"He changed his name to Treyherne when he moved out here, Rex. He really did walk away from his old life."

Rex looked as if he agreed with that analysis.

The second letter in the folder had an earlier date. It was addressed to Jonathan Feathergill at an address in New York. Nick read it quickly.

Dear Mr. Feathergill:

I regret to inform you that I fear there is no hope for a cure. The insanity that afflicted your father has been passed down to your brother, Edward. We have attempted several forms of treatment but nothing has proven effective.

He is, and will always be, a danger to others. All I can offer you is the guarantee of a safe, secure environment here at Maple Tree Farm.

As you know we maintain the highest levels of discretion. The details of your brother's medical condition as well as his location will not be divulged to anyone except the members of his immediate family. I understand that you are his only living relation . . .

The letter was signed Dr. Clement Hulton.

There was one more note from Hulton.

Dear Mr. Feathergill:

I write to inform you of news of the most serious nature. Edward Feathergill was reported missing three days ago. We have conducted an exhaustive search of the grounds and the surrounding woods. We have found no trace of him. We believe he attempted to leave our remote location by means of a small rowboat during the recent storm. The vessel no doubt capsized in the high seas. I and the members of my staff are convinced that Edward perished. Please accept my condolences but under the circumstances perhaps it is for the best . . .

Nick put the letters back into the folder. He fired up the Packard and drove to the nearest phone booth. He arranged several stacks of coins on the small tray beneath the phone and dialed the operator.

"Long distance, please," he said.

When the long-distance operator came on the line he gave her the name and address of Maple Tree Farm. She, in turn, told him the initial charges. He fed the coins into the slots.

It took a few minutes to put through the call but eventually a man came on the line. He sounded like a secretary or clerk.

"Maple Tree Farm. How may I assist you?"

"This is Jonathan Feathergill calling for Dr. Hulton."

"Yes, of course, Mr. Feathergill. I'll connect you immediately."

A moment later a polished, professional male voice came on the line.

"Mr. Feathergill, I must say, this is a surprise. What can I do for you?"

"A year and a half ago you informed me that my brother died while trying to escape Maple Tree Farm."

"That is correct." Hulton's voice tightened. "We assumed he perished at sea. What is this about? Has there been some news?"

"Edward Feathergill not only survived that storm, he made it out to California and adopted a new identity. He called himself Morris Deverell and, as far as I can tell, he murdered at least three people before he was finally caught while attempting to kill a fourth victim. He tried to escape. This time he didn't make it. You may have seen the stories in the press. The papers labeled him the Dagger Killer."

There was a short, fraught silence on the other end of the line. Then Hulton heaved a weary sigh.

"I did see something about the Dagger Killer murders in the press," he said. "It caught my attention, as I'm sure you can imagine. But there were no photos in the local newspaper. It considers itself a family paper. It does not print sordid pictures of deranged murderers. But I did check the name of the killer. When I realized the name was unfamiliar, I set my concerns aside."

"Why did the story catch your attention?" Nick asked.

"Why, because of the daggers, of course. I remember very clearly that when you brought Edward to Maple Tree Farm you explained that your brother had used an antique dagger from your father's collection to murder your mother. One doesn't forget that sort of detail."

Nick hung up the phone and called Raina Kirk in Burning Cove. He told her what he wanted. "You can reach me at the Pacific Horizon Hotel in Adelina Beach. That's where Vivian and Lyra and I are staying while Vivian looks for a new place to rent."

"It's going to take some time to track down the people who might have the answers you're looking for," Raina warned.

"Do whatever you have to do. Please call me as soon as you've got something."

"Of course," Raina said. "How's the shoulder?"

Nick glanced at his right shoulder. His shirtsleeve covered the bandage. "Better, thanks. Stitches will come out next week."

"Lucky it was just a twenty-two. Not much stopping power."

"I'm hearing that a lot."

"Oh, one more thing," Raina said. "You can tell Vivian I happened to walk past the Ashwood Gallery this morning on my way into the office. One of her photos was in the window."

"She'll be thrilled."

"She certainly knows some interesting men," Raina said.

"Don't remind me."

Chapter 43

The following afternoon Nick was drinking coffee with Vivian and Lyra in the hotel gardens when he heard his name.

"Long distance for Mr. Sundridge." A page dressed in a snappy little cap and the livery of the Pacific Horizon Hotel strode briskly across the terrace, an ornate telephone in his gloved hands. "Long distance for Mr. Sundridge."

Nick put down his cup and signaled the page. The young man hurried forward, set the telephone on the table, and plugged the cord into a nearby wall jack. He paused to give Rex a couple of pats and then sped off.

Nick picked up the receiver. "This is Sundridge. What have you got for me, Raina?"

Vivian and Lyra put down their cups and listened intently.

"I've got some answers," Raina said, cool satisfaction edging her polished voice. "Luther is here with me. We just finished going through my notes. Jonathan and Edward were the two sons of Harold Feathergill, a wealthy New Yorker from an old, established family. Harold evidently took his own life when the boys were in their teens."

"Evidently? The authorities aren't sure of the cause of death?"

"Officially his death was an accident. He fell from a high window at his summer home. But my contact at a New York newspaper told me that rumors of suicide circulated widely at the time. You know how it is when it comes to suicide. Families go out of their way to cover it up."

"Right."

"My contact said there were a few other rumors about Harold Feathergill as well," Raina continued. "Looks like he may have murdered a housemaid. Her death was listed as accidental, too, but the maid's family refused to believe it. They claimed he killed the girl with, get this, an antique dagger. He owned a large collection of blades. After his death the collection went to his eldest son, Edward."

"Who became Morris Deverell," Nick said. "Like father, like son."

"It was shortly after the housemaid's death that Harold Feathergill apparently jumped out a window. However, Mrs. Feathergill was found dead a few months later. This time there was no doubt that it was murder. She was killed by a dagger from her husband's collection."

"Edward murdered his own mother."

"According to the authorities, a madman broke into the house and attacked Mrs. Feathergill, who was home alone at the time. But my contact says people who were acquainted with the family were sure Edward was the madman who murdered her."

"Were there any rumors about the brother's mental health?"

"According to my source, Jonathan Feathergill was supposed to be the stable son," Raina said. "It was said he appeared to have escaped the family curse."

Nick closed his eyes and took a couple of deep breaths. Raina was just using a casual turn of phrase. He didn't have a curse, he had very strong *intuition*. The Sundridge intuition had its downside but a few nightmares and visions did not constitute a curse. He had that on good authority, first Caleb Jones's old journal and recently from Vivian. Vivian saw beneath the surface. She would know a curse if she encountered one.

"Nick?" Raina said into his ear. "Are you still there?"

He opened his eyes and found Vivian watching him intently.

She smiled.

The California sunlight got a little warmer, a shade more golden. The Pacific sparked and flashed and dazzled. The elegantly manicured hotel gardens appeared more lush. The scents of flowers and the sea stirred his senses.

Everything that was important to him now was in Vivian's smile—trust, friendship, understanding, acceptance, approval. She believed in him. And maybe, just maybe, she loved him. He devoutly hoped so because he was sure he would be doomed if she didn't.

He knew now that the jolt of unfamiliar sensations that had blindsided him the first day when she opened her door and found him on her front step was not a sign of lack of sleep. The rush of exhilaration he had experienced was his Sundridge intuition telling him she was the one he had been waiting for.

He forced himself to focus on what mattered at that moment.

"I'm here," he said to Raina. "Go on."

"We know from his poems that Jonathan was every bit as mad as his brother but he was a lot better at concealing his crazy side," Raina said. "He was in the murder-for-hire business in New York for at least two years before he moved to California."

"Not crazy. Just plain evil."

"What?" It was Raina's turn to fall silent for a beat or two. "Oh, yes. I see what you mean. *Evil* is the right word, isn't it? It's just that, in the modern era, we're supposed to believe that human motives and emotions can be explained by psychological theories."

"We're not there yet," Nick said.

"No," Raina said. Her voice was very firm now. "Not yet. To continue with the history of the Feathergill family, Edward Feathergill vanished from society shortly after his mother was murdered. He was said to be on an extended voyage around the world. Eventually he was declared lost at sea."

"Instead, Jonathan had him locked up in a private sanitarium, Maple Tree Farm," Nick said. "Then, with his brother safely out of the way, Jonathan moved to California, reinvented himself under the name Jonathan Treyherne, and went back into the murder-for-hire business."

"It must have come as a shock when his brother escaped and tracked him down in L.A.," Raina said. "But there wasn't much Jonathan could do. Then Edward started killing again. He finally got arrested for murder, thanks to Vivian. Jonathan must have been frantic. He could not afford to have his brother talking to the police."

"So he smuggled Edward out of the hospital, drove him to a lonely highway, and ran him down," Nick said.

On the other side of the table, sudden comprehension lit Vivian's eyes.

"That bastard Treyherne blamed *me*," she said. "He convinced himself I was the reason he had to murder his own brother."

"Yes," Nick said. "That fits. He blamed you and he wanted revenge."

"I heard that," Raina said. "We finally have a motive that explains why Vivian's name is in the journal. In his own twisted way, Jonathan was determined to avenge his brother's death."

"That's why there was no client named in the final entry in the journal," Nick said. "The Poet *was* the client."

"Hang on," Raina said. "Luther wants to talk to you."

Luther came on the line.

"It's over," he said. "I'm going to give the journal and your uncle's transcriptions of the poems to someone I know in the Bureau. The FBI and the Los Angeles police will probably conduct their own investigations into the murders that have already occurred."

"It's going to be hard to reopen any of those cases," Nick said. "The Poet was very, very good at making the deaths looks like accidents or natural causes."

"Don't worry," Luther said. "The most spectacular cases will be tried in the press. I'm sure there will be a few convictions. Regardless, those other crimes are not our problem. Our job was to stop the open commission, the murder that was still in the planning stage. Thanks to you, Vivian Brazier is alive. Nice work, Nick."

Nick hung up the phone and looked at Vivian and Lyra.

"Luther says it's over," he said.

Lyra shuddered. "I still can't believe that my sister was the target of not one but two killers. The fact that they were brothers makes it even more bizarre."

"Yes, but it does explain the coincidence factor," Nick said. "We now know why Vivian was attacked twice within the same month."

Vivian looked thoughtful. "One thing I still don't understand. How did Jonathan Treyherne, or Feathergill or whatever his name was, figure out that Toby Flint would know how to find me?"

Lyra waved a hand in a casual gesture. "According to Nick, the Poet had a history of stalking his victims for a full month before he acted. He collected information about them. If he was watching your beach cottage he would have seen Flint stop by to borrow some film or gas money. It wouldn't have taken much research to discover Flint was always in need of cash."

Vivian sighed. "In exchange for a few dollars, Toby would have been happy to answer a couple of seemingly innocent questions. I guess that explains it. Coincidences do happen.

"That," Nick said, "has not been my experience."

Chapter 44

Late that afternoon Nick eased the Packard to the curb and shut off the engine. For a moment he sat quietly, studying the run-down boardinghouse Toby Flint had called home. There was a faded ROOM FOR RENT sign in a downstairs window.

He got out of the car and went up the cracked path to the front door. He clanged the knocker several times before someone finally responded.

There was some shuffling in the hallway and the door opened. A middle-aged woman in a floral-patterned housedress, her hair in an old-fashioned marcel wave, peered out.

"If you've come about the vacancy I'll warn you right now the rent has to be paid in advance at the start of every week and I don't allow men to take women upstairs," she announced. "This is a respectable establishment."

"I'll keep that in mind," Nick said. He took out his wallet and removed a couple of bills. "But I'm not looking for a room. I wanted to ask you a few questions about one of your previous boarders. Toby Flint."

"You're looking for Flint?" The woman was briefly distracted by the sight of the bills. She looked up quickly, eyes narrowing. "All I can say is, good luck to you. He skipped out on the rent a few days ago. Haven't seen him since."

"Flint is dead," Nick said. "He was hit by a car in Burning Cove."

"Huh. Would have thought Burning Cove was too expensive for the likes of Flint. He was always short of cash. Well, that explains why he didn't come back for his things."

"He left his belongings behind?"

"Yeah. I cleaned out his room this morning. Not a lot of stuff. He pawned everything except his darkroom equipment and the short-wave radio. I took the radio. Figured it would cover a couple of weeks' rent."

"What did you do with the rest of his possessions?" Nick asked.

"Put 'em in a box. I was going to take them to a secondhand shop to see if I could get a few bucks for the photography equipment."

"I'll give you twenty dollars for the box."

The landlady narrowed her eyes. "What would you want with Flint's things?"

"I've got a friend who's interested in photography. She might be able to use some of his equipment."

"Uh-huh. I'll take the twenty bucks first. No changing your mind if it turns out you don't want anything in the box."

"You've got yourself a deal, ma'am."

Nick handed her the money. She made it disappear inside the bodice of the housedress.

"Follow me," she said. "The box is in a closet at the end of the hall."

A short time later Nick settled the box that contained Flint's worldly belongings into the trunk of the Packard, got behind the wheel, and drove back to the hotel.

The front desk clerk looked up when he saw Nick come through the door.

"Mr. Sundridge," he said. "Let me get a bellhop to take care of that box for you."

"Never mind," Nick said. "I've got it. Would you ring Miss Brazier's room and let her know I'm back?"

"Both Miss Braziers went out while you were gone," the clerk said. "Shopping?"

"No." A flash of excitement lit the clerk's eyes. "Mr. Ripley Fleming the movie actor sent a limo around to fetch Miss Lyra. I believe there was something said about a tour of the studio followed by tea. As for Miss Vivian, she got a phone call and immediately took off in Miss Lyra's car."

Nick paused, thinking. Ripley Fleming was no longer a suspect. At least it was no longer possible to suspect him of being the assassin for hire. And the real killer had been his own client so there was no mysterious client left to identify. Lyra was safe with Fleming.

"Do you know who telephoned Vivian Brazier?" he asked.

"A secretary who said she was calling from the Penfield Gallery here in town. Miss Vivian appeared to be quite excited when she left a short time later."

"Did she have her portfolio with her?"

"A flat leather case? Why, yes, as a matter of fact."

Nick relaxed. "Sounds like she's been invited to show her work to the Penfield Gallery again. That's very good news."

So why was he suddenly sensing ice-cold fingers on the back of his neck?

Damn Sundridge intuition.

He and Rex went through the lobby and up the main staircase to the second floor. He let himself into his room, set the box on the table near the window, and took off his jacket. After arranging a couple of sheets of notepaper and a pen on the table, he went to work.

Sorting through the belongings of a man who had gambled away everything of value including, in the end, his own life, proved a depressing business.

Nick set the handful of personal effects out on the table and contemplated them for a long time, searching for connections. There were several envelopes marked with dates. They were stuffed with negatives and prints. The oldest packet was the smallest. It was dated six years earlier.

Nick picked up the envelope with the most recent date and dumped the contents onto the table. Dozens of negatives fell out. He sifted through them. Bodies. Fires. Movie stars partying in nightclubs. There were also a few prints of pictures that had obviously been taken from a distance. One featured two women and a famous male film star naked together on a beach. Another was a picture of two men embracing. Evidently at some point in the not too distant past Toby had decided to try his hand at blackmail in an attempt to pay off his gambling debts.

So much for the most recent images. There wasn't much point going through the other packets. Probably more of the same.

Still, in his experience answers were frequently locked in the past.

He picked up the first envelope, the one dated six years earlier. He unsealed it and emptied the prints and negatives onto the table.

And there it was, right in front of him, the connection that made the picture complete.

"Shit."

He had to be certain.

He picked up the telephone and asked for long distance. "The Brazier residence in San Francisco, please."

The housekeeper answered a short time later. Nick identified himself. The housekeeper said she knew who he was because she had spoken with Lyra and Vivian that morning.

"I'm so glad you're all safe," the housekeeper said. "I can't imagine what Mr. and Mrs. Brazier will say when they get home."

"I have a question," Nick said. "It's very important. I know that Lyra took a phone call from someone here in Adelina Beach who wanted to know where Vivian was."

"Really? How odd. Shortly after Lyra left town I took a call as well from someone who said he was looking for Vivian. A very nice man. Sounded quite posh. He was trying to find Vivian because he wanted her to do his portrait. He had heard about the fire at the beach house, you see. He said no one knew where Vivian had gone afterward. He assumed that she was staying in a hotel until she could find another house to rent. I had just spoken with Vivian and offered to call her to tell her about the commission but the man said it would be faster if he talked to her directly. He was in a hurry. Something about a funeral."

"Did you tell him where Vivian was?"

"Fortunately Miss Lyra had written the number of the Burning Cove Hotel down on the notepad next to the telephone. I gave it to the gentleman. Does that answer your question?"

"Yes. Yes, it does. Good-bye, ma'am."

Nick tossed the receiver into the cradle and headed for the door with his keys and his holstered gun, moving fast. The hot acid of something akin to panic sluiced through his veins. He fought it with every ounce of willpower he possessed. He had to stay in control because he had to get to Vivian.

Chapter 45

know you don't like landscapes," Vivian said. "At least not the photographic kind. But that's all that I have available at the moment."

Fenella Penfield gazed at the two prints for a long time before she raised her head. Vivian braced herself for another rejection.

They were in Fenella's back room facing each other across a long workbench that was littered with framing tools and materials. They were the only people in the gallery. The shop had been in the process of closing just as Vivian parked Lyra's racy little speedster at the far end of the block. She had arrived in time to see the salesclerks leaving and was sure her brief moment of opportunity had closed.

But Fenella had stayed behind to view the pictures. It was obvious she was irritated and, evidently, rather desperate. One of her artists was not going to be able to deliver two pictures that had been promised for an upcoming show. Fenella needed something to go on the walls.

"I've changed my mind about the landscapes," Fenella said. "And also your *Finding California*. Your pictures are certainly not fine art but I do have a few clients with less cultivated tastes who might like them.

There are always a few unsophisticated types, the nouveau riche, at my shows. They'll buy whatever I tell them to buy. I'm sure I can unload these."

Talk about damning with faint praise, Vivian thought.

A tide of anger rose up, threatening to choke her. She went hot and cold all over. It was too much. On top of everything else that had happened in the past several days, the rude dismissal of her art was just *too much*.

She gave Fenella her most dazzling smile.

"Thank you, but I've changed my mind," she said. She gathered up the prints and slipped them into the portfolio. "I'm afraid I won't have time to develop any pictures for you."

Fenella looked shocked. "What are you talking about? Last week you were begging me to hang those landscapes."

"I did not beg you. I offered them to you. You rejected them."

Fenella watched angrily as Vivian closed the portfolio. "Hold on. I need those pictures for my next exhibition."

"Too bad. You can't have them. By the way, I recently spent a few days in Burning Cove. I spoke to the proprietor of the Ashwood Gallery. I believe you know her?"

"Joan Ashwood?" Fenella appeared wary now. "Yes, I know her in a professional capacity. She has attended some of my exhibitions. Occasionally we compete for the same artists and photographers. Winston Bancroft, for example."

"Yes, I know."

Fenella frowned. "Why did you ask me if I knew Joan?"

Vivian flashed another bright smile. "Miss Ashwood was gracious enough to accept a couple of pictures from my Men series for her gallery."

Fenella stiffened. "Is that right? Well, it's no secret that Joan Ashwood caters to a much *different* clientele. Mobsters, celebrities, rich people with too much money and no taste." She paused for emphasis.

"And now, apparently, clients with prurient interests. Pay attention, Miss Brazier. If you don't let me have those images for my show, you will never hang another picture in a respectable gallery anywhere in L.A. Your career as an artist will be ruined."

"Face it, you've already done your best to destroy my career. I really don't think there's anything else you can do to ruin me."

Fenella stared at her. "What are you talking about?"

Vivian hoisted the portfolio case off the workbench. "In the course of our conversation Miss Ashwood informed me that the reason I have run into so much trouble trying to persuade galleries around here to hang my work isn't because my pictures aren't good but because of certain rumors about me."

Fenella looked at first as if she was going to deny any knowledge of the gossip but whatever she saw in Vivian's expression must have convinced her that it was time for the truth. She looked deeply pained.

"I suppose you are referring to the gossip about your work as a newspaper photographer," she said.

"Yes. Rumors which you no doubt helped spread. You certainly didn't do anything to squelch them. I'm starting to wonder if you're the one who started them. Maybe it wasn't Kempton, after all."

Fenella sighed. "The art world can be very harsh on artists who dabble in commercial work."

"Even when they do it to pay the rent?"

"I'm afraid so. Everyone knows that all successful artists do some commercial work along the way but they are supposed to keep it a secret. Those, such as yourself, who are working in the medium of photography have an especially difficult time. The line between cheap, five-dollar-a-shot crime scene photos and true art is already extremely blurry."

"In other words, so-called sophisticated gallery owners such as yourself, the people who make the rules, are afraid to trust their own instincts when it comes to judging art photography. Admit it."

Fenella drew herself up and straightened her sharp shoulders. "Gallery owners must maintain their credibility with their clientele. If it got out that they were marketing photographs that anyone could take with a Brownie, well, you can see the problem."

"It's all about maintaining an image of exclusivity."

"I'm sorry, but that's the way it is."

"In that case," Vivian said, "why were you willing to hang my pictures?"

Fenella looked hesitant. Then she sighed. "If you must know, the artist who failed to deliver the pictures for my show was Winston Bancroft. I need to hang a couple of examples of art photography to round out the show. Your work is . . . good enough."

"No," Vivian said. She started toward the door between the back room and the sales floor. "My work is too good for your gallery."

She could feel Fenella's eyes burning holes between her shoulder blades all the way across the shadowed showroom. She did not take a deep breath until she was outside on the tree-shaded sidewalk. Her anger faded as she walked halfway down the block to where she had parked Lyra's speedster. She put the portfolio in the trunk and got behind the wheel.

She had just put the last nail in the coffin of her Adelina Beach career, but now that she knew about the rumors, she realized there had never been any hope in the first place. All was not lost. She was going to have two pictures from her Men series in the Ashwood Gallery show. If they got some positive attention and maybe even sold, she would have a chance in the world of fine art.

She was still sitting behind the wheel, trying to get a handle on her plans for the future, when a cab pulled up in front of the gallery. Fenella walked out of the shop and got into the back of the taxi. The vehicle sped off.

Vivian was so preoccupied with her thoughts that it took her a moment to realize she was getting a weird feeling on the back of her neck.

A tiny whisper of ghostly energy. It occurred to her that there was something wrong with the street scene in front of her.

She realized she was focusing on the empty parking space in front of the gallery entrance. *What's wrong with the composition of this picture?* she thought. Something was off. The sidewalks were empty. There was virtually no traffic in the street. The elegant shops and boutiques had closed for the day.

It finally struck her that Fenella Penfield had gone home in a taxi, not her prized Duesenberg. The elegant sedan had not been parked in front of the gallery that day.

Fenella liked to be seen driving through town in the big car. She used it as a marketing device, a visual indication of the classiness of the Penfield Gallery. It sent a clear message. But evidently she had not driven the sedan to work that day. Perhaps it was in a garage for some routine maintenance.

Or repairs.

The small chill on the back of Vivian's neck turned to ice. *Don't let your imagination run wild.* Nevertheless, she could not shake the ominous sensation that was welling up from the shadows. A thought surfaced and burned in her mind—to her knowledge the Burning Cove Police had not yet found the car that had killed Toby Flint. The vehicle Jonathan Treyherne had been driving the night he attacked Nick had shown no indications of having been in an accident. The theory was that Treyherne had used a stolen car to murder Flint but as of yet there was no evidence to support that notion.

The Dagger Killer had been one of Fenella's clients. Vivian reminded herself that was not an odd coincidence. Deverell-Feathergill had been wealthy and he had lived in Adelina Beach. Wealthy people in Adelina Beach bought art from Fenella Penfield. It made perfect sense that he had shopped at the Penfield Gallery.

Another little electric thrill swept through Vivian. The authorities had found some photographic equipment at the Deverell-Feathergill mansion, but there had been no report of any negatives or prints having been discovered in there.

She had been certain that when the police found the Dagger Killer they would find a portfolio of the death scenes.

A prickling sensation raised the fine hairs on her arms. *Something wicked this way comes.*

Probably not a good time to be recalling that particular quote from Shakespeare. But it ignited yet another memory. Toby Flint had mentioned that at one time he'd had dreams of a career in art photography. He had been living in Adelina Beach when he'd had those dreams. He would have encountered Fenella Penfield.

Again, so what?

Her thoughts continued to circle but they kept coming back to the simple fact that the car that had been used to murder Toby Flint had not been found.

And now the Duesenberg that was always parked in front of the Penfield Gallery was—if not missing—unaccounted for. Fenella Penfield had gone home in a taxi.

She thought about the rage in Fenella's eyes when she had called the Men series porn.

Why do you hate me so much, Fenella Penfield? Because I'm the future of photography and you're the past?

Vivian turned the key in the ignition and eased the speedster away from the curb. She motored sedately to the corner, turned right, and cruised slowly past the entrance to the alley behind the Penfield Gallery. There was one lone delivery truck parked behind a shop.

The fashionable street of boutiques and galleries had once been a block of stylish houses. The homes had each had garages that opened onto the alley. Most had no doubt been converted into storage facilities for the shops.

She drove on a short distance, pulled into a parking space, and stopped, trying to decide what to do next. There would be nothing illegal about taking a quick look through the window of the garage behind the Penfield Gallery. It wasn't as if she would be breaking into the shop. You couldn't get arrested for looking into a garage window, could you?

And surely you couldn't get arrested for taking a photo of whatever you saw when you looked through that window, assuming you noticed something of interest.

She got out, opened the trunk, and picked up the Speed Graphic. It was already loaded with film and a fresh flashbulb. Every photographer who covered crimes and fires made sure to keep a camera handy and ready to go.

She slung the strap of the camera over one shoulder and walked briskly to the entrance of the alley. She arrived just in time to see a deliveryman emerge from the rear door of a shop. He jumped up into the front seat of his truck and drove off toward the far end of the narrow lane.

She waited until she was sure he was gone and then went quickly toward the garage behind the Penfield Gallery. Her anxiety spiked with each step. Once again she reminded herself that what she planned to do was not illegal. It was, however, very likely a waste of time.

She hurried to the grimy window on the side of the garage and peered into the gloom-filled space. The Duesenberg was inside. The stylish hood ornament was bent and twisted to one side. One front headlight was broken. There was a crack in the windshield.

Vivian got a little light-headed. She stepped back and tried to think clearly. First things first. She had to take a photo and get out of the alley. There was a phone booth on the corner. She would call Nick immediately.

A footstep behind her was all the warning she got before Fenella spoke.

"Turn around," Fenella said. "Slowly. One false move and I'll pull the trigger."

Vivian shivered, a wave of shock and panic icing her nerves. Her mouth got very dry. She turned around and saw Fenella, gun in hand, standing a few feet away.

"I saw you leave in the cab," Vivian said.

"I got out as soon as the taxi turned the corner. I told the driver it was such a nice day I had decided to walk home. Did you think I didn't notice you in that blue speedster at the end of the block? I'm not a fool. I knew you were getting suspicious. Inside. Now. Or I will pull this trigger."

"That would be stupid," Vivian said. "People will hear the shot."

"Unlikely. The neighborhood is deserted at this time of day. Even if someone did happen to hear it, the sound would be dismissed as a backfire. Go on, into my shop. Don't worry. I left the door open for you."

Vivian briefly contemplated making a run for it, but Fenella was too close and the strange glitter in her eyes made it clear that she was more than willing to pull the trigger.

"If you're going to kill me anyway, why not shoot me now?" Vivian asked.

"Shut up and go inside. There is something I want you to see."

Vivian went up the back steps, opened the door, and moved into the shadows of Fenella's back room. She understood why people obeyed when someone held a gun on them. It was all about buying time.

"I assume this means you never really intended to display my pictures in your next exhibition," Vivian said.

Chapter 46

Y ou're wrong," Fenella said. "I had every intention of exhibiting your photographs in my next show."

"Why? I can't believe you would have done me any favors just because Winston Bancroft failed to deliver a couple of pictures."

"That was something of a story, I'm afraid. Bancroft has already delivered his photos. But I needed to convince you that I really did want your pictures for the exhibition. I wanted to make sure you were in the gallery that evening so that you could witness your failure as an artist."

"You just assumed my photographs would not get any attention? That no one would buy them?"

"Exactly. Later you were going to take your own life. The plan was for you to retreat here to my back room and put a bullet in your head. Everyone would have assumed you could not handle the pain of finding out for certain that you were a failure."

"You had the whole scene composed in your mind."

"Yes. I had it all worked out."

"Do you really think the people who know me would have believed your ridiculous story for even sixty seconds?"

"Why not?" Fenella's voice tightened. "You call yourself an *artist*. They're notoriously dramatic and emotional. Unstable."

"Nick Sundridge and my family would never have bought that version of events, trust me."

"It doesn't matter because plans have changed. The stairs. Go on. What I have to show you is in the room at the top."

The overhead fixtures were off in the back room of the gallery and the blinds were closed but the staircase that led to the balcony on the floor above was illuminated by a couple of narrow windows.

Vivian started up the steps, moving as slowly as she dared, trying to buy time to come up with a strategy. Fenella followed close behind but not so close that Vivian could risk trying to shove her down the stairs.

The one thing that was clear now was that Fenella did not want to pull the trigger until after the so-called private viewing.

"Why murder Toby Flint?" Vivian asked.

"I needed him to find you after you and Sundridge disappeared," Fenella said. "Toby never missed a meeting of the Adelina Beach Photography Club. I waited for him in his car that night. When he came out of the meeting hall I did a deal with him. I offered to pay off his gambling debts if he could find you. It didn't take him long to discover that you and Sundridge were in Burning Cove."

"He called my sister in San Francisco. She told him where I was. But that wasn't enough for you, was it? You made him go to Burning Cove. You told him he had to do one more thing to get his money. He had to place the phone call that would draw me out of the hotel that night. You wanted me on that empty street so that you could run me down with your car."

"I couldn't think of any other way to get you out of the hotel. I knew you and Toby were friends. You trusted him."

"Yes," Vivian said. A sense of sadness flitted through her. "I did trust him. I thought he called me to warn me that I was in danger. But I guess he needed the money too much."

"He needed the money all right. His life was at stake. I paid him a thousand dollars in cash. There was to be another thousand afterward. But that bastard betrayed me."

"What do you mean? He made the call to the hotel, just as you paid him to do."

"He telephoned you *two hours* before he was supposed to do it," Fenella said, her voice rising to a shrill pitch. "I had a feeling I couldn't trust him. I followed him that night when he left that cheap auto court where he was staying. When he went into that phone booth I knew he had decided to warn you. When he went back to his car I saw my chance to get rid of him and I took it. I knew then I'd lost the opportunity to get you. I had to drive back to Adelina Beach that night because I had to do something about the car. There was so much damage. I had no idea it would be that bad. When I read in the papers that Deverell had been struck and killed by a car it sounded so simple, so easy."

"Nick was right—there was a connection between the murders of Deverell and Flint. It wasn't a coincidence. You got the idea for using a car from the newspapers. You copied the technique."

"The drive back to Adelina Beach was a nightmare with only one headlight and a cracked windshield. I didn't dare wait until daylight because I was afraid someone here in town would see the car and ask questions."

"You hid your damaged car in the garage behind your shop."

"I didn't know what to do with it. Do you have any idea how hard it is to conceal a well-known automobile that has sustained so much damage? I couldn't take it to a local repair shop. I didn't dare drive it to my home. The housekeeper and the gardener would have noticed. I decided to leave it in the old garage behind the gallery until I could figure out what to do with it."

"You think your car is going to be a problem?" Vivian reached the landing and stopped. "Wait until you have to figure out how to get rid of my body."

"That's going to be the easy part, thanks to your snooping around. Open that door."

Vivian walked halfway along the balcony and stopped in front of the door. She tried the knob.

"It's locked," she said.

"Of course it is. Here's the key."

Fenella tossed a key onto the floor. Vivian picked it up and inserted it in the lock. She got the door open and took two steps into a long, dark chamber.

"The light switch is to your right," Fenella said as she stepped in and closed the door. "Turn it on."

Vivian groped for the switch, found and flipped it. Most of the room remained in shadow but three carefully positioned and focused lights winked on. They illuminated three large, elegantly framed photographs on the wall.

Vivian tried to steel herself because she was almost certain now that she knew what Fenella wanted her to see. But that did nothing to mitigate the shock of raw horror that slammed through her.

She recognized all three pictures. She had shot the same scenes while surrounded by homicide detectives, uniformed officers, and other news photographers. But her front-page photos had revealed the harsh, gritty reality of violent death. The three death scenes on the wall had been manipulated using every trick in the pictorial photographer's repertoire to make them appear to be paintings.

"You were the photographer who composed the pictures," Vivian said. "Not Morris Deverell. There were two Dagger Killers, not one."

"You're wrong. Until I was forced to get rid of Toby Flint I'd never actually killed anyone. I was the *artist*. Deverell was just my assistant. I chose the subjects and booked the evening appointments. While we discussed new acquisitions for their art collections I put a little something into their drinks to make them go to sleep. Deverell helped me set up my camera and arrange the lighting. When all was ready, he used his dagger. He loved that part. When I looked through the lens and saw true perfection I took the picture."

"No wonder you got nervous when you found out the police were looking for a photographer working in the pictorial tradition."

"Nervous? I was frantic. I couldn't believe someone had figured it out."

Vivian studied the image of Clara Carstairs's body. It was rendered in sepia tones. The picture had been printed using a variety of special effects and tints. The modern furniture behind the ornate sofa in the Carstairs mansion had been painted out and replaced with the scene of an ancient Greek temple.

The photos of the Attenbury and Washfield murders had been manipulated in a similar manner. Attenbury appeared to have been killed in an ancient Roman bath. Washfield looked as if he had been stabbed in an Egyptian pyramid.

"I call the series Dreams of Antiquity," Fenella said.

"Such a terribly old-fashioned, outmoded style," Vivian said.

"It's *art*," Fenella hissed. "*Fine* art. The real thing. I do not make sleazy photos for the front page of a scandal sheet."

"How did you and Deverell come to know each other?"

"The first time he walked into my gallery there was a spark between us, a certain something. I showed him some of my early work, imaginary death scenes. He had the eye of an experienced collector. He saw my potential but he sensed that my vision could only be truly realized if it was inspired by the reality of death."

"I get it. He seduced you by pretending to praise your talent."

"He was my *muse*."

"No, he used you as an accomplice to his own crazy murders. You had the connections he needed to get into the homes of his chosen celebrity victims." Vivian turned to face her. "I suppose it was easy to convince him to go after me."

"He was thrilled at the thought of killing you. I admit he was becoming very unstable there at the end. I knew the time had come to get rid of him but I thought the least he could do was remove you first."

"You must have panicked all over again when you found out he had not only failed, he had also managed to get himself arrested."

"That night was the worst night of my life," Fenella said grimly. "I thought my only hope was to disappear. I packed a bag and drove to a hotel in L.A. I checked in under another name. I kept the radio on all night. At dawn I heard that Morris had been struck by a hit-and-run driver while attempting to escape. The case was closed. I could hardly believe my good luck."

"You're going to botch the job of killing me, you know. You lack the skills needed to cover your tracks."

"Shut up."

"Look at how you bungled the business of murdering Toby Flint. You can't even figure out how to get rid of your damaged car."

"You were the reason everything went wrong," Fenella shrieked. "You deserve to pay."

"You've been jealous of me from the first moment you viewed my pictures."

"That's a lie. You're not a real artist. You're a fraud."

Vivian smiled. "You know I'm good, a lot better than you ever were, and what's more, I'm working in the modern style. You're the one who started the rumors about my crime scene photography, aren't you?"

"I couldn't let the other galleries hang your pictures. The only way to stop them was to make it clear that you were just a scandal sheet reporter with a camera."

"I'm assuming it was Toby Flint who told you about that side of my career."

"He came to me for money one day shortly after you'd turned him down. He was still mad at you. He said something about how much he'd done for you and now you wouldn't even give him a small loan."

"Why would Toby think you would give him money? How well did you two know each other?"

"We were lovers once a long time ago. We both had dreams of becoming true artists with our cameras. Toby actually sold a couple of pictures in good galleries. But in the end his gambling addiction destroyed him."

"You never made it as an artist, either. That's why you ended up running a gallery, isn't it?"

"The damned modernists have ruined photography. The so-called experts don't appreciate true art. Curators and galleries wouldn't even look at my work."

"Hey, trust me, I know the feeling." Vivian glanced at the door at the end of the gallery. "Is that your darkroom?"

"Yes."

"Mind if I take a look?"

"Yes, I mind. This has gone far enough. Time for you to stage your dramatic exit."

"How do you plan to manage that?"

"Simple. There's going to be another fire. My gallery this time. When they find your body in the ashes, no one will notice the bullet hole."

Fenella raised the pistol.

Vivian averted her eyes, aimed, and triggered the flash of her camera in a single, practiced move.

The magnesium filament flared, a brilliant, dazzling, white-hot explosion of light in the shadowed room. For a critical few seconds Fenella was effectively blinded.

Vivian threw herself toward the nearest painting on the wall, the framed image of the Clara Carstairs murder scene. She was pretty sure the very last thing Fenella would do was shoot holes in her elaborately manipulated work of art.

Fenella pulled the trigger of the gun once and then a second time. But she was firing blind, the gun aimed vaguely in the direction of where Vivian had been standing a few seconds earlier. Both shots struck the back wall.

Fenella paused, blinking furiously in an effort to clear her vision. She started to turn toward the wall of paintings.

Vivian hurled the sturdy Speed Graphic as if it were a medieval weapon.

Fenella's vision returned in time for her to see the heavy object flying toward her. She screeched and reeled back, instinctively raising a hand to block the blow.

The big camera did no serious damage but it threw her off balance. She yelped and lurched to the side, stumbling a little in her pumps.

Vivian launched herself at Fenella, who was now so panic-stricken she seemed to have forgotten how to work the gun. She bolted for the door and succeeded in getting it open.

Vivian managed to grab a fistful of Fenella's jacket.

"Let me go," Fenella screamed.

She stumbled out onto the balcony, dragging Vivian with her. Fenella whipped around and clawed at Vivian's face.

Vivian let go of the jacket an instant before Fenella's nails raked her eyes.

Fenella was unprepared for the sudden release. She lost her balance and fell hard against the old railing. The rusty metal fasteners groaned in protest. There was a wrenching, splintering sound. An entire section of the rotten railing gave way.

Fenella was unable to stop herself. Her momentum sent her over the edge.

She did not even have time to scream before she struck some object below and then fell again, this time onto the floor.

An acute silence ensued.

Vivian picked up her camera, moved cautiously farther out onto the balcony, and looked down. There was enough light seeping in through the cracks in the blinds to reveal Fenella sprawled on the floor next to a massive bronze statue of a nude female goddess. The gun had landed some distance away.

Glass shattered somewhere in the salesroom at the front of the shop.

"Vivian." Nick's voice roared through the old house.

Rex barked excitedly.

"In here," Vivian called. But the words sounded thin and breathless. She took a deep breath and tried again. "Nick. I'm in here."

She started down the stairs, hugging the wall because in her shaky condition she needed support and she knew now she could not trust the old railing.

Nick and Rex raced through the door that separated the salesroom from the back room. Rex bounded toward the staircase to give Vivian his customary greeting.

Nick hit the light switch and raked the scene in a glance.

"Vivian?" he said.

"I'm all right. Honestly." She sat down on a step and hugged Rex. "I'm okay."

Nick grabbed a sheet of paper off a nearby workbench and used it to pick up the pistol. He set it on a table.

"There should be prints," he said. "She's not wearing gloves."

"Yes," Vivian said.

Nick crouched next to Fenella and felt for a pulse.

Vivian held her breath.

Nick rose, shaking his head. "Looks like she struck her head on the statue on the way down."

He crossed the room and started up the stairs.

Vivian got to her feet and fell into his arms.

"Nick," she said.

"You're sure you're all right?" he said.

"Yes," she said. "She's the one who murdered Toby. Used her Duesenberg. I found it in the garage out back. Lots of damage."

"That explains a few things."

Sirens sounded in the distance.

"How did you know about Fenella?" Vivian asked.

"A few loose ends have been bothering me," Nick said. "Before he died Treyherne gave me a lot of information. He talked freely that night. I think he was having a nervous breakdown. But he never mentioned Flint or the fact that he'd killed Flint. A murder is a big thing to leave out of that kind of conversation."

"You never got to ask him if he'd used Toby to find me because Treyherne jumped off the cliff."

"This afternoon I called your family's home in San Francisco. Your housekeeper said someone who convinced her he was a potential portrait client had telephoned asking how he could get in touch with you. She gave him the number of the Burning Cove Hotel."

Vivian winced. "Of course. Dorothy would have assumed she was doing me a favor. But that means both Toby Flint and Treyherne tracked me down the same way—by calling my home in San Francisco. Lyra took the call from Toby. Dorothy got the one from Treyherne."

"Yes, but I was still left with the fact that someone had used Flint to find you. If it wasn't Treyherne, who was it? Another thing that's been bothering me is that the police never found the Dagger Killer's photos. They discovered some photography equipment but no pictures."

Vivian glanced up at the gallery door. "I knew there would be a gallery of the death scenes."

"Today I found some of Flint's early pictures, the ones he did when he first arrived here in Adelina Beach. Art photos, not spot news work."

"Toby once had dreams of doing art photography," Vivian said.

"Fenella was his model. Her name and the dates of the photographs were in the envelope with the pictures. She also took some shots of him

that he kept. The fact that there had once been a close connection between the two of them was the missing piece of the puzzle."

"What do you mean?" Vivian asked.

"If Treyherne hadn't used Flint to find you, that meant Flint was
working for someone else. Someone who was in the picture but not
obvious. I couldn't overlook the fact that you and Flint and Fenella
Penfield were connected."

"And we know you don't like coincidences."

"There was one other coincidence I didn't like. The desk clerk at
the hotel mentioned that you had gone off to the Penfield Gallery with
your portfolio."

"All those factors came together to spark your intuition?"

"It would be more accurate to say they scared the living hell out
of me."

The sirens were louder now.

"You called the police?" Vivian asked.

"No, I didn't want to take the time," Nick said. "On my way through
the lobby I told the hotel clerk to telephone Detective Archer and send
him here."

The sound of vehicles braking sharply in the street and the sudden
cessation of the sirens announced the arrival of the police.

Nick looked up at the broken balcony railing. Then he fixed his
gaze on Vivian.

"What the hell happened up there?" he asked.

"A lot," Vivian said. "I'll wait until Archer gets here. Meanwhile,
would you kindly step out of the way? You're blocking the light and
casting a shadow."

She reached into her pocket for a fresh flashbulb and readied the
camera. The Speed Graphic had been through some rough handling,
but it had been built for the real world of news photography. It worked
flawlessly.

Eddy, the photo editor at the *Adelina Beach Courier*, allowed her to use the paper's darkroom in exchange for an exclusive.

The sensational photo of the owner of one of the most respected art galleries in Southern California dead on the floor of her own back room, with Detective Archer and an imposing bronze nude gazing on somberly, went national.

Some of the family newspapers cropped out various portions of the nude goddess's anatomy.

Regardless, this time there was a photo credit—Vivian Brazier.

Chapter 47

Vivian thought the day would never end but eventually she found herself in the hotel dining room with Lyra and Nick. She wasn't hungry but Lyra was anxious that she eat something. Fortified by a couple of sidecars, she managed to nibble her way through most of the whole artichoke served with hollandaise and some of the baked fresh halibut that followed. She drew the line at dessert, preferring to sip on an after-dinner brandy while Lyra and Nick finished the ice cream.

She was dreading the thought of going upstairs to the room she shared with Lyra because she knew she would not be able to sleep. She would probably be up all night, and that meant Lyra wouldn't get any sleep, either.

"Why don't you and Nick have another brandy in the bar," Lyra said. "Take your time. No rush. I won't worry about you unless you don't show up for breakfast."

"You just read my mind, didn't you?" Vivian said.

Lyra smiled. "That's what sisters do. Take good care of her, Nick."

"I will," Nick vowed.

Lyra gave Vivian a hug and crossed the lobby to the staircase that led to the upper floors.

When she was gone, Nick took Vivian's arm.

"Do you want that brandy now or would you prefer to take Rex for a walk along the beach?"

"Let's get Rex and go for a walk."

A short time later the three of them were on the beach path. The night was clear. The ocean was paved in moonlight. Strings of lights illuminated the pier.

For a time there was silence but Vivian found it a comfortable silence. She did not have to make conversation with Nick. Rex paced alongside them, content just to be with Nick. *Like me,* Vivian thought. *I'm content to be with Nick, too.* Tonight she would not allow herself to contemplate the possibility that tomorrow or the next day or the day after Nick would be going home to San Francisco.

"I wish I could say something reassuring," he said. "Something comforting about what you've been through lately. But the truth is, I don't think you ever get over the shock of knowing someone wants to kill you and is prepared to do it."

"But eventually you get some perspective, right?"

"Eventually. Doesn't mean you won't have some bad dreams now and again."

"You were attacked. Shot. Think you'll have bad dreams?"

"Maybe. But I've had them before."

"She never even screamed, Nick."

"Fulton Gage didn't scream when he went off the roof of that hotel."

They walked in silence for a while. When they reached the pier they followed the strings of lights past the closed hot dog stand and the darkened carousel to the far end. There they stood close together looking out over the moon-silvered sea.

"Are you sure you're over Patricia?" Vivian asked.

"Absolutely positive. Are you sure you're over Winston Bancroft?"

"Yep."

"There are a few things you should probably know about me," Nick said. "I'm going to keep doing this investigation work because it's the one thing I'm pretty good at. I can't think of any other way to use my talent, and Uncle Pete says if I don't use it, my talent will destroy me."

"It might not destroy you but you would probably be a very unhappy man if you did not use your talent."

"I've got it under control for the most part but sometimes I still have nightmares."

"I expect to have a few of those myself."

"And then there's the annulment," Nick said.

"I already know about that."

"What kind of private eye is so incompetent that he marries a woman who is married to another man?"

Vivian smiled and touched his hand. "A man who was born to be a hero. Why are you telling me all these things?"

"Damned if I know," Nick said. "No, that's not true. I know exactly why I'm telling you this stuff. I want you to know that I am probably not good husband material."

She took her hand off his, turned to face the moon-swept sea, and gripped the pier railing.

"As long as we're on the subject of marriage," she said, "I don't think anyone would consider me good wife material. I was involved in a scandalous affair with a renowned artist. I turned down the one marriage proposal that I received from a suitable gentleman. My neighbors in Adelina Beach will be happy to tell you they watched a parade of attractive, partially clothed men come and go from my cottage. On top of that I spent a few days at a resort hotel where I shared a room with a man who was not my husband."

"Vivian—"

"Furthermore, I seem to be on the brink of launching a career in photography with a series of pictures of naked men. Pictures, I might add, that were labeled pornographic by the proprietor of one of the most respected galleries in California. In addition, rumors abound that I have betrayed my artistic ambitions by shooting crime photos for the press. And, last but not least, I was recently involved in a murder investigation."

She finally ran down. She did not realize how tense she was until Nick gently pried her fingers one by one off the railing and turned her to face him.

"If you're trying to convince me that I shouldn't fall in love with you, you're going about it all wrong," he said. "It's too late for the warning anyway. I fell in love with you the first time I saw you."

A quiet sense of joy rose from somewhere deep inside, filling her to the brim. She raised her fingertips to frame his face.

"I am very glad to hear that because I love you with all my heart and I think you are *excellent* husband material. In fact, I think you would be the perfect husband for me."

Nick smiled his slow, breathtaking smile, the smile that heated his eyes and hit her senses like a glass of champagne. She suddenly felt fizzy and bubbly and excited and glorious.

"Are you asking me to marry you?" he said.

"Yes." She wrapped her arms around his neck. "I am asking you to marry me. I know it's much too soon to think about the future. We've been through a lot of drama recently. The wisest course of action is to wait. Give things time to return to normal. I just wanted you to know how I felt—"

He silenced her with a kiss that burned through any other reasonable, conventional arguments in favor of delay that she might have managed to dredge up from the depths.

By the time he raised his head she was breathless.

"In case you're wondering," he said, "my answer is yes."

Chapter 48

"Why did you do it?" Lyra asked. "Why did you make the papers give you a photo credit for the picture of Fenella Penfield on the floor of her gallery? You always said if it got out you were shooting crime scenes it would ruin your chances of making it as an art photographer."

Vivian picked up the pot and poured herself another cup of tea. "There's no point trying to keep my night shift work a secret. I decided I might as well try to build a new career. I'm thinking of billing myself as a documentary photographer."

Lyra gave that a moment of thought. "Well, it does sound a little classier than crime scene photographer."

"That's my theory," Vivian said.

She and Lyra were sitting in the hotel tearoom, drowning their sorrows in oolong tea while they ate their way through a full tray of scones and dainty sandwiches. Originally they had intended to head straight for the bar and order a pitcher of martinis but it was only three o'clock in the afternoon. They had decided to save the martinis until five o'clock. Even a couple of wild women had to maintain a few standards.

"You think you've got problems?" Lyra helped herself to a tiny lemon square from the tiered serving tray in the center of the table. "I'm the one who has to tell the parents that I canceled the wedding to Prince Charming while they were out of town. Also, I've got to explain that story in *Whispers*."

Vivian glanced at the afternoon copy of *Hollywood Whispers* lying on the table. The headline was in large, bold font. WHO IS THE NEW MYSTERY WOMAN IN RIPLEY FLEMING'S LIFE? The photo showed the actor dancing with Lyra at the Paradise Club in Burning Cove.

"If it's any consolation, you do look like a real mystery woman," Vivian said.

Lyra looked pleased. "I do, don't I? You've gotta love Hollywood. You can be anyone you dare to be."

"I understand the problem of trying to explain the canceled wedding," Vivian said. "I'm the one who turned down Hamilton's first offer of marriage, remember? Father was furious. Mother said I had ruined my life."

Lyra winced. "I can't believe that at the time I thought it was a lucky break for me."

"I suppose we should look on the bright side," Vivian said.

"There's a bright side? I mean, apart from me having found out the truth before the wedding?"

"Of course there's a bright side. Mr. Perfect wasn't guilty of trying to have me murdered."

Lyra hoisted her teacup. "Here's to Hamilton Merrick. He may be a lying, cheating, two-timing bastard but he doesn't hire professional killers."

"Obviously a man of high principles," Vivian said. She raised her cup, took a healthy swallow of tea, and thought longingly of the martinis that had been postponed until five. With a small sigh of regret she set the cup carefully onto the saucer. "You're sure your heart isn't broken?"

"Nope. I got over Hamilton during the drive from San Francisco to Burning Cove. Nothing like a road trip to give a woman a new perspective. Dating a famous movie star is just icing on the cake."

Vivian hesitated. "You do realize that handsome, talented movie stars probably don't make the best husband material, right?"

"Of course. I don't have any illusions on the subject. And you needn't worry that Ripley Fleming is trying to seduce me, either."

"Is that so?"

Lyra winked. "You could say that Ripley and I find our current association mutually convenient. We're both having fun together but that's it."

"I realize Mr. Fleming felt he owed me a favor. I assumed that entertaining my heartbroken sister while we were in Burning Cove was his way of paying off the debt."

"Ripley had the best of intentions, believe me," Lyra said. "But the situation has proven useful to him, as well."

"What do you mean?"

Lyra picked up her cup and looked at Vivian over the rim. "Let's just say that Ripley Fleming is a great admirer of your artistic approach to the nude male figure."

Vivian perked up. "He saw one of my Men series and liked it?"

"In the window of that gallery in Burning Cove."

"That's so nice to hear. Thank you. I keep thinking that if I could just get my work into a few more of the right galleries—"

Lyra leaned forward across the small table and lowered her voice. "Listen up, Sister, you're missing my point."

"There was a point?"

"Oh, for pity's sake. Stop thinking about your no-longer-failed art career and focus on what I just said. Ripley is a big admirer of the nude male figure. In fact, he prefers it to the nude female figure."

Vivian stared at her. "I don't—" Comprehension finally struck. She started to smile and then she laughed. "I see. I suppose that does explain why he wanted to call off the wedding with Clara Carstairs."

"It was supposed to be just another studio marriage arranged by the publicists but Clara had begun to take things seriously. She fell in love with Ripley. No surprise. He really is a very nice person."

"I see," Vivian said.

"When it became apparent that Clara expected a real marriage, Ripley decided that he could not go through with it."

"Ripley tried to do the right thing."

"Yes," Lyra said. She smiled. "Now you can understand why you don't have to be afraid I'll fall head over heels for him. Between you and me, I was serious when I said I won't ever marry."

"I used to think I would never marry, either," Vivian said.

Lyra's brows rose. "But?"

"But now I've changed my mind."

Lyra smiled again. "Nick Sundridge."

It was not a question.

Vivian felt the heat rise in her cheeks. "Is it that obvious?"

"Only to your sister, who has known you her entire life. If it makes you feel any better, I'm pretty sure he feels the same way about you."

"What are you going to do, Lyra? After you tell the parents that you won't be marrying Hamilton, that is?"

"I don't know," Lyra admitted, "but I'm sure of one thing: I'm not going back to San Francisco. After I've explained the situation to Mother and Father I'm going to do what I should have done a long time ago—find my passion and pursue it."

"Where?"

Lyra smiled. "Burning Cove looks like an excellent place for an ambitious woman with a few dreams."

"What will you do?"

"I haven't decided. I suppose I could always open an art gallery and show my sister's fine art photography. But something tells me that won't be necessary. You're already hanging in a very fine gallery there."

Vivian laughed.

A page in the hotel livery walked through the tearoom. He had a telephone in his hands.

"Long distance for Miss Vivian Brazier. Long distance for Miss Vivian Brazier."

Vivian raised one hand. The page hurried over. He put the telephone on the table and plugged the cord into a wall jack.

"Thank you." Vivian picked up the receiver. "This is Vivian Brazier."

"Joan Ashwood of the Ashwood Gallery in Burning Cove."

Vivian froze. "If you're calling to tell me that under the circumstances you feel you can no longer display my pictures—"

"I'm calling to inform you I have recently sold the two pictures from your Men series that you left with me."

"Really?" Vivian tightened her grip on the receiver. "Who bought them?"

"A collector who wishes to remain anonymous."

"I see," Vivian said.

"I believe you said you planned to create twelve limited-edition photographs in that series?"

"Yes, that's right."

"If you have not already promised them to another gallery I would like to take all of them. Sixteen signed, limited editions, each. Standard contract terms."

Vivian stared at Lyra speechless.

"Miss Brazier?" Joan said, sounding concerned. "Are you there?"

Vivian pulled herself together. "Yes. Yes, I'm here."

"The show is next week. I realize it's very short notice but if you could have a couple more large prints from that series ready by then I would love to exhibit them."

"I can manage to have two or three ready in time," Vivian said. She cleared her throat. "About my name."

"What about it?" Joan asked.

"I'm sure by now you've seen the photo I took of Fenella Penfield."

"Oh, yes, it's in all the papers. Excellent shot, by the way. The outflung hand. The massive statue and the police detective gazing down at the body. The context told the whole story. No words needed."

Vivian was horrified. "I assure you, it wasn't posed."

"I never thought it was. I just said it was a very evocative photograph."

"My point is, not only was my name in the story, I also got the photo credit. That means I no longer have any hope of concealing my crime scene work. Perhaps I should use a pseudonym for my art photography?"

"Not in Burning Cove. Here we live by the First Law of Marketing: *Any publicity is good publicity.* That's one of the reasons why I want to get some more of your work into my upcoming exhibition rather than wait for the next one. Strike while the iron is hot and all that."

"Okay. If you think that's for the best."

"Trust me, I know what I'm doing."

Vivian hung up, dazed.

"Well?" Lyra said.

"The Ashwood Gallery in Burning Cove wants more pictures from my Men series."

Lyra's eyes sparkled with excitement. "That's fantastic news."

Vivian got a little thrill of awareness and turned her head to see Nick walking toward the table where she sat with Lyra. Rex was with him. He stopped in front of them, brows slightly elevated.

"What did I miss?" he asked.

"Have a seat," Lyra said. "We're celebrating because Vivian just got some very good news. The Ashwood Gallery in Burning Cove is going to hang the rest of the pictures from her Men series. Evidently the first two pictures were snapped up by an anonymous collector."

"My art career rises from yet another near-death experience and lurches forward once more," Vivian said.

Nick sat down and helped himself to a dainty salmon and cucumber sandwich. "Congratulations. That's great news. Can't say I'm surprised, though. I knew it was just a matter of time before someone recognized your talent."

Vivian went very still, a dark thought crowding out some of her delight.

"You're not the anonymous collector who bought those pictures from the Burning Cove gallery, are you?" she asked.

Nick put the entire sandwich into his mouth and gave her one of his patented enigmatic looks.

"Why?" he said around the sandwich.

She cleared her throat, not wanting to hurt his feelings. "While it would be a lovely gesture and much appreciated, it wouldn't be quite the same as a genuine sale to a real collector."

Nick nodded, swallowed, and reached for another sandwich. "I thought about buying those pictures anonymously but I knew it wouldn't give you the validation you wanted. So, no, I didn't buy them and I don't know who did."

Vivian relaxed. "Good. Thanks."

Lyra chuckled. "See? Those sales were the real deal."

Nick groaned. "I suppose this means I'm going to have to live with a steady stream of half-naked Muscle Beach men wandering in and out of Vivian's studio."

Vivian got a warm, giddy feeling. Across the table Lyra met her eyes and winked.

"I intend to finish the Men series," Vivian said. "But after that I'm moving on to another subject."

"I'm afraid to ask what that will be," Nick said.

"Good, because I haven't decided yet," Vivian said.

"As it happens, I've got a little good news myself," Nick said. "Raina called to let me know she checked with the front desk staff of the Burning Cove Hotel. Ripley Fleming's secretary booked his room there a full month before the events here in Adelina Beach. He stays there frequently and prefers one particular villa."

"Hah." Vivian smiled. "So there is such a thing as coincidence, after all. If you want more proof, just look at how the two of us met."

Nick smiled. His eyes heated. "That wasn't coincidence. That was fate."

Lyra jumped to her feet and stole a cup and saucer from a nearby table. Seating herself again, she poured tea for Nick. Then she raised her cup in a toast.

"Here's to wild women everywhere," she said.

Nick smiled at Vivian once more. "I'll drink to that."

Chapter 49

I look forward to hanging the rest of the pictures in your Men series," Joan Ashwood said. She surveyed the glamorous crowd that filled her gallery. "I've already sold the three images on display here tonight and I've got orders for most of the limited-edition prints. I will definitely be raising the price on your next series."

"I can hardly believe it," Vivian said. "I can't thank you enough for this opportunity."

As the night of the Ashwood Gallery show approached she had grown increasingly anxious. Nothing Nick or Lyra said could reassure her. On the day of the event she had been convinced she was doomed to a humiliating public failure. The knowledge that said failure would likely take place in front of Winston Bancroft did not help her nerves.

But when the doors opened, Luther Pell and Raina Kirk had been among the first to arrive. Oliver Ward and his wife, Irene, had soon joined them. A short time later, Ripley Fleming, Lyra on his arm, strolled into the room, making the kind of entrance that only a true star could manage. They had been accompanied by a couple of studio publicists.

Ripley paused to congratulate her. He winked before moving on with Lyra to examine a large abstract sculpture made of gleaming chrome.

Vivian smiled at Joan. "I think I know the identity of the anonymous collector who bought the first two pictures in my Men series."

Joan chuckled. "I believe there was some mention of a debt that needed to be repaid. But the circumstances aren't important. What matters is that a collector snatched up those first pictures. That automatically tripled the price on the next ones."

Several press photographers were gathered on the sidewalk outside the entrance, lighting up the night with their camera flashbulbs as they took pictures of the fashionable celebrities and socialites who were arriving.

The only person who had not yet appeared was Winston Bancroft.

Joan had instructed Vivian to stay close, at least for the first hour, so that Joan could introduce her to everyone. Every time the door opened on a new arrival, Vivian took a deep breath and waited to see if Winston would appear. After an hour she began to hope that he might not show up. Maybe he had a bad cold. Or a flat tire.

When there was a slight lull in the wave of introductions, Vivian could not stand the suspense any longer. She looked at Joan.

"Evidently Mr. Bancroft has been delayed," she said, trying not to sound too relieved.

"Winston?" Joan chuckled. "Don't worry, he'll show up. He's definitely not the reclusive, socially awkward, painfully shy artistic type. And when he does finally walk into the room, you'll know it. He'll make an entrance that will rival Ripley Fleming's."

"Right," Vivian said.

Joan's brows rose. "Have you met him?"

"Took a course in photography from him in San Francisco."

"I see. Interesting. You obviously went on to develop your own style. Most of the photographers I know who took a course from him try to imitate his approach and techniques. Imitation is usually a mistake when it comes to art."

"Mr. Bancroft is . . . very confident. In a classroom setting he can be somewhat intimidating."

Joan smiled. "Obviously you weren't intimidated by him. Your work is very, very different."

"Yes, but my last news photo was a picture of a dead woman," Vivian said.

"No, it wasn't," Joan said. "Your last photograph was a picture of a dead *murderess*, a staggeringly evil woman who just happened to be the Dagger Killer's partner in crime. Your photo told a story of insanity hidden behind the mask of respectability and the gloss of artistic pretension."

"Wow." Vivian was lost in admiration. "No wonder you're good at selling art."

"It's more fun than selling hats, that's for sure."

Vivian was about to respond but at that moment the front door opened again. A slight hush fell over the crowd. Everyone turned to look at the new arrivals.

A tall, dramatically handsome man with shoulder-length dark hair brushed straight back from a sharp widow's peak strode into the room and stopped just inside the entrance. He was not alone. A very pretty, very tiny blonde clung to his arm.

"About time he got here," Joan said. "Come with me, Miss Brazier. I'm sure you'll want to say hello to Winston."

Not really, Vivian thought. But she dutifully followed Joan through the crowded room to where Winston stood surrounded by a group of admirers. Occupied with playing the role of the Great Artist, he did not appear to notice Joan and Vivian until Joan spoke.

"Winston, I'm so glad you could make it," Joan said. "I was starting to think you might have been delayed."

Winston made a show of turning toward Joan, his vampire eyes flashing with his trademark smoldering sensuality. He tried to pretend he had not noticed Vivian but she caught the faint telltale narrowing of his gaze.

He kissed the back of Joan's hand and smiled his charming smile, the one that showed the dimple. "Miss one of your shows, Joan? Not in a million years. I understand you have some pictures by one of my former students on display tonight. I'm interested to see if she has made any progress since she left the classroom."

Joan started to make the introductions but Vivian forestalled her.

"Hello, Winston," she said.

"Vivian, darling, how nice to see you again." Winston's eyes glittered. "I understand you've had a rather exciting time of it lately."

"Yes." Vivian smiled at the blonde. "Are you going to introduce me to your companion?"

Winston frowned, evidently having forgotten about the woman on his arm.

"I'm Ginny," the blonde said in a soft voice. "I'm one of Winston's models."

"I see," Vivian said. "That must be very interesting work."

"Yes, it is." Ginny glowed. "I was the model for the pictures on display here tonight."

Before Vivian could respond, Winston gave her an icy smile.

"Your photo of Fenella Penfield lying dead on the floor of her gallery was in all the papers. So you're pursuing a career in news photography on the side? A wise choice, considering your lack of appreciation for fine art photography."

There was a short silence during which everyone, including Joan, seemed nonplussed. Before Vivian could come up with a suitable response to the unveiled insult, Nick made his way into the circle around Winston. He had a glass of champagne in his hand. He gave it to Vivian.

"Here you go," he said. He gave no indication that he had noticed Winston. "Figured you could use this."

"Thank you," Vivian said. "You're right. I did need this."

"By the way, there are 'sold' cards under all three of your photographs," Nick continued in a conversational tone.

"Yes," Vivian said, going for demure. "Miss Ashwood said they were snapped up by one of her clients."

Winston's brows rose in a parody of amazement. "Congratulations. I suppose it's not surprising that there are a few people here in Burning Cove who are comfortable with your sentimental greeting card approach to your subjects."

It seemed to Vivian that the entire room was holding its breath. She gave Winston a steely smile and reminded herself that the last thing she wanted to do tonight was escalate the situation into a scene that would embarrass Joan.

"Lucky me," she said evenly.

Satisfied, Winston smirked and started to turn away.

Nick spoke into the breathless silence. "I don't know much about art but I'm not surprised that the images from your Men series are outselling those old-fashioned pictures of naked women on the other side of the gallery."

Stunned horror leveled the room. Winston looked as if he had been struck by lightning. His eyes stopped smoldering.

"You're right," he said with a savage smile. "You don't know much about art. It's always a good idea for a man to know his limitations."

"What I know," Nick said, "is that the images in the Woman in the Window series remind me of the collection of dirty postcards I found in Uncle Pete's attic. He said he picked them up in Paris on his way home from the Great War."

"Your uncle evidently taught you everything you know about art, which amounts to absolutely nothing," Winston shot back.

The scene was getting out of hand. Vivian was torn between laughter and outright panic.

Pete materialized out of the crowd. There was an unholy gleam in his eyes that looked very familiar. There was a remarkably similar glint in Nick's eyes.

"Someone mention my name?" Pete asked.

"We were discussing dirty postcards and your name came up," Nick said.

Pete got a reminiscent look. "I do have a nice collection up in the attic. Those pictures of naked ladies on the other side of the gallery remind me of some of those postcards."

The entire room was electrified now. Winston turned on Joan.

"I expected to encounter a more sophisticated clientele here tonight," he said.

"Eye of the beholder and all that," Joan said. She spoke in soothing tones. "Don't worry, Winston. I have clients clamoring for your pictures. Now, why don't you get a glass of champagne and mingle. I see a crowd of admirers gathering around your pictures. This would be an excellent opportunity for you to explain the artistic values of pictorialism."

"Right." Winston exhaled a theatrical sigh. "I suppose it is my job to help educate the masses."

Satisfied that he'd had the last word, he stalked toward the far side of the gallery. The crowd parted for him. He was soon surrounded by a gaggle of admirers.

He had apparently forgotten about Ginny. For a moment she just stood there, stricken. She finally pulled herself together and fixed Vivian with an unreadable look.

"I apologize for the scene my friends just made," Vivian said. She shot Nick and Pete a quelling glance and turned back to Ginny. "That was uncalled-for."

Ginny blinked and then she started to smile. The smile turned into a mischievous laugh.

"No apologies necessary," she said. "He had it coming. Between you and me, I thought the pictures looked a lot like dirty postcards, too. But I told myself I was working for a real artist so it had to be real art."

"You are working for a real artist," Vivian said. "Winston really is brilliant in his own way."

"Do you really think so?" Ginny looked unsure.

"I'm positive," Vivian said. "His style is different from mine, that's all."

Pete snagged a glass of champagne off a passing tray. "A glass of champagne, ma'am?"

Ginny brightened. She took the glass and emptied half of it in a single swallow. She smiled at Pete.

"Thank you," she said.

"Anytime." Pete cleared his throat. "Would you care to tour the pictures on display with me? I'm sure you know a lot more about art than I do."

Ginny's smile got a few watts hotter. "It would be my pleasure."

She slipped a graceful hand around his arm. Pete escorted her through the crowd.

Vivian groaned. "I'm sorry, Joan."

"Don't be," Joan said, radiating satisfaction. "There is nothing more entertaining than a loud argument about what constitutes true art. You'll notice that no one is walking out the door. Mr. Sundridge and his uncle have guaranteed that this show will make tomorrow's edition of the *Herald*. My gallery will be the talk of the town tomorrow."

Vivian shot Nick another ferocious glare. "I just hope they didn't hurt your gallery's reputation."

"Nope, not a chance," Joan said. She gave Nick a speculative look. "Out of curiosity, do you really think that Miss Brazier's Men will outsell Winston's Woman in the Window series?"

"Damned if I know," Nick said. "I was being honest when I said I didn't know much about art. All I can tell you is that it's clear from Bancroft's pictures that he doesn't really like women. If they have secrets, he doesn't care about them. He shoots them the way you'd shoot a doll or a statue. Vivian cares about her subjects and it shows. She knows they all have secrets and she knows how to make sure the viewer understands that, too."

Joan nodded. "I agree."

Vivian thought about that for approximately thirty seconds.

"And therein lies my problem," she said. "You know what? I think Fenella Penfield and Winston Bancroft are right."

Joan and Nick both looked at her.

"What do you mean?" Joan said.

"I do try to capture something real and personal about my subjects. I'm not going for an idealized composition or lighting. I'm not creating an abstract vision that must be appreciated on purely aesthetic grounds. I'm interested in hinting at a subject's secrets because those secrets are what make us human."

Joan laughed again. "Got news for you. A lot of people would call that art. I certainly do. And here is what I know for certain: I can sell it."

Chapter 50

Nick picked up the bottle of champagne that he had just opened and filled the two crystal flutes.

"I don't know about you, but this has been a thrilling day for me," he said. "My first real wedding. And my first real honeymoon."

Vivian smiled. "I'm pretty thrilled myself."

The wedding had been a simple affair at the Burning Cove courthouse followed by a small reception at the Burning Cove Hotel. The guests had included Ripley Fleming, Oliver and Irene Ward, Luther Pell, Raina Kirk, and of course Lyra and Uncle Pete. Lyra had taken charge of the wedding photos.

A telegram had been sent to London informing Mr. and Mrs. Brazier that their eldest daughter was at long last a respectably married woman.

It had been a glorious day, Vivian thought, a perfect day for a wedding with the golden sun and the diamond-bright Pacific Ocean providing the setting.

It was almost midnight. Their guests had moved on to the hotel's lounge to enjoy the jazz trio. She and Nick had slipped away to walk back through the lush gardens to the honeymoon suite.

They were on the patio savoring the scented night together. Vivian smiled at the sight of Nick in his elegant black-and-white formal clothes. He looked so good, she thought. Solid. Strong. A man a woman could depend on.

She was still in the ankle-length, silver satin gown that Lyra had chosen for her.

Rex was under the table, relaxing after another meal of steak and eggs.

"We look a lot more respectable now than we did the first time we checked into the Burning Cove," she said.

"True." Nick sat down on the edge of a chaise lounge and touched the rim of his flute to her glass. "But I will always have good memories of that morning."

"Even though someone had tried to murder us the night before?"

"No first date ever goes smoothly."

"True." Vivian smiled. "It's what happens afterward that matters."

Nick smiled. His eyes burned in the shadows. Joy and a deep sense of certainty thrilled her senses.

They finished their champagne and set the flutes on the table. Vivian reached out and slowly, deliberately loosened the knot of Nick's black bow tie.

He got to his feet and scooped her up off the lounger. The silver skirts of her wedding gown cascaded over his arm, gleaming in the moonlight.

"What happened afterward is that we got married," Nick said. "For real."

Vivian touched the side of his face with her fingertips.

"Yes," she said. "For real."

"And forever."

"Forever," she whispered.

He carried her into the shadows of the honeymoon suite.

Out on the patio, Rex settled down for the night. The steak-and-eggs life was good, but as long as he was with his humans, he was content.

Discover a brand new gripping
romantic suspense series from
Jayne Ann Krentz ...

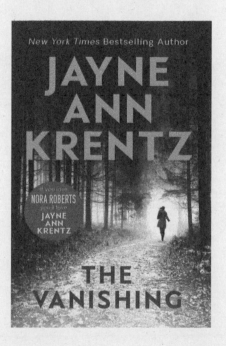